BOSTON NOIR 2
THE CLASSICS

BOSTON NOIR 2
THE CLASSICS

EDITED BY DENNIS LEHANE,
MARY COTTON & JAIME CLARKE

Published by Akashic Books
©2012 Akashic Books

Series concept by Tim McLoughlin and Johnny Temple
Boston map by Aaron Petrovich

Hardcover ISBN-13: 978-1-61775-137-0
Paperback ISBN-13: 978-1-61775-136-3
Library of Congress Control Number: 2012939265
All rights reserved

Grateful acknowledgment is made for permission to reprint the stories in this anthology. *Bait* (excerpt) by Kenneth Abel was originally published by Delacorte Press in 1994, © 1994 by Kenneth Abel; *Blanche Cleans Up* (excerpt) by Barbara Neely was originally published by Viking Penguin in 1998, © 1998 by Barbara Neely; *Infinite Jest* (excerpt) by David Foster Wallace, Copyright © 1996 by David Foster Wallace Literary Trust, reprinted by permission of Little, Brown and Company, New York, NY, all rights reserved; "Driving the Heart" by Jason Brown was originally published in *Driving the Heart & Other Stories* (New York: W.W. Norton & Company, Inc., 1999), © 1999 by Jason Brown; "Home Sweet Home" by Hannah Tinti was originally published in *Animal Crackers: Stories*, used by permission of The Dial Press/Dell Publishing, a division of Random House, Inc., © 2004 by Hannah Tinti; "Townies" by Andre Dubus was originally published in *Finding a Girl in America*, reprinted by permission of David R. Godine, Publisher, Inc. and Open Road Integrated Media, Copyright © 1980 by Andre Dubus; "Lucky Penny" by Linda Barnes is reprinted by permission of the Gina Maccoby Literary Agency, Copyright © 1985 by Linda Barnes, "Lucky Penny" was originally published in *New Black Mask Quarterly*, No. 3, 1985; "Mushrooms" by Dennis Lehane was originally published in *Coronado* (New York: William Morrow, 2006), © 2006 by Dennis Lehane; "Night-Side" by Joyce Carol Oates was originally published in *Night-Side* (New York: Vanguard Press, Inc., 1977), © 1977 by Joyce Carol Oates; "Surrogate" by Robert B. Parker was originally published in *Surrogate* (Northridge, CA: Lord John Press, 1982), © 1982 by Robert B. Parker; "The 5:22" by George Harrar was originally published in *Story* magazine, Autumn 1998, © 1998 by George Harrar; "The Balance of the Day" by George V. Higgins, Copyright © Loretta Cubberley Higgins, first published in *GQ* magazine, November 1985, reprinted with the permission of the Albert LaFarge Literary Agency; "The Marriage Privilege" by Chuck Hogan was originally published in *Boston College* magazine, Summer 2006, © 2006 by Chuck Hogan; "At Night" by David Ryan was originally published in *BOMB* magazine, Fall 1998, © 1998 by David Ryan.

First printing

Akashic Books | PO Box 1456 | New York, NY 10009
info@akashicbooks.com | www.akashicbooks.com

ALSO IN THE AKASHIC BOOKS NOIR SERIES

BALTIMORE NOIR, edited by LAURA LIPPMAN

BARCELONA NOIR (SPAIN), edited by ADRIANA V. LÓPEZ & CARMEN OSPINA

BOSTON NOIR, edited by DENNIS LEHANE

BRONX NOIR, edited by S.J. ROZAN

BROOKLYN NOIR, edited by TIM McLOUGHLIN

BROOKLYN NOIR 2: THE CLASSICS, edited by TIM McLOUGHLIN

BROOKLYN NOIR 3: NOTHING BUT THE TRUTH, edited by TIM McLOUGHLIN & THOMAS ADCOCK

CAPE COD NOIR, edited by DAVID L. ULIN

CHICAGO NOIR, edited by NEAL POLLACK

COPENHAGEN NOIR (DENMARK), edited by BO TAO MICHAËLIS

D.C. NOIR, edited by GEORGE PELECANOS

D.C. NOIR 2: THE CLASSICS, edited by GEORGE PELECANOS

DELHI NOIR (INDIA), edited by HIRSH SAWHNEY

DETROIT NOIR, edited by E.J. OLSEN & JOHN C. HOCKING

DUBLIN NOIR (IRELAND), edited by KEN BRUEN

HELSINKI NOIR (FINLAND), edited by JAMES THOMPSON

HAITI NOIR, edited by EDWIDGE DANTICAT

HAVANA NOIR (CUBA), edited by ACHY OBEJAS

INDIAN COUNTRY NOIR, edited by SARAH CORTEZ & LIZ MARTÍNEZ

ISTANBUL NOIR (TURKEY), edited by MUSTAFA ZIYALAN & AMY SPANGLER

KANSAS CITY NOIR, edited by STEVE PAUL

KINGSTON NOIR (JAMAICA), edited by COLIN CHANNER

LAS VEGAS NOIR, edited by JARRET KEENE & TODD JAMES PIERCE

LONDON NOIR (ENGLAND), edited by CATHI UNSWORTH

LONE STAR NOIR, edited by BOBBY BYRD & JOHNNY BYRD

LONG ISLAND NOIR, edited by KAYLIE JONES

LOS ANGELES NOIR, edited by DENISE HAMILTON

LOS ANGELES NOIR 2: THE CLASSICS, edited by DENISE HAMILTON

MANHATTAN NOIR, edited by LAWRENCE BLOCK

MANHATTAN NOIR 2: THE CLASSICS, edited by LAWRENCE BLOCK

MEXICO CITY NOIR (MEXICO), edited by PACO I. TAIBO II

MIAMI NOIR, edited by LES STANDIFORD

MOSCOW NOIR (RUSSIA), edited by NATALIA SMIRNOVA & JULIA GOUMEN

MUMBAI NOIR (INDIA), edited by ALTAF TYREWALA

NEW JERSEY NOIR, edited by JOYCE CAROL OATES

NEW ORLEANS NOIR, edited by JULIE SMITH

ORANGE COUNTY NOIR, edited by GARY PHILLIPS

PARIS NOIR (FRANCE), edited by AURÉLIEN MASSON

PHILADELPHIA NOIR, edited by CARLIN ROMANO

PHOENIX NOIR, edited by PATRICK MILLIKIN

PITTSBURGH NOIR, edited by KATHLEEN GEORGE

PORTLAND NOIR, edited by KEVIN SAMPSELL

QUEENS NOIR, edited by ROBERT KNIGHTLY

RICHMOND NOIR, edited by ANDREW BLOSSOM, BRIAN CASTLEBERRY & TOM DE HAVEN

ROME NOIR (ITALY), edited by CHIARA STANGALINO & MAXIM JAKUBOWSKI

ST. PETERSBURG NOIR (RUSSIA), edited by NATALIA SMIRNOVA & JULIA GOUMEN

SAN DIEGO NOIR, edited by MARYELIZABETH HART

SAN FRANCISCO NOIR, edited by PETER MARAVELIS

SAN FRANCISCO NOIR 2: THE CLASSICS, edited by PETER MARAVELIS

SEATTLE NOIR, edited by CURT COLBERT

STATEN ISLAND NOIR, edited by PATRICIA SMITH

TORONTO NOIR (CANADA), edited by JANINE ARMIN & NATHANIEL G. MOORE

TRINIDAD NOIR (TRINIDAD & TOBAGO), edited by LISA ALLEN-AGOSTINI & JEANNE MASON

TWIN CITIES NOIR, edited by JULIE SCHAPER & STEVEN HORWITZ

VENICE NOIR (ITALY), edited by MAXIM JAKUBOWSKI

WALL STREET NOIR, edited by PETER SPIEGELMAN

FORTHCOMING

BOGOTÁ NOIR (COLOMBIA), edited by ANDREA MONTEJO

BUFFALO NOIR, edited by BRIGID HUGHES & ED PARK

JERUSALEM NOIR, edited by SAYED KASHUA

LAGOS NOIR (NIGERIA), edited by CHRIS ABANI

MANILA NOIR (PHILIPPINES), edited by JESSICA HAGEDORN

PRISON NOIR, edited by JOYCE CAROL OATES

SEOUL NOIR (KOREA), edited by BS PUBLISHING CO.

TEL AVIV NOIR (ISRAEL), edited by ETGAR KERET

For Max

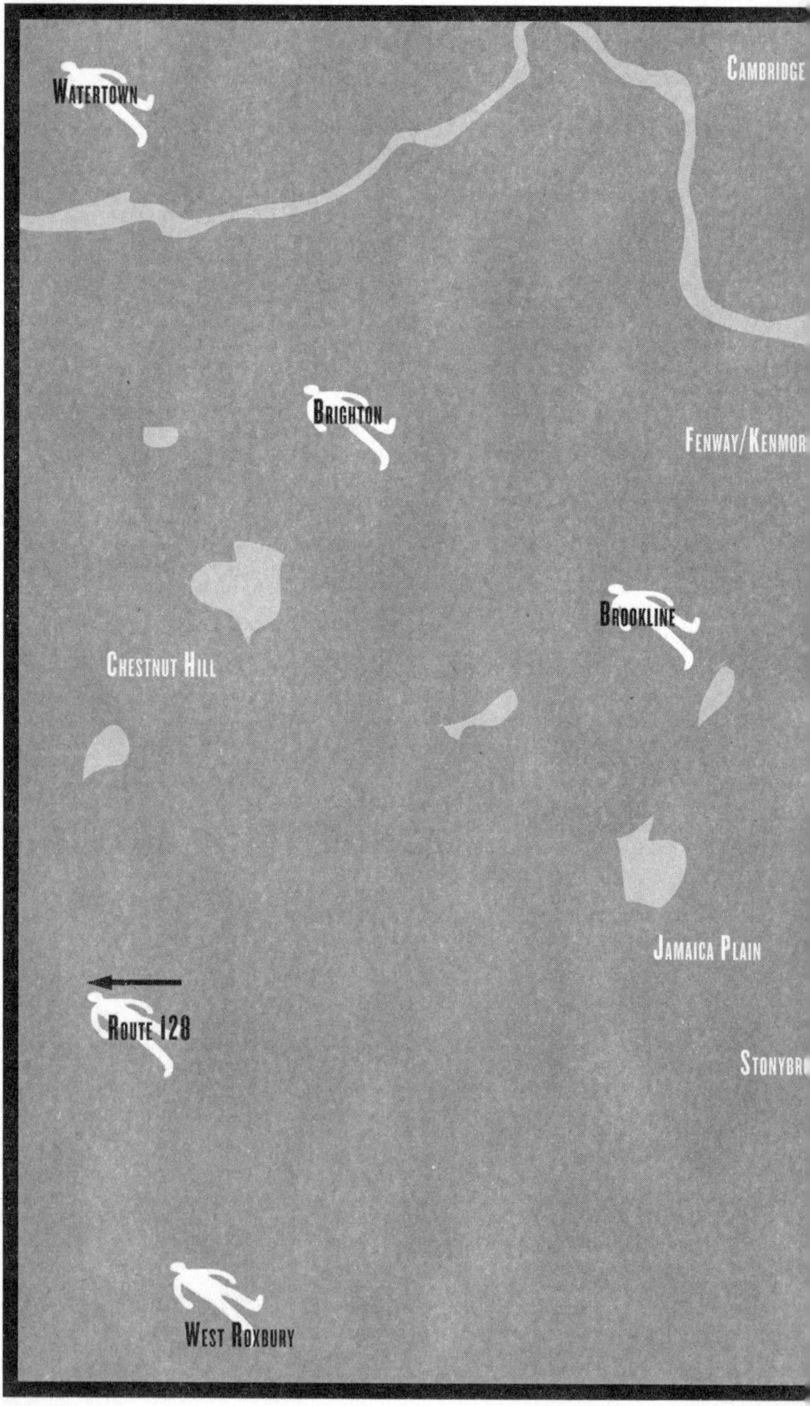
Watertown
Cambridge
Brighton
Fenway/Kenmor
Brookline
Chestnut Hill
Jamaica Plain
Route 128
Stonybr
West Roxbury

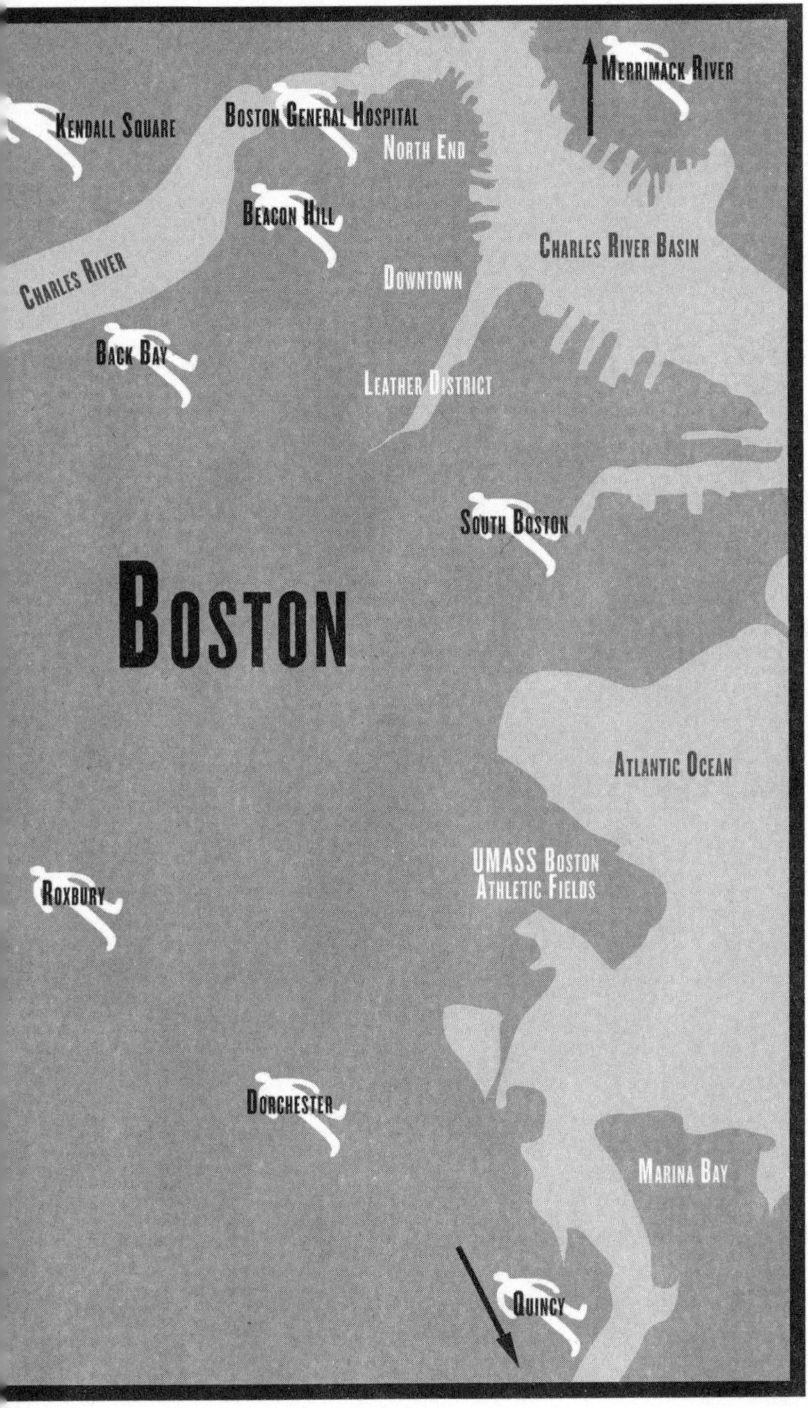

Merrimack River
Kendall Square
Boston General Hospital
North End
Beacon Hill
Charles River Basin
Charles River
Downtown
Back Bay
Leather District
South Boston
Boston
Atlantic Ocean
UMASS Boston
Athletic Fields
Roxbury
Dorchester
Marina Bay
Quincy

TABLE OF CONTENTS

PART III: VOYEURS & OUTSIDERS

INTRODUCTION
They Look Like You and Me

There's a mysterious phenomenon particular to Boston involving the network of underground and above-ground trains that form the spiderweb of the Massachusetts Bay Transportation Authority, known colloquially as the T. The city's subway employs a directional concept known as Inbound and Outbound, which confounds and baffles tourists and transient college students alike, since it's not readily evident what exactly Inbound and Outbound are in relation to. Any number of theories persist: toward the Atlantic Ocean means Inbound, away means Outbound; toward the gold- capped State House in Beacon Hill designates Inbound, away from it is Outbound, and on and on. All guesses are reduced to just that when the Inbound train you're riding on suddenly and inexplicably transforms into an Outbound train by passing through some magical plane of existence.

What is noir and what is not inhabits a similarly gray area. Its definition is continually expanding from the previous generation's agreed-upon notion that noir involves men in fedoras smoking cigarettes on street corners. Noir alludes to crime, sure, but it also evokes bleak elements, danger, tragedy, sleaze, all of which is best represented by its root French definition: black. We used this idea as our guide for this sequel to the best-selling *Boston Noir* anthology, which was originally published in 2009. Whereas *Boston Noir* comprised brand-new pieces commissioned for the anthology, our charge here was to scour the body of Boston literature for previously published short stories and novel excerpts that best illuminate the dark corners of the Hub.

While the tales told within take place in the Boston metro area and its exburbs, the first story we agreed should be included unfolds north of the city, Andre Dubus's "Townies." One of the modern short story masters, Dubus's work is filled with grim circumstances and ersatz characters. His fiction could fill an entire volume of noir, and the unforgettable protagonist of "Townies" and his irrevocable act are as haunting as any ghost story.

Our search deep into the archives of Boston fiction turned up a priceless find: Robert B. Parker's short story "Surrogate," which features an early appearance of Spenser, his famous detective. It's rumored that "Surrogate" was commissioned by *Playboy* but never published there, appearing only in a limited-edition volume, then later in an anthology published in England. You're among the first to read it in a very long time.

We uncovered other gems as well: "The Marriage Privilege" by Chuck Hogan, which was previously published in the Boston College alumni magazine; and Linda Barnes's short story "Lucky Penny," which won a 1985 Anthony Award and also marked the first appearance of the towering cop-turned–private detective Carlotta Carlyle, who would star in ten of Barnes's hard-boiled detective novels; and Joyce Carol Oates writing occult fiction. You read that right.

The vast treasure trove of George V. Higgins's work made for long stretches of interesting and entertaining reading and when the arguing was over, "The Balance of the Day" became our favorite, second only to our desire to reprint Higgins's entire novel *The Friends of Eddie Coyle*.

Barbara Neely's four novels featuring Blanche White, a

sharp-tongued, middle-aged black cleaning woman, are sadly out of print. The excerpt from *Blanche Cleans Up* anthologized here features an amateur private detective in the unique position to investigate the death of a young black man from the inside of the Boston Brahmin politician's house she's currently cleaning.

Kenneth Abel's novel *Bait*, also unfairly out of print, shows us a gritty Boston populated by fascinating characters: brilliant (and not so brilliant) mob bosses and thugs, recovering alcoholic cops and the women who love them, and government officials trying desperately to look like they know what they're doing.

The late David Foster Wallace's novel *Infinite Jest* is set partly in Enfield, a fictional Brighton. (Wallace lived for a time in Boston.) The novel is full of comedy, but is also filled with blackness, and the excerpt we've chosen is singular in its depravity.

Knowing that Hannah Tinti grew up in Salem, Massachusetts, the witch-burning capital of the country, won't prepare you for the grand noir soap opera she unfurls in her story "Home Sweet Home."

In the gradations of noir, the stories by Jason Brown, George Harrar, and David Ryan are perhaps on the subtle end, but they fall in the final act of this volume because they are deeply unsettling. That's fair warning.

For those of us lucky enough to call Boston home, the commonwealth is an endless source of fascinating landscapes: the autumnal light spreading across the Charles River; the ice floes in the wintry Boston Harbor; a spring air tantalizing leaves in Harvard Yard; the salty taste of summer as sunbathers peer into the horizon, shielding their eyes from the glare, squinting into the middle distance. Beyond the postcard fabric, though, lies a community populated by broken families, criminal minds, voyeurs, and outsiders. They look like you and me. These are their stories.

Jaime Clarke, Mary Cotton & Dennis Lehane
Boston, MA
September 2012

PART I

BROKEN FAMILIES

THE MARRIAGE PRIVILEGE

BY CHUCK HOGAN

West Roxbury

(Originally published in 2006)

At home in Beverly Farms, sitting in his father's study, Miles Bard Jr. looked small in the oversized calfskin chair. Fellowes, the attorney, said yes to a whiskey, but hadn't touched it yet. The father, Miles Bard Sr., owner of Bard Industries, walked around and around them, remaining on the periphery of the problem.

"Motor vehicle homicide, operating under the influence," said Fellowes. "This is not going to go away. You are looking at eight hard years, minimum. *Minimum*. That is, if you plea out. If the media heat doesn't inspire the DA to go after you with straight-up murder. And if your previous DWIs are allowed in? Then much more. You got into a fight earlier that night."

"It wasn't a fight," said Miles. "We passed this wedding reception. I went in, asked if I could kiss the bride."

"It was a gay wedding and you popped the guy on the button. Hilarious. Juries love rich kids. They'll laugh right along with you."

"I was drunk. Blame the state of Massachusetts."

"Yes. We'll put the state on trial. Your personal distress over same-sex marriages caused you to go out and consume eleven Stoli-and-Sprites over a four-hour period and jump the median, killing a man in a Sentra."

Miles Bard shrugged. He was a pretty kid of twenty-three,

sharp-featured, hair shiny and black as the wings of a crow. The soft brace on his arm was all he had to show for the head-on collision.

Fellowes said, "The man you killed was a newlywed. Home from his honeymoon less than two weeks. Married his college sweetheart."

"Dumb-ass should have swerved."

"Maybe you should have stayed awake."

"A deer ran out."

"Yes. A deer on Massachusetts Avenue. The first such sighting in Cambridge since the advent of the motor car."

"It's my word against hers."

"Ah. The victim's sister. Do you know where they were coming from? Do you have any idea? An alumni Mass at Boston College. They were driving home from church, brother and sister. You, mister Stoli-and-Sprites? Your word against hers?"

Fellowes eased his grip on the chair back. This was not what he was paid to do. Lecture. Admonish. That was the father's responsibility. Whether he realized it or not.

"A man is dead, and his twin sister is paralyzed from the waist down," said Fellowes. "A twenty-six-year-old woman, a social worker, confined to a wheelchair for life, pointing her finger at you in open court? Have I painted the picture? There is nothing any lawyer in the country, myself included, can do to inoculate you against that. You are going to prison, young Miles. All I can do is gum up the process. Delay the inevitable. Giving you maybe a year or so of freedom."

The chair groaned as Miles sat up, searching out his father. "I had enough trouble in lockup," he said. "This face, what are they going to do to me in prison?"

At least young Bard was afraid of something. Fellowes

looked at the father, who had stopped his circuit of the room.

Ice cracked in Bard Sr.'s glass. He nodded.

Fellowes reached for his whiskey, downed it, then transferred the check from his folder into his suit pocket. "Maybe there is something you can do," said the lawyer. "Maybe one thing. A longshot. One in a million, perhaps. But your only chance."

Miles looked up at him, then at his father. A scared little boy, his hands clawing plump armrests. "We're going to kill her?"

Fellowes had never seen a father look at his own offspring with such disgust.

The morning Nicole was released from the Spinal Cord Injury Program at Spaulding Rehabilitation, she returned to her rented West Roxbury house to find a brand-new, fully customized, wheelchair-accessible Toyota Rampvan idling at the curb. The driver, upon her inquiry, explained that he was there at her service. But after learning who had hired him, Nicole angrily declined the ride.

Every morning the van would pull up, the driver tipping his cap, and every morning Nicole refused his offer—sometimes rudely, though the driver's courtesy never wavered. She insisted on taking a taxi van for the disabled to her various appointments: physical therapy, occupational therapy, counseling.

Friends visited frequently, bringing dinners, movies. A small circle, they even set up a schedule to ensure that Nicole would be occupied nightly. The drop-off in participation, which her friends pledged would never occur, inevitably did.

Miles mailed Nicole a letter every day. The first arrived from a drug and alcohol rehabilitation center in Arizona; later, from his father's home in Beverly Farms.

Depression came and went in cycles, each one stealing away another little piece of the old Nicole.

One hot day, the taxi van did not show up. The Rampvan driver was so patient, so pleasant, Nicole decided to accept his ride, just this once.

A gentlemanly retiree with an ailing wife, he and Nicole struck up a rapport. Nicole accepted another ride, and another, and soon began relying on the van full-time.

Miles stopped mailing his letters, instead trusting them to the driver to be hand-delivered. Nicole accepted them wordlessly, and, if she opened them, never did so in the driver's presence.

Six months after the accident, Fellowes petitioned the court and somehow got Miles's driver's license reinstated.

One morning, as Nicole rolled up the side ramp, she noticed that the regular driver was not there. Realization bloomed into horror as she recognized Miles and, shaking, demanded to be let out. Miles went around to help but she yelled at him to get away, demanding that he call her a taxi van.

The driver's wife was ill, Miles told her. But Nicole would not look at him. She would not speak to him. The taxi arrived and she wheeled aboard.

She refused the Rampvan for the next few days, punishing the driver for his absence, but eventually resumed their comfortable routine.

Two weeks later, Miles was back at the wheel. "Please," he said.

Nicole would not get inside.

"Have you been reading my letters?"

"Why are you doing this?" she said. "Haven't you the human decency to stay away?"

Three weeks later, he was back again.

"What is it you want?" she demanded to know.

"To help you."

It was late. Waiting for a taxi van to be dispatched would mean missing therapy. "Don't you talk to me," she said, as the ramp lowered. "Don't look at me."

Her physical therapy session took place at a local gym. From his stool at the juice bar, Miles saw her through the glass door. Saw her struggling.

"If you want a better therapist," he said, on the way home, "I could get you one."

"Leave me alone."

"Please. Let me do something for you. Anything."

"Stay away. And you can keep your van."

"This van is yours. The driver too."

"You can't buy your way out of this."

"I don't want to. I mean—I don't intend to. I don't expect anything. Please. Just let me help."

Nicole said, "You killed my brother."

Miles remained patient and penitent. Every now and then he drove. One day Nicole returned home to find the bumpy, insurer-provided front-door ramp gone, and a smoother, wider ramp built in its place. Miles watched her stop before it, then roll up to her door without a word.

Another day, the Rampvan broke down. Furious at having to spend time with him, Nicole occupied herself by grocery shopping. "You seem to be getting around better," Miles said.

She was at the deli counter, trying to get the server's attention. "Don't talk to me."

In the cereal aisle, he said, "I was terrified of going to prison."

"Good."

"But not anymore. I just mean that I no longer dread it. It's an opportunity. That's how I look at everything now. Every day, every minute."

A taxi van returned them to West Roxbury. The grocery bags were too heavy to hang on the baßck of her chair, so, for the first time, Miles set foot inside her home. Old and small-windowed, with push-button light switches and iron radiators that hissed. Miles noticed gouge marks on the narrow walls, from her chair. "May I use your bathroom?"

"No."

But she did let him. He saw the seat in the tub, the railing installed over the toilet.

She was sitting in the sunlight of the front windows when he emerged. "You hate me," he said. "And you have every right. I can't change or fix what happened, what I did. I can only act in the here and now. Please, let me be of some service to you."

She refused, but for the moment appeared less certain of him.

He began coming inside some afternoons. Straightening up the place. Changing lightbulbs, fetching things from the basement, clearing out high closet shelves. He was something of a butler. Few words passed between them.

One afternoon, Nicole's doorbell brought Miles face-to-face with Thea, her sister-in-law, the widow of the man Miles had killed. Thea stared at him, the CorningWare pan exploding with a crack as the casserole slipped from her hands.

"What are you doing here?" she shouted, pushing past him to check on Nicole. "What are you *thinking*, Nicole?" Thea dialed 911 as Nicole watched from her chair in the corner of the room. "You're getting a restraining order!"

* * *

But Nicole did not get a restraining order. Miles began bringing her movies, and occasionally watched a few minutes with her. One time they caught themselves laughing at the same thing, and then Nicole became very quiet, and Miles got up and left the room.

He replaced the seat pad and armrests on Nicole's motorized chair. Lifting her back into it was the first time he ever touched her. The frail thinness of her dead legs shocked him. Nicole stared straight ahead the entire time.

Thea never stopped by again. Miles sensed that she and Nicole were no longer talking. Letters from Nicole's lawyers and the district attorney arrived in the mail, but he never looked at them.

Miles was learning how to cook, and began preparing meals for her. He ate in the kitchen, Nicole sitting alone in the dining room, until one night he joined her. Their conversations were generally confined to movies and television shows. At some point she began calling him Miles. The one time he ever brought up her dead brother, he received a quiet yet harsh rebuke. "Never speak Greg's name to me again," Nicole said, shaking. "Not out of your mouth. Never."

He never again did. A few days later they were back on speaking terms.

Together they attended the driver's wife's funeral. Nicole wept at the interment, and Miles did too. At one point he rested his hand upon her shoulder, and she reached up and touched his fingers. Then both hands fell away.

She agreed to let him take her to a small Italian restaurant on the way home. He ordered a soft drink with his meal, explaining how he had not tasted a drop of alcohol since that day. "You do seem to have changed," she said.

"All due to you. For allowing me the opportunity. And by your example."

"My example?"

"Moving on. Facing such adversity and making yourself into something new. And by allowing me to serve you. It gives my life some meaning."

It was late when they arrived home, the latest they had been together. Nicole was exhausted, and Miles removed her shoes so she wouldn't have to, then bid her good night.

The trial date, after two protracted delays, was set to begin in five weeks.

Nicole grew more and more nervous, and Miles sought to reassure her. "All you have to do is tell them what happened that night."

"I can never forgive you," she told him later.

He said, "I wouldn't let you if you tried."

"But it's no secret. I've come to rely on you. I don't know what I'll do after. It will be lonely around here."

He assured her that he felt the same. Then, with just two weeks until the trial, and still so much unsaid between them, Miles broke down one night at dinner. "I have a terrible confession to make. All this—at first—was my father's lawyer's suggestion."

"All what?"

"The Rampvan. The letters. But you must believe me that, over time, everything has changed."

"What suggestion?" she said.

"It's something called the 'Marriage Privilege.' Massachusetts law exempts a person from testifying against his or her spouse, even about events that occurred prior to their marriage. He told me it was my only chance to stay free. The man is a crook—they're all crooks, my father included. Scoundrels and thieves. But I have no fear of prison now. It is only right that I should atone. As I have tried to do here, in serving you." Nicole remained still as Miles went on. "This is very awkward, what I am saying. But I can't imagine leaving you now. I don't exist anywhere else, except here, in this house. With you. If it was just me, I wouldn't care about prison. I'd welcome it. But . . . what about you?"

After some time, Nicole said, "Marriage?"

"I could provide for you. At the very least. My father's money, my place in his company. I could build us a bigger house. All the special things you need. Of course, I would never expect you to love me. But there are reasons to marry beyond love—don't you think?"

She stared, thunderstruck.

"I know," he said. "And it would be so awkward for you, what others would think. My fate is entirely in your hands— as it should be, as it has been ever since that terrible night. It is for you to decide. What is best and right for you—and you alone."

The case was dismissed with a single crack of the gavel. "A terrible violation of ordinary moral decency," decreed the judge. But Nicole just sat there, unmoved.

Bailiffs held Thea back as she fought to get to the defense table, swearing wildly at Miles. Her cursing faded to anguished sobs as Miles wheeled Nicole away through a side door. They sat alone together in a clerk's room, holding hands, not saying anything, waiting for the Rampvan to pull around to the rear exit so they could avoid the media.

Miles began to feel that a great weight had been lifted.

Fellowes watched Miles Bard Sr. read about his son in the newspaper, while the genuine article sat before his desk.

The father said, "I don't know whether to congratulate you or spit on you."

"No prenup," Fellowes reminded Bard Sr. "You're exposed here. Miles's shares in the company, the personal family assets in his name. A divorce will be costly, much more so than a Rampvan and some home improvements." He looked at the son sitting deeply in the dimpled leather chair. "How long are you willing to play this out?"

"Six months," said young Miles. "Then I'll get the marriage annulled. She's paralyzed from the waist down, right? And all the charges have been summarily dismissed." On Fellowes's look, he said, "She can keep the house."

The newspaper rustled as it was folded and set aside. "If only you'd applied yourself to the company with such ruthless determination," said Bard Sr. "But that doesn't hold your interest, does it? The legitimate world."

The old man had come late to fatherhood, building a corporation instead of raising a son, and this was the result. Someone he did not know; a creature with half his genes and none of his respect. A creature who frightened him. And to whom he could never say *No* again.

Fellowes watched Miles cross to the mirror-backed bar. "Should you?" said Fellowes.

Miles toasted himself with a glass of bourbon. "I earned this."

For the first few days, everything was the same between them. It was decided that Miles would sleep at his father's while the

Dover house remodeling continued. Nicole began to notice that his afternoon errands were taking longer. One Friday evening he came in muttering to himself and fell asleep on her sofa.

Dinners together dropped off. Miles cooked less and ordered takeout more. He didn't always stay and keep her company. On some days, there was no dinner at all.

He chauffeured her to her appointments, but was not always there waiting when she finished. "Where were you?" she would ask, when he returned.

"Nowhere," he would answer, with an empty smile.

Her home grew shabby as Miles let his cleaning duties slide. Nicole did most of the packing for the move.

"You've changed," she told him, confronting him one rainy afternoon. "Do you think I don't know you're drinking again?"

Miles bared a knife-blade smile. Nicole could see, behind his eyes, every hateful thing he wanted to say to her. He went out, staying away for days.

When he returned, he pretended nothing had happened. He expected relief from her, maybe even forgiveness, but Nicole did not crumble. Instead, she watched him all the time. Judging him. He feigned indifference, but his discomfort was evident. Her gaze haunted him.

Moving day was a joyless affair. Miles spent much of it talking on his phone to people Nicole had never met. The ride from West Roxbury to Dover passed in silence, and she felt herself crossing a line that she could never cross back over. An onlooker might have thought they were downgrading from a fully accessible three-bedroom showplace to an underfurnished rental, rather than the other way around.

Inside her new home, Nicole rode the brass-gated lift to

the second floor. She rolled along the wide and silent hallway into the master bedroom suite, where her steel-framed hospital bed looked small.

Had Miles looked in on her that first evening, he would have seen that the only item Nicole had unpacked was a framed photograph of herself and Greg, the twins laughing and dancing at Greg's wedding. Instead, he retired directly to the bed in the guest room.

Miles awoke to find his wrists bound behind his back. He tried to stand, but a cord around his neck tethered him to the headboard.

The lamps came on brightly inside the newly painted room. Miles squinted and blinked at the intruder. She wore a black sweatsuit and pale latex gloves, her hair tucked up inside a knit cap.

Thea, the widow. A small silver revolver trembled in her hand.

"Nicole!" Miles called out, when he could dislodge the word from his throat.

Thea's jaw quivered as she pulled a photograph from her pocket and showed it to Miles from the foot of the bed. Her wedding photo.

Thea told him about her life with Greg. How they met, what his hobbies were, his favorite movies, sports, foods. She took Miles through their wedding day, from breakfast with her parents to the farewell dance. She told him all about Bermuda, what they did each hour of their honeymoon. And the last time she saw Greg, kissing him goodbye that afternoon in the kitchen of their Somerville apartment. She swiped angry tears on her sleeve at the end, the revolver trembling all the more.

Miles saw that she was working herself up into a killing.

"You'll never get away with this!" he cried, through the choking neck cord. "Even if you kill us both!"

Thea said, "You haven't figured it out by now?"

Tires whispered over carpet as Nicole rolled in through the wide door. She wore a long, sheer white nightgown, barefoot and delicate-looking in the chair, even lovely.

Thea never broke aim on Miles. "Nine months ago, I bought this gun. Never fired it. Reported it stolen in a break-in two months later. I have an alibi for tonight, not foolproof, but good enough. These gloves hide my fingerprints, the hat keeps in my hair. Leaving only Nicole as a witness. She will tell the police the truth of what she sees here tonight. Because we want your father to know who will be running Bard Industries alongside him from now on. And who will inherit everything after he is gone. The same two women who avenged their own losses by murdering his degenerate son."

"Inherit everything . . . ?" The cord was too tight.

"'There are reasons to marry beyond love,'" said Nicole, sitting ghostlike in the chair. "Your own words, Miles. Couldn't one of those reasons be revenge?"

Thea said, "Without any proof that I was ever inside this house, my criminal conviction will hang on one thing. Nicole's eyewitness testimony in a court of law. Which she will be exempted from giving." The revolver stopped trembling as Thea aimed it at Miles's heart. "You got away with murder. Why can't we?"

"You see, Miles," explained Nicole, "Thea and I, we are going to be married."

NIGHT-SIDE

BY JOYCE CAROL OATES

Quincy

(Originally published in 1977)

To Gloria Whelan

> *6 February 1887. Quincy, Massachusetts. Montague House.*

Disturbing experience at Mrs. A——'s home yesterday evening. Few theatrics—comfortable though rather pathetically shabby surroundings—an only mildly sinister atmosphere (especially in contrast to the Walpurgis Night presented by that shameless charlatan in Portsmouth: the Dwarf Eustace who presumed to introduce me to Swedenborg himself, under the erroneous impression that I am a member of the Church of the New Jerusalem—*I!*). Nevertheless I came away disturbed, and my conversation with Dr. Moore afterward, at dinner, though dispassionate and even, at times, a bit flippant, did not settle my mind. Perry Moore is of course a hearty materialist, an Aristotelian-Spencerian with a love of good food and drink, and an appreciation of the more nonsensical vagaries of life; when in his company I tend to support that general view, as I do at the University as well—for there is a terrific pull in my nature toward the gregarious that I cannot resist. (That I do not wish to resist.) Once I am alone with my thoughts, however, I am accursed with doubts about my own position and nothing seems more precarious than my intellectual "convictions."

The more hardened members of our Society, like Perry Moore, are apt to put the issue bluntly: Is Mrs. A—— of Quincy a conscious or unconscious fraud? The conscious frauds are relatively easy to deal with; once discovered, they prefer to erase themselves from further consideration. The unconscious frauds are not, in a sense, "frauds" at all. It would certainly be difficult to prove criminal intention. Mrs. A——, for instance, does not accept money or gifts so far as we have been able to determine, and both Perry Moore and I noted her courteous but firm refusal of the Judge's offer to send her and her husband (presumably ailing?) on holiday to England in the spring. She is a mild, self-effacing, rather stocky woman in her mid-fifties who wears her hair parted in the center, like several of my maiden aunts, and whose sole item of adornment was an old-fashioned cameo brooch; her black dress had the appearance of having been homemade, though it was attractive enough, and freshly ironed. According to the Society's records she has been a practicing medium now for six years. Yet she lives, still, in an undistinguished section of Quincy, in a neighborhood of modest frame dwellings. The A——s' house is in fairly good condition, especially considering the damage routinely done by our winters, and the only room we saw, the parlor, is quite ordinary, with overstuffed chairs and the usual cushions and a monstrous horsehair sofa and, of course, the oaken table; the atmosphere would have been so conventional as to have seemed disappointing had not Mrs. A—— made an attempt to brighten it, or perhaps to give it a glamorously occult air, by hanging certain watercolors about the room. (She claims that the watercolors were "done" by one of her contact spirits, a young Iroquois girl who died in the 1770s of smallpox. They are touchingly garish—mandalas and triangles and stylized eyeballs and even a transparent Cosmic Man with Indian-black hair.)

At last night's sitting there were only three persons in addition to Mrs. A——. Judge T—— of the New York State Supreme Court (now retired); Dr. Moore; and I, Jarvis Williams. Dr. Moore and I came out from Cambridge under the aegis of the Society for Psychical Research in order to make a preliminary study of the kind of mediumship Mrs. A—— affects. We did not bring a stenographer along this time though Mrs. A—— indicated her willingness to have the sitting transcribed; she struck me as being rather warmly cooperative, and even interested in our formal procedures, though Perry Moore remarked afterward at dinner that she had struck him as "noticeably reluctant." She was, however, flustered at the start of the séance and for a while it seemed as if we and the Judge might have made the trip for nothing. (She kept waving her plump hands about like an embarrassed hostess, apologizing for the fact that the spirits were evidently in a "perverse uncommunicative mood tonight.")

She did go into trance eventually, however. The four of us were seated about the heavy round table from approximately six fifty p.m. to nine p.m. For nearly forty-five minutes Mrs. A—— made abortive attempts to contact her Chief Communicator and then slipped abruptly into trance (dramatically, in fact: her eyes rolled back in her head in a manner that alarmed me at first), and a personality named Webley appeared. "Webley's" voice appeared to be coming from several directions during the course of the sitting. At all times it was a least three yards from Mrs. A——; despite the semidark of the parlor I believe I could see the woman's mouth and throat clearly enough, and I could not detect any obvious signs of ventriloquism. (Perry Moore, who is more experienced than I in psychical research, and rather more casual about the whole phenomenon, claims he has witnessed feats of ventriloquism that would make poor Mrs. A—— look quite shabby in comparison.) "Webley's" voice was raw, singsong, peculiarly disturbing. At times it was shrill and at other times so faint as to be nearly inaudible. Something brattish about it. Exasperating. "Webley" took care to pronounce his final *g*'s in a self-conscious manner, quite unlike Mrs. A——. (Which could be, of course, a deliberate ploy.)

This Webley is one of Mrs. A——'s most frequent manifesting spirits, though he is not the most reliable. Her Chief Communicator is a Scots patriarch who lived "in the time of Merlin" and who is evidently very wise; unfortunately he did not choose to appear yesterday evening. Instead, Webley presided. He is supposed to have died some seventy-five years ago at the age of nineteen in a house just up the street from the A——s'. He was either a butcher's helper or an apprentice tailor. He died in a fire—or by a "slow dreadful crippling disease"—or beneath a horse's hooves, in a freakish accident; during the course of the sitting he alluded self-pityingly to his death but seemed to have forgotten the exact details. At the very end of the evening he addressed me directly as Dr. Williams of Harvard University, saying that since I had influential friends in Boston I could help him with his career—it turned out he had written hundreds of songs and poems and parables but none had been published; would I please find a publisher for his work? Life had treated him so unfairly. His talent—his genius—had been lost to humanity. I had it within my power to help him, he claimed, was I not *obliged* to help him . . . ? He then sang one of his songs, which sounded to me like an old ballad; many of the words were so shrill as to be unintelligible, but he sang it just the same, repeating the verses in a haphazard order:

This ae nighte, this ae nighte,
   —Every nighte and alle,
Fire and fleet and candle-lighte,
   And Christe receive thy saule.

When thou from hence away art past,
   —Every nighte and alle,
To Whinny-muir thou com'st at last:
   And Christe receive thy saule.

From Brig o' Dread when thou may'st pass,
   —Every nighte and alle,
The whinnes sall prick thee to the bare bane:
   And Christe receive thy saule.

The elderly Judge T—— had come up from New York City in order, as he earnestly put it, to "speak directly to his deceased wife as he was never able to do while she was living"; but Webley treated the old gentleman in a high-handed, cavalier manner, as if the occasion were not at all serious. He kept saying, "Who is there tonight? *Who* is there? Let them introduce themselves again—I don't *like* strangers! I tell you I don't *like* strangers!" Though Mrs. A—— had informed us beforehand that we would witness no physical phenomena, there were, from time to time, glimmerings of light in the darkened room, hardly more than the tiny pulsations of light made by fireflies; and both Perry Moore and I felt the table vibrating beneath our fingers. At about the time when Webley gave way to the spirit of Judge T——'s wife, the temperature in the room seemed to drop suddenly and I remember being gripped by a sensation of panic—but it lasted only an instant and I was soon myself again. (Dr. Moore claimed not to have noticed any drop in temperature and Judge T—— was so rattled after the sitting that it would have been pointless to question him.)

The séance proper was similar to others I have attended. A spirit—or a voice—laid claim to being the late Mrs. T——; this spirit addressed the survivor in a peculiarly intense, urgent manner, so that it was rather embarrassing to be present. Judge T—— was soon weeping. His deeply creased face glistened with tears like a child's.

"Why Darrie! *Darrie!* Don't cry! Oh don't cry!" the spirit said. "No one is dead, Darrie. There is no death. No death! . . . Can you hear me, Darrie? Why are you so frightened? So upset? No need, Darrie, no need! Grandfather and Lucy and I are together here—happy together. Darrie, look up! Be brave, my dear! My poor frightened dear! We never knew each other, did we? My poor dear! My love! . . . I saw you in a great transparent house, a great burning house; poor Darrie, they told me you were ill, you were weak with fever; all the rooms of the house were aflame and the staircase was burnt to cinders, but there were figures walking up and down, Darrie, great numbers of them, and you were among them, dear, stumbling in your fright—so clumsy! Look up, dear, and shade your eyes, and you will see me. Grandfather helped me—did you know? Did I call out his name at the end? My dear, my darling, it all happened so quickly—we never knew each other, did we? Don't be hard on Annie! Don't be cruel! Darrie? Why are you crying?" And gradually the spirit voice grew fainter; or perhaps something went wrong and the channels of communication were no longer clear. There were repetitions, garbled phrases, meaningless queries of "Dear? Dear?" that the Judge's replies did not seem to placate. The spirit spoke of her gravesite, and of a trip to Italy taken many years before, and of a dead or unborn baby, and again of Annie—evidently Judge T——'s daughter; but the jumble of words did not always make sense and it was a great relief when Mrs. A—— suddenly woke from her trance.

Judge T—— rose from the table, greatly agitated. He wanted to call the spirit back; he had not asked her certain crucial questions; he had been overcome by emotion and had found it difficult to speak, to interrupt the spirit's monologue. But Mrs. A—— (who looked shockingly tired) told him the spirit would not return again that night and they must not make any attempt to call it back.

"The other world obeys its own laws," Mrs. A—— said in her small, rather reedy voice.

We left Mrs. A——'s home shortly after nine p.m. I too was exhausted; I had not realized how absorbed I had been in the proceedings.

Judge T—— is also staying at Montague House, but he was too upset after the sitting to join us for dinner. He assured us, though, that the spirit was authentic—the voice had been his wife's, he was certain of it, he would stake his life on it. She had never called him "Darrie" during her lifetime, wasn't it odd that she called him "Darrie" now?—and was so concerned for him, so loving?—and concerned for their daughter as well? He was very moved. He had a great deal to think about. (Yes, he'd had a fever some weeks ago—a severe attack of bronchitis and a fever; in fact, he had not completely recovered.) What was extraordinary about the entire experience was the wisdom revealed: There is no death.

There is no death.

Dr. Moore and I dined heartily on roast crown of lamb, spring potatoes with peas, and buttered cabbage. We were served two kinds of bread—German rye and sour-cream rolls;

the hotel's butter was superb; the wine excellent; the dessert—crepes with cream and toasted almonds—looked marvelous, though I had not any appetite for it. Dr. Moore was ravenously hungry. He talked as he ate, often punctuating his remarks with rich bursts of laughter. It was his opinion, of course, that the medium was a fraud—and not a very skillful fraud, either. In his fifteen years of amateur, intermittent investigations he had encountered far more skillful mediums. Even the notorious Eustace with his levitating tables and hobgoblin chimes and shrieks was cleverer than Mrs. A——; one knew of course that Eustace was a cheat, but one was hard pressed to explain his method. Whereas Mrs. A—— was quite transparent.

Dr. Moore spoke for some time in his amiable, dogmatic way. He ordered brandy for both of us, though it was nearly midnight when we finished our dinner and I was anxious to get to bed. (I hoped to rise early and work on a lecture dealing with Kant's approach to the problem of Free Will, which I would be delivering in a few days.) But Dr. Moore enjoyed talking and seemed to have been invigorated by our experience at Mrs. A——'s.

At the age of forty-three Perry Moore is only four years my senior, but he has the air, in my presence at least, of being considerably older. He is a second cousin of my mother, a very successful physician with a bachelor's flat and office in Louisburg Square; his failure to marry, or his refusal, is one of Boston's perennial mysteries. Everyone agrees that he is learned, witty, charming, and extraordinarily intelligent. Striking rather than conventionally handsome, with a dark, lustrous beard and darkly bright eyes, he is an excellent amateur violinist, an enthusiastic sailor, and a lover of literature—his favorite writers are Fielding, Shakespeare, Horace, and Dante. He is, of course, the perfect investigator in spiritualist matters since he is detached from the phenomena he observes and yet he is indefatigably curious; he has a positive love, a mania, for facts. Like the true scientist he seeks facts that, assembled, may possibly give rise to hypotheses: he does not set out with a hypothesis in mind, like a sort of basket into which certain facts may be tossed, helter-skelter, while others are conveniently ignored. In all things he is an empiricist who accepts nothing on faith.

"If the woman is a fraud, then," I say hesitantly, "you believe she is a self-deluded fraud? And her spirits' information is gained by means of telepathy?"

"Telepathy indeed. There can be no other explanation," Dr. Moore says emphatically. "By some means not yet known to science . . . by some uncanny means she suppresses her conscious personality . . . and thereby releases other, secondary personalities that have the power of seizing upon others' thoughts and memories. It's done in a way not understood by science at the present time. But it will be understood eventually. Our investigations into the unconscious powers of the human mind are just beginning; we're on the threshold, really, of a new era."

"So she simply picks out of her clients' minds whatever they want to hear," I say slowly. "And from time to time she can even tease them a little—insult them, even: she can unloose a creature like that obnoxious Webley upon a person like Judge T—— without fear of being discovered. Telepathy. . . . Yes, that would explain a great deal. Very nearly everything we witnessed tonight."

"*Everything*, I should say," Dr. Moore says.

In the coach returning to Cambridge I set aside Kant and my lecture notes and read Sir Thomas Browne: *Light that makes*

all things seen, makes some things invisible. The greatest mystery of
Religion is expressed by adumbration.   •

19 March 1887. Cambridge. 11 p.m.

Walked ten miles this evening; must clear cobwebs from mind.

Unhealthy atmosphere. Claustrophobic. Last night's sitting in Quincy—a most unpleasant experience.

(Did not tell my wife what happened. Why is she so curious about the Spirit World?—about Perry Moore?)

My body craves more violent physical activity. In the summer, thank God, I will be able to swim in the ocean: the most
strenuous and challenging of exercises.

Jotting down notes re the Quincy experience:

I. Fraud

Mrs. A——, possibly with accomplices, conspires
to deceive: she does research into her clients' lives
beforehand, possibly bribes servants. She is either
a very skillful ventriloquist or works with someone who is. (Husband? Son? The husband is a
retired cabinet-maker said to be in poor health;
possibly consumptive. The son, married, lives in
Waterbury.)

Her stated wish to avoid publicity and her de-
clining of payment may simply be ploys; she may
intend to make a great deal of money at some future time.

(Possibility of blackmail?—might be likely in
cases similar to Perry Moore's.)

II. Non-fraud

Naturalistic

1. Telepathy. She reads minds of clients.
2. "Multiple personality" of medium. Aspects of her own buried psyche are released as her conscious personality is suppressed. These secondary beings are in mysterious rapport with the "secondary" personalities of the clients.

Spiritualistic
1. The controls are genuine communicators, intermediaries between our world and the world of the dead. These spirits give way to other spirits, who then speak through the medium; or
2. These spirits *influence* the medium, who relays their messages using her own vocabulary. Their personalities are then filtered through and limited by hers.
3. The spirits are not those of the deceased; they are perverse, willful spirits. (Perhaps demons? But there are no demons.)

III. Alternative hypothesis
Madness: the medium is mad, the clients are mad, even the detached, rationalist investigators are mad.

Yesterday evening at Mrs. A——'s home, the second sitting Perry Moore and I observed together, along with Miss Bradley, a stenographer from the Society, and two legitimate clients— a Brookline widow, Mrs. P——, and her daughter Clara, a handsome young woman in her early twenties. Mrs. A—— exactly as she appeared to us in February; possibly a little stouter. Wore black dress and cameo brooch. Served Lapsang tea, tiny sandwiches, and biscuits when we arrived shortly after six p.m. Seemed quite friendly to Perry, Miss Bradley, and me; fussed over us, like any hostess; chattered a bit about the cold spell. Mrs. P—— and her daughter arrived at six thirty and the sitting began shortly thereafter.

Jarring from the very first. A babble of spirit voices. Mrs. A—— in trance, head flung back, mouth gaping, eyes rolled upward. Queer. Unnerving. I glanced at Dr. Moore but he seemed unperturbed, as always. The widow and her daughter, however, looked as frightened as I felt.

Why are we here, sitting around this table?

What do we believe we will discover?

What are the risks we face . . . ?

"Webley" appeared and disappeared in a matter of minutes. His shrill, raw, aggrieved voice was supplanted by that of a creature of indeterminate sex who babbled in Gaelic. This creature in turn was supplanted by a hoarse German, a man who identified himself as Felix; he spoke a curiously ungrammatical German. For some minutes he and two or three other spirits quarreled. (Each declared himself Mrs. A——'s Chief Communicator for the evening.) Small lights flickered in the semidark of the parlor and the table quivered beneath my fingers and I felt, or believed I felt, something brushing against me, touching the back of my head. I shuddered violently but regained my composure at once. An unidentified voice proclaimed in English that the Spirit of our Age was Mars: there would be a catastrophic war shortly and most of the world's population would be destroyed. All atheists would be destroyed. Mrs. A—— shook her head from side to side as if trying to wake. Webley appeared, crying "Hello? Hello? I can't see anyone! Who is there? Who has called me?" but was again supplanted by another spirit who shouted long strings of words in a foreign language. [Note: I discovered a few days later that this language was Walachian, a Romanian dialect. Of course Mrs. A——, whose ancestors are English, could not possibly have known Walachian, and I rather doubt that the woman has even heard of the Walachian people.]

The sitting continued in this chaotic way for some minutes. Mrs. P—— must have been quite disappointed, since she had wanted to be put in contact with her deceased husband. (She needed advice on whether or not to sell certain pieces of property.) Spirits babbled freely in English, German, Gaelic, French, even in Latin, and at one point Dr. Moore queried a spirit in Greek, but the spirit retreated at once as if not equal to Dr. Moore's wit. The atmosphere was alarming but at the same time rather manic; almost jocular. I found myself suppressing laughter. Something touched the back of my head and I shivered violently and broke into perspiration, but the experience was not altogether unpleasant; it would be very difficult for me to characterize it.

And then—

And then, suddenly, everything changed. There was complete calm. A spirit voice spoke gently out of a corner of the room, addressing Perry Moore by his first name in a slow, tentative, groping way. "Perry? Perry . . . ?" Dr. Moore jerked about in his seat. He was astonished; I could see by his expression that the voice belonged to someone he knew.

"Perry . . . ? This is Brandon. I've waited so long for you, Perry, how could you be so selfish? I forgave you. Long ago. You couldn't help your cruelty and I couldn't help my innocence. Perry? My glasses have been broken—I can't see. I've been afraid for so long, Perry, please have mercy on me! I can't bear it any longer. I didn't *know* what it would be like. There are crowds of people here, but we can't see one another, we don't know one another, we're strangers, there is a universe of strangers—I can't see anyone clearly—I've been lost for twenty years, Perry, I've been waiting for you for twenty years! You don't dare turn away again, Perry! Not again! Not after so long!"

Dr. Moore stumbled to his feet, knocking his chair aside. "No— Is it— I don't believe—"

"Perry? Perry? Don't abandon me again, Perry! Not again!"

"What is this?" Dr. Moore cried.

He was on his feet now; Mrs. A—— woke from her trance with a groan. The women from Brookline were very upset and I must admit that I was in a mild state of terror, my shirt and my underclothes drenched with perspiration.

The sitting was over. It was only seven thirty.

"Brandon?" Dr. Moore cried. "Wait. Where are—? Brandon? Can you hear me? Where are you? Why did you do it, Brandon? Wait! Don't leave! Can't anyone call him back— Can't anyone help me—"

Mrs. A—— rose unsteadily. She tried to take Dr. Moore's hands in hers but he was too agitated.

"I heard only the very last words," she said. "They're always that way—so confused, so broken—the poor things— Oh, what a pity! It wasn't murder, was it? Not murder! Suicide—? I believe suicide is even worse for them! The poor broken things, they wake in the other world and are utterly, utterly lost—they have no guides, you see—no help in crossing over— They are completely alone for eternity—"

"Can't you call him back?" Dr. Moore asked wildly. He was peering into a corner of the parlor, slightly stooped, his face distorted as if he were staring into the sun. "Can't someone help me? . . . Brandon? Are you here? Are you here somewhere? For God's sake, can't someone help!"

"Dr. Moore, please, the spirits are gone—the sitting is over for tonight—"

"You foolish old woman, leave me alone! Can't you see I—I—I must not lose him— Call him back, will you? I insist! I insist!"

"Dr. Moore, please— You mustn't shout—"

"I said call him back! At once! *Call him back!*"

Then he burst into tears. He stumbled against the table and hid his face in his hands and wept like a child; he wept as if his heart had been broken.

And so today I have been reliving the séance. Taking notes, trying to determine what happened. A brisk windy walk of ten miles. Head buzzing with ideas. Fraud? Deceit? Telepathy? Madness?

What a spectacle! Dr. Perry Moore calling after a spirit, begging it to return—and then crying, afterward, in front of four astonished witnesses.

Dr. Perry Moore of all people.

My dilemma: whether I should report last night's incident to Dr. Rowe, the president of the Society, or whether I should say nothing about it and request that Miss Bradley say nothing. It would be tragic if Perry's professional reputation were to be damaged by a single evening's misadventure; and before long all of Boston would be talking.

In his present state, however, he is likely to tell everyone about it himself.

At Montague House the poor man was unable to sleep. He would have kept me up all night had I had the stamina to endure his excitement.

There *are* spirits! There have always been spirits!

His entire life up to the present time has been misspent!

And of course, most important of all—there is no death!

He paced about my hotel room, pulling at his beard nervously. At times there were tears in his eyes. He seemed to want a response of some kind from me but whenever I started to speak he interrupted; he was not really listening.

"Now at last I know. I can't undo my knowledge," he said in a queer hoarse voice. "Amazing, isn't it, after so many years . . . so many wasted years . . . Ignorance has been my lot, darkness . . . and a hideous complacency. My God, when I consider my deluded smugness! I am so ashamed, so ashamed. All along people like Mrs. A—— have been in contact with a world of such power . . . and people like me have been toiling in ignorance, accumulating material achievements, expending our energies in idiotic transient things . . . But all that is changed now. Now I know. I *know*. There is no death, as the Spiritualists have always told us."

"But, Perry, don't you think— Isn't it possible that—"

"I *know*," he said quietly. "It's as clear to me as if I had crossed over into that other world myself. Poor Brandon! He's no older now than he was *then*. The poor boy, the poor tragic soul! To think that he's still living after so many years . . . Extraordinary . . . It makes my head spin," he said slowly. For a moment he stood without speaking. He pulled at his beard, then absently touched his lips with his fingers, then wiped at his eyes. He seemed to have forgotten me. When he spoke again his voice was hollow, rather ghastly. He sounded drugged. "I . . . I had been thinking of him as . . . as dead, you know. As dead. Twenty years. Dead. And now, tonight, to be forced to realize that . . . that he isn't dead after all . . . It was laudanum he took. I found him. His rooms on the third floor of Weld Hall. I found him, I had no real idea, none at all, not until I read the note . . . and of course I destroyed the note . . .

I had to, you see: for his sake. For his sake more than mine. It was because he realized there could be no . . . no hope . . . Yet he called me cruel! You heard him, Jarvis, didn't you? Cruel! I suppose I was. Was I? I don't know what to think. I must talk with him again. I . . . I don't know what to . . . what to think. I . . ."

"You look awfully tired, Perry. It might be a good idea to go to bed," I said weakly.

". . . recognized his voice at once. Oh at once: no doubt. None. What a revelation! And my life so misspent . . . Treating people's *bodies*. Absurd. I know now that nothing matters except that other world . . . nothing matters except our dead, our beloved dead . . . who are *not dead*. What a colossal revelation . . . ! Why, it will change the entire course of history. It will alter men's minds throughout the world. You were there, Jarvis, so you understand. You were a witness . . ."

"But—"

"You'll bear witness to the truth of what I am saying?"

He stared at me, smiling. His eyes were bright and threaded with blood.

I tried to explain to him as courteously and sympathetically as possible that his experience at Mrs. A——'s was not substantially different from the experiences many people have had at séances. "And always in the past psychical researchers have taken the position—"

"You were *there*," he said angrily. "You heard Brandon's voice as clearly as I did. Don't deny it!"

"—have taken the position that—that the phenomenon can be partly explained by the telepathic powers of the medium—"

"That was Brandon's *voice*," Perry said. "I felt his presence, I tell you! *His*. Mrs. A—— had nothing to do with it—nothing at all. I feel as if . . . as if I could call Brandon back by myself . . . I feel his presence even now. Close about me. He isn't dead, you see; no one is dead, there's a universe of . . . of people who are not dead . . . Parents, grandparents, sisters, brothers, everyone . . . everyone . . . . How can you deny, Jarvis, the evidence of your own senses? You were there with me tonight and you know as well as I do . . ."

"Perry, I don't *know*. I did hear a voice, yes, but we've heard voices before at other sittings, haven't we? There are always voices. There are always 'spirits.' The Society has taken the position that the spirits could be real, of course, but that there are other hypotheses that are perhaps more likely—"

"Other hypotheses indeed!" Perry said irritably. "You're like a man with his eyes shut tight who refuses to open them out of sheer cowardice. Like the cardinals refusing to look through Galileo's telescope! And you have pretensions of being a man of learning, of science . . . Why, we've got to destroy all the records we've made so far; they're a slander on the world of the spirits. Thank God we didn't file a report yet on Mrs. A——! It would be so embarrassing to be forced to call it back . . ."

"Perry, please. Don't be angry. I want only to remind you of the fact that we've been present at other sittings, haven't we?—and we've witnessed others responding emotionally to certain phenomena. Judge T——, for instance. He was convinced he'd spoken with his wife. But you must remember, don't you, that you and I were not at all convinced . . . ? It seemed to us more likely that Mrs. A—— is able, through extrasensory powers we don't quite understand, to read the minds of her clients, and then to project certain voices out into the room so that it sounds as if they are coming from other people . . . You even said, Perry, that she wasn't a very skillful ventriloquist. You said—"

"What does it matter what, in my ignorance, I said?" he cried. "Isn't it enough that I've been humiliated? That my entire life has been turned about? Must you insult me as well—sitting there so smugly and insulting *me*? I think I can make claim to being someone whom you might respect."

And so I assured him that I did respect him. And he walked about the room, wiping at his eyes, greatly agitated. He spoke again of his friend, Brandon Gould, and of his own ignorance, and of the important mission we must undertake to inform men and women of the true state of affairs. I tried to talk with him, to reason with him, but it was hopeless. He scarcely listened to me.

". . . must inform the world . . . crucial truth . . . There is no death, you see. Never was. Changes civilization, changes the course of history. Jarvis?" he said groggily. "You see? *There is no death.*"

25 March 1887. Cambridge.

Disquieting rumors re Perry Moore. Heard today at the University that one of Dr. Moore's patients (a brother-in-law of Dean Barker) was extremely offended by his behavior during a consultation last week. Talk of his having been drunk—which I find incredible. If the poor man appeared to be excitable and not his customary self, it was not because he was *drunk*, surely.

Another far-fetched tale told me by my wife, who heard it from her sister Maude: Perry Moore went to church (St. Aidan's Episcopal Church on Mount Street) for the first time in a decade, sat alone, began muttering and laughing during the sermon, and finally got to his feet and walked out, creating quite a stir. *What delusions! What delusions!*—he was said to have muttered.

I fear for the poor man's sanity.

31 March 1887. Cambridge. 4 a.m.

Sleepless night. Dreamed of swimming . . . swimming in the ocean . . . enjoying myself as usual when suddenly the water turns thick . . . turns to mud. Hideous! Indescribably awful. I was swimming nude in the ocean, by moonlight, I believe, ecstatically happy, entirely alone, when the water turned to mud. . . . Vile, disgusting mud; faintly warm; sucking at my body. Legs, thighs, torso, arms. Horrible. Woke in terror. Drenched with perspiration: pajamas wet. One of the most frightening nightmares of my adulthood.

A message from Perry Moore came yesterday just before dinner. Would I like to join him in visiting Mrs. A—— sometime soon, in early April perhaps, on a noninvestigative basis . . . ? He is uncertain now of the morality of our "investigating" Mrs. A—— or any other medium.

4 April 1887. Cambridge.

Spent the afternoon from two to five at William James's home on Irving Street, talking with Professor James of the inexplicable phenomenon of consciousness. He is robust as always, rather irreverent, supremely confident in a way I find enviable; rather like Perry Moore before his conversion. (Extraordinary eyes—so piercing, quick, playful; a graying beard liberally threaded with white; close-cropped graying hair; a large, curving, impressive forehead; a manner intelligent and graceful and at the same time rough-edged, as if he anticipates or perhaps even hopes for recalcitration in his listeners.) We both find conclusive the ideas set forth in Binét's *Alterations of Personality* . . . unsettling as these ideas may be to the rationalist position. James speaks of a *peculiarity* in the constitution of human nature: that is, the fact that we inhabit not only our ego-consciousness but a wide field of psychological experience (most clearly represented by the phenomenon of memory, which no one can adequately explain) over which we have no control whatsoever. In fact, we are not generally aware of this field of consciousness.

We inhabit a lighted sphere, then; and about us is a vast penumbra of memories, reflections, feelings, and stray uncoordinated thoughts that "belong" to us theoretically, but that do not seem to be part of our conscious identity. (I was too timid to ask Professor James whether it might be the case that we do not inevitably own these aspects of the personality—that such phenomena belong as much to the objective world as to our subjective selves.) It is quite possible that there is an element of some indeterminate kind: oceanic, timeless, and living, against which the individual being constructs temporary barriers as part of an ongoing process of unique, particularized survival; like the ocean itself, which appears to separate islands that are in fact not "islands" at all, but aspects of the earth firmly joined together below the surface of the water. Our lives, then, resemble these islands . . . All this is no more than a possibility, Professor James and I agreed.

James is acquainted, of course, with Perry Moore. But he declined to speak on the subject of the poor man's increasingly eccentric behavior when I alluded to it. (It may be that he knows even more about the situation than I do—he enjoys a multitude of acquaintances in Cambridge and Boston.) I brought our conversation round several times to the possibility of the *naturalness* of the conversion experience in terms of the individual's evolution of self, no matter how his family, his colleagues, and society in general viewed it, and Professor James appeared to agree; at least he did not emphatically disagree. He maintains a healthy skepticism, of course, regarding Spiritualist claims, and all evangelical and enthusiastic religious movements, though he is, at the same time, a highly articulate foe of the "rationalist" position and he believes that psychical research of the kind some of us are attempting will eventually unearth riches—revealing aspects of the human psyche otherwise closed to our scrutiny.

"The fearful thing," James said, "is that we are at all times vulnerable to incursions from the 'other side' of the personality . . . We cannot determine the nature of the total personality simply because much of it, perhaps most, is hidden from us . . . When we are invaded, then, we are overwhelmed and surrender immediately. Emotionally charged intuitions, hunches, guesses, even ideas may be the least aggressive of these incursions; but there are visual and auditory hallucinations, and forms of automatic behavior not controlled by the conscious mind . . . Ah, you're thinking I am simply describing insanity?"

I stared at him, quite surprised.

"No. Not at all. Not at all," I said at once.

Reading through my grandfather's journals, begun in East Anglia many years before my birth. Another world then. Another language, now lost to us. *Man is sinful by nature. God's justice takes precedence over His mercy.* The dogma of Original Sin: something brutish about the innocence of that belief. And yet consoling . . .

Fearful of sleep since my dreams are so troubled now. The voices of impudent spirits (Immanuel Kant himself come to chide me for having made too much of his categories—!), stray shouts and whispers I cannot decipher, the faces of my own beloved dead hovering near, like carnival masks, insubstantial and possibly fraudulent. Impatient with my wife, who questions me too closely on these personal matters; annoyed from time to time, in the evenings especially, by the silliness of the children. (The eldest is twelve now and should know better.) Dreading to receive another lengthy letter—sermon, really—from Perry Moore re his "new position," and yet perversely hoping one will come soon.

I must know.

(Must know *what . . . ?*)

I must know.

        10 April 1887. Boston. St. Aidan's Episcopal Church.
Funeral service this morning for Perry Moore; dead at forty-three.

        17 April 1887. Seven Hills, New Hampshire.
A weekend retreat. No talk. No need to think.

Visiting with a former associate, author of numerous books. Cartesian specialist. Elderly. Partly deaf. Extraordinarily kind to me. (Did not ask about the Department or about my work.) Intensely interested in animal behavior now, in observation primarily; fascinated with the phenomenon of hibernation.

He leaves me alone for hours. He sees something in my face I cannot see myself.

The old consolations of a cruel but just God: ludicrous today.

In the nineteenth century we live free of God. We live in the illusion of freedom-of-God.

Dozing off in the guest room of this old farmhouse and then waking abruptly. *Is someone here? Is someone here?* My voice queer, hushed, childlike. *Please: is someone here?*

Silence.

* * *

Query: Is the penumbra outside consciousness all that was ever meant by "God"?

Query: Is inevitability all that was ever meant by "God"?

God—the body of fate we inhabit, then; no more and no less.

God pulled Perry down into the body of fate: into Himself. (Or Itself.) As Professor James might say, Dr. Moore was "vulnerable" to an assault from the other side.

At any rate he is dead. They buried him last Saturday.

25 April 1887. Cambridge.

Shelves of books. The sanctity of books. Kant, Plato, Schopenhauer, Descartes, Hume, Hegel, Spinoza. The others. All. Nietzsche, Spencer, Leibniz (on whom I did a torturous Master's thesis). Plotinus. Swedenborg. *The Transactions of the American Society for Psychical Research.* Voltaire. Locke. Rousseau. And Berkeley: the good Bishop adrift in a dream.

An etching by Halbrecht above my desk, The Thames 1801. Water too black. Inky-black. Thick with mud . . . ? Filthy water in any case.

Perry's essay, forty-five scribbled pages. "The Challenge of the Future." Given to me several weeks ago by Dr. Rowe, who feared rejecting it for the *Transactions* but could not, of course, accept it. I can read only a few pages at a time, then push it aside, too moved to continue. Frightened also.

The man had gone insane.

Died insane.

Personality broken: broken bits of intellect.

His argument passionate and disjointed, with no pretense of objectivity. Where some weeks ago he had taken the stand that it was immoral to investigate the Spirit World, now he took the stand that it was imperative we do so. We are on the brink of a new age . . . new knowledge of the universe . . . comparable to the stormy transitional period between the Ptolemaic and the Copernican theories of the universe . . . More experiments required. Money. Donations. Subsidies by private institutions. All psychological research must be channeled into a systematic study of the Spirit World and the ways by which we can communicate with that world. Mediums like Mrs. A——— must be brought to centers of learning like Harvard and treated with the respect their genius deserves. Their value to civilization is, after all, beyond estimation. They must be rescued from arduous and routine lives where their genius is drained off into vulgar pursuits . . . they must be rescued from a clientele that is mainly concerned with being put into contact with deceased relatives for utterly trivial, self-serving reasons. Men of learning must realize the gravity of the situation. Otherwise we will fail, we will stagger beneath the burden, we will be defeated, ignobly, and it will remain for the twentieth century to discover the existence of the Spirit Universe that surrounds the Material Universe, and to determine the exact ways by which one world is related to another.

Perry Moore died of a stroke on the eighth of April; died instantaneously on the steps of the Bedford Club shortly after two p.m. Passersby saw a very excited, red-faced gentleman with an open collar push his way through a small gathering at the top of the steps—and then suddenly fall, as if shot down.

In death he looked like quite another person: his features sharp, the nose especially pointed. Hardly the handsome Perry Moore everyone had known.

He had come to a meeting of the Society, though it was suggested by Dr. Rowe and by others (including myself) that he stay away. Of course he came to argue. To present his "new position." To insult the other members. (He was contemptuous of a rather poorly organized paper on the medium Miss E—— of Salem, a young woman who works with objects like rings, articles of clothing, locks of hair, et cetera; and quite angry with the evidence presented by a young geologist that would seem to discredit, once and for all, the claims of Eustace of Portsmouth. He interrupted a third paper, calling the reader a "bigot" and an "ignorant fool.")

Fortunately the incident did not find its way into any of the papers. The press, misunderstanding (deliberately and maliciously) the Society's attitude toward Spiritualism, delights in ridiculing our efforts.

There were respectful obituaries. A fine eulogy prepared by Reverend Tyler of St. Aidan's. Other tributes. A *tragic loss . . . Mourned by all who knew him . . .* (I stammered and could not speak. I cannot speak of him, of it, even now. Am I mourning, am I aggrieved? Or merely shocked? Terrified?) Relatives and friends and associates glossed over his behavior these past few months and settled upon an earlier Perry Moore, eminently sane, a distinguished physician and man of letters. I did not disagree, I merely acquiesced; I could not make any claim to have really known the man.

And so he has died, and so he is dead . . .

Shortly after the funeral I went away to New Hampshire for a few days. But I can barely remember that period of time now. I sleep poorly, I yearn for summer, for a drastic change of climate, of scene. It was unwise for me to take up the responsibility of psychical research, fascinated though I am by it; my classes and lectures at the University demand most of my energy.

How quickly he died, and so young: so relatively young.

No history of high blood pressure, it is said.

At the end he was arguing with everyone, however. His personality had completely changed. He was rude, impetuous, even rather profane; even poorly groomed. (Rising to challenge the first of the papers, he revealed a shirtfront that appeared to be stained.) Some claimed he had been drinking all along, for years. Was it possible . . . ? (He had clearly enjoyed the wine and brandy in Quincy that evening, but I would not have said he was intemperate.) Rumors, fanciful tales, outright lies, slander . . . It is painful, the vulnerability death brings.

Bigots, he called us. Ignorant fools. Unbelievers—atheists—traitors to the Spirit World—heretics. Heretics! I believe he looked directly at me as he pushed his way out of the meeting room: his eyes glaring, his face dangerously flushed, no recognition in his stare.

After his death, it is said, books continue to arrive at his home from England and Europe. He spent a small fortune on obscure, out-of-print volumes—commentaries on the Kabbala, on Plotinus, medieval alchemical texts, books on astrology, witchcraft, the metaphysics of death. Occult cosmologies. Egyptian, Indian, and Chinese "wisdom." Blake, Swedenborg, Cozad. *The Tibetan Book of the Dead*. Datsky's *Lunar Mysteries*. His estate is in chaos because he left not one but several wills, the most recent made out only a day before his death, merely a few lines scribbled on scrap paper, without witnesses. The family will contest, of course. Since in this will he left his money and property to an obscure woman living in Quincy, Massachusetts, and since he was obviously not in his right mind at the time, they would be foolish indeed not to contest.

Days have passed since his sudden death. Days continue to pass. At times I am seized by a sort of quick, cold panic; at other times I am inclined to think the entire situation has been exaggerated. In one mood I vow to myself that I will never again pursue psychical research because it is simply too dangerous. In another mood I vow I will never again pursue it because it is a waste of time and my own work, my own career, must come first.

Heretics, he called us. Looking straight at me.

Still, he was mad. And is not to be blamed for the vagaries of madness.

19 June 1887. Boston.

Luncheon with Dr. Rowe, Miss Madeleine van der Post, young Lucas Matthewson; turned over my personal records and notes re the mediums Dr. Moore and I visited. (Destroyed jottings of a private nature.) Miss van der Post and Matthewson will be taking over my responsibilities. Both are young, quick-witted, alert, with a certain ironic play about their features; rather like Dr. Moore in his prime. Matthewson is a former seminary student now teaching physics at Boston University. They questioned me about Perry Moore, but I avoided answering frankly. Asked if we were close, I said *No.* Asked if I had heard a bizarre tale making the rounds of Boston salons— that a spirit claiming to be Perry Moore has intruded upon a number of séances in the area—I said honestly that I had not; and I did not care to hear about it.

Spinoza: *I will analyze the actions and appetites of men as if it were a question of lines, of planes, and of solids.*

It is in this direction, I believe, that we must move. Away from the phantasmal, the vaporous, the unclear; toward lines, planes, and solids.

Sanity.

8 July 1887. Mount Desert Island, Maine.
Very early this morning, before dawn, dreamed of Perry Moore: a babbling gesticulating spirit, bearded, bright-eyed, obviously mad. Jarvis? Jarvis? Don't deny me! he cried. I am so . . . so bereft . . .

Paralyzed, I faced him: neither awake nor asleep. His words were not really *words* so much as unvoiced thoughts. I heard them in my own voice; a terrible raw itching at the back of my throat yearned to articulate the man's grief.

Perry?

You don't dare deny me! Not now!

He drew near and I could not escape. The dream shifted, lost its clarity. Someone was shouting at me. Very angry, he was, and baffled—as if drunk—or ill—or injured.

Perry? I can't hear you—

—our dinner at Montague House, do you remember? Lamb, it was. And crepes with almond for dessert. You remember! You remember! You can't deny me! We were both nonbelievers then, both abysmally ignorant—you can't deny me!

(I was mute with fear or with cunning.)

—that idiot Rowe, how humiliated he will be! All of them! All of you! The entire rationalist bias, the—the conspiracy of—of fools—bigots— In a few years— In a few short years— Jarvis, where are you? Why can't I see you? Where have you gone? —My eyes can't focus: will someone help me? I seem to have lost my way. Who is here? Who am I talking with? You remember me, don't you?

(He brushed near me, blinking helplessly. His mouth was a hole torn into his pale ravaged flesh.)

Where are you? Where is everyone? I thought it would

be crowded here but—but there's no one— I am forgetting so much! My name—what was my name? Can't see. Can't remember. Something very important—something very important I must accomplish—can't remember— Why is there no God? No one here? No one in control? We drift this way and that way, we come to no rest, there are no landmarks—no way of judging—everything is confused—disjointed— Is someone listening? Would you read to me, please? Would you read to me?—anything!—that speech of Hamlet's—*To be or not*—a sonnet of Shakespeare's—any sonnet, anything—*That time of year thou may in me behold*—is that it?—is that how it begins? *Bare ruin'd choirs where the sweet birds once sang.* How does it go? Won't you tell me? I'm lost—there's nothing here to see, to touch—isn't anyone listening? I thought there was someone nearby, a friend: isn't anyone here?

(I stood paralyzed, mute with caution: he passed by.)

—*When in the chronicle of wasted time*—*the wide world dreaming of things to come*—is anyone listening?—can anyone help?—I am forgetting so much—my name, my life—my life's work—to penetrate the mysteries—the veil—to do justice to the universe of—of what—what had I intended?—am I in my place of repose now, have I come home? Why is it so empty here? Why is no one in control? My eyes—my head—mind broken and blown about—slivers—shards—annihilating all that's made to a—a green thought—a green shade—Shakespeare? Plato? Pascal? Will someone read me Pascal again? I seem to have lost my way—I am being blown about— Jarvis, was it? My dear young friend Jarvis? But I've forgotten your last name—I've forgotten so much—

(I wanted to reach out to touch him—but could not move, could not wake. The back of my throat ached with sorrow. Silent! Silent! I could not utter a word.)

—my papers, my journal—twenty years—a key somewhere
hidden—where?—ah yes: the bottom drawer of my desk—do
you hear?—my desk—house—Louisburg Square—the key is
hidden there—wrapped in a linen handkerchief—the strongbox is—the locked box is—hidden—my brother Edward's
house—attic—trunk—steamer trunk—initials R.W.M.—Father's trunk, you see—strongbox hidden inside—my secret
journals—life's work—physical and spiritual wisdom—must
not be lost—are you listening?—is anyone listening? I am forgetting so much, my mind is in shreds—but if you could locate
the journal and read it to me—if you could salvage it—me—I
would be so very grateful—I would forgive you anything, all
of you— Is anyone there? Jarvis? Brandon? No one? —My
journal, my soul: will you salvage it? Will—

(He stumbled away and I was alone again.)

Perry—?

But it was too late: I awoke drenched with perspiration.

Nightmare.

Must forget.

Best to rise early, before the others. Mount Desert Island
lovely in July. Our lodge on a hill above the beach. No spirits
here: wind from the northeast, perpetual fresh air, perpetual
waves. Best to rise early and run along the beach and plunge
into the chilly water.

Clear the cobwebs from one's mind.

How beautiful the sky, the ocean, the sunrise!

No spirits here on Mount Desert Island. Swimming: skillful exertion of arms and legs. Head turned this way, that way.
Eyes half shut. The surprise of the cold rough waves. One
yearns almost to slip out of one's human skin at such times . . . !

Crude blatant beauty of Maine. Ocean. Muscular exertion of body. How alive I am, how living, how invulnerable; what a triumph in my every breath . . .

Everything slips from my mind except the present moment. I am living, I am alive, I am immortal. Must not weaken: must not sink. Drowning? No. Impossible. Life is the only reality. It is not extinction that awaits but a hideous dream-like state, a perpetual groping, blundering—far worse than extinction—incomprehensible: so it is life we must cling to, arm over arm, swimming, conquering the element that sustains us.

Jarvis? someone cried. *Please hear me—*

How exquisite life is, the turbulent joy of life contained in flesh! I heard nothing except the triumphant waves splashing about me. I swam for nearly an hour. Was reluctant to come ashore for breakfast, though our breakfasts are always pleasant rowdy sessions: my wife and my brother's wife and our seven children thrown together for the month of July. Three boys, four girls: noise, bustle, health, no shadows, no spirits. No time to think. Again and again I shall emerge from the surf, face and hair and body streaming water, exhausted but jubilant, triumphant. Again and again the children will call out to me, excited, from the day-side of the world that they inhabit.

I will not investigate Dr. Moore's strongbox and his secret journal; I will not even think about doing so. The wind blows words away. The surf is hypnotic. I will not remember this morning's dream once I sit down to breakfast with the family. I will not clutch my wife's wrist and say *We must not die! We dare not die!*—for that would only frighten and offend her.

Jarvis? she is calling at this very moment.

And I say *Yes—? Yes, I'll be there at once.*

HOME SWEET HOME

BY HANNAH TINTI

Route 128

(Originally published in 2004)

Pat and Clyde were murdered on pot roast night. The doorbell rang just as Pat was setting the butter and margarine (Clyde was watching his cholesterol) on the table. She was thinking about James Dean. Pat had loved him desperately as a teenager, seen his movies dozens of times, written his name across her notebooks, carefully taped pictures of him to the inside of her locker so that she would have the pleasure of seeing his tortured, sullen face from *East of Eden* as she exchanged her French and English textbooks for science and math. When she graduated from high school, she took down the photos and pasted them to the inside cover of her yearbook, which she perused longingly several times over the summer and brought with her to the University of Massachusetts, where it sat, unopened, alongside her thesaurus and abridged collegiate dictionary until she met Clyde, received her M.R.S. degree, and packed her things to move into their two-bedroom ranch house on Bridge Street.

Before she put the meat in the oven that afternoon, Pat had made herself a cup of tea and turned on the television. Channel 56 was showing *Rebel without a Cause*, and as the light slowly began to rise through the screen of their old Zenith, she saw James Dean on the steps of the planetarium, clutching at the mismatched socks of a dead Sal Mineo and crying. She put down her tea, slid her warm fingertips inside the V neck of her dress, and held her left breast. Her heart was suddenly pounding, her nipple hard and erect against the palm of her hand. It was like seeing an old lover, like remembering a piece of herself that no longer existed. She watched the credits roll and glanced outside to see her husband mowing their lawn. He had a worried expression on his face and his socks pulled up to his knees.

That evening before dinner, as she arranged the butter and margarine side by side on the table—one yellow airy and light, the other hard and dark like the yolk of an egg—she wondered how she could have forgotten the way James Dean's eyebrows curved. *Isn't memory a strange thing*, she thought. *I could forget all of this, how everything feels, what all of these things mean to me.* She was suddenly seized with the desire to grab the sticks of butter and margarine in her hands and squeeze them until her fingers went right through, to somehow imprint their textures and colors on her brain like a stamp, to make them something that she would never lose. And then she heard the bell.

When she opened the door, Pat noticed that it was still daylight. The sky was blue and bright and clear and she had a fleeting, guilty thought that she should not have spent so much time indoors. After that she crumpled backward into the hall as the bullet from a .38-caliber Saturday Night Special pierced her chest, exited below her shoulder blade, and jammed into the wood of the stairs, where it would later be dug out with a pen knife by Lieutenant Sales and dropped gingerly into a transparent plastic baggie.

Pat's husband, Clyde, was found in the kitchen by the back door, a knife in his hand (first considered a defense against his attacker and later determined to be the carver of the roast).

He had been shot twice—once in the stomach and once in the head—and then covered with cereal, the boxes lined up on the counter beside him and the crispy golden contents of Cap'n Crunch, cornflakes, and Special K emptied out over what remained of his face.

Nothing had been stolen.

It was a warm spring evening full of summer promises. Pat and Clyde's bodies lay silent and still while the orange sunset crossed the floors of their house and the streetlights clicked on. As darkness came and the skunks waddled through the backyard and the raccoons crawled down from the trees, they were still there, holding their places, suspended in a moment of quiet blue before the sun came up and a new day started and life went on without them.

It was Clyde's mother who called the police. She dialed her son's number every Sunday morning from Rhode Island. These phone calls always somehow perfectly coincided with breakfast, or whenever Pat and Clyde were on the verge of making love.

Thar she blows, Clyde would say, and take his hot coffee with him over to where the phone hung on the wall, or slide out of bed with an apologetic glance at his wife. The coffee and Pat would inevitably cool, and in this way his mother would ruin every Sunday. It had been years now since they had frolicked in the morning, but once, when they were first married and Pat was preparing breakfast, she had heard the phone, walked over to where her husband was reading the paper, dropped to her knees, pulled open his robe, and taken him in her mouth. *Let it ring*, she thought, and he had let it ring. Fifteen minutes later the police were on their front porch with smiles as Clyde, red-faced, bathrobe bulging, answered their questions at the door.

In most areas of her life Clyde's mother was a very nice person. She behaved in such a kind and decorous manner that people would often remark, having met her, *What a lovely woman.* But with Clyde she lost her head. She was suspicious, accusing, and tyrannical. After her husband died, she became even worse. Once she got through her grief, her son became her man. She pushed this sense of responsibility through him like fishhooks, plucking on the line, reeling him back in when she felt her hold slipping, so that the points became embedded in his flesh so deep that it would kill him to take them out.

She dialed the police after trying her son thirty-two times, and because the lieutenant on duty was a soft touch, his own mother having recently passed, a cruiser was dispatched to Pat and Clyde's on Bridge Street, and because one of the policemen was looking to buy in the neighborhood, the officers decided to check out the back of the house after they got no answer, and because there was cereal blowing around in the yard, the men got suspicious, and because it was a windy day and because the hinges had recently been oiled and because the door had been left unlocked and swung open and because one of them had seen a dead body before, a suicide up in Hanover, and knew blood and brain and bits of skull when he saw them, he made the call back to the station, because his partner was quietly vomiting in the rosebushes, and said, *We've got trouble.*

Earlier that morning Mrs. Mitchell had let her dog out with a sad, affectionate pat on his behind. Buster was a Labrador retriever and treated all the yards on Bridge Street as if they were his own, making his way leisurely through flower beds, pausing for a drink from a sprinkler, tearing into garbage bags, and relieving himself among patches of newly planted rutabagas. Before long he was digging a hole in Pat and Clyde's backyard.

There were small golden flakes scattered on the grass. Buster licked one up and crunched. The flakes were food, and the dog followed the promise of more across the lawn, through the back door, and over to Clyde, stiff and covered with flies, the remaining cereal a soggy wet pile of pink plaster across his shoulders. The rug underneath the kitchen table was soaked in blood. Buster left red paw prints as he walked around the body and sniffed at the slippers on the dead man's feet. The dog smelled Clyde's last moment, curled into the arch of his foot.

The doorbell had chimed just as Clyde pierced the roast with the carving fork, releasing two streams of juice, which ran down the sides of the meat until they were captured by the raised edge of the serving plate. He paused then as he lifted the knife, waiting to hear and recognize the voices of his wife and whoever had come to visit. His stomach tightened in the silence. He was hungry. When the shot exploded he felt it all at once and everywhere—in the walls, in his eyes, in his chest, in his arms, in the utensils he was holding, in the piece of meat he was carving, in the slippers that placed him on the floor, in the kitchen, before their evening meal.

Buster pulled off one of the slippers and sank his teeth into it. He worked on removing the stuffing of the inner lining and kept his eye on the dead man, who used to shoo-shoo him away from garbage bags, from munching the daffodils that lined the walk, from humping strays behind the garage. Once, after catching the dog relieving himself in the middle of the driveway, Clyde had dragged him by the collar all the way down Bridge Street. *Listen to me, pooch*, Mr. Mitchell had said after Clyde left, one hand smoothing where the collar had choked and the other hand vigorously scratching the dog's behind. *You shit wherever you feel like shitting.*

When the dog decided to leave the house, he took the slipper with him. He dragged it over to the hole he'd already started and threw it in. Buster walked back and forth over the spot once it was filled, then lifted his leg to mark it.

The Mitchells had brought their dog with them when they moved into the neighborhood. Three years later, a son arrived—not a newborn baby decked out in bonnets but a thin, dark boy of indiscriminate age. His name was Miguel, and it was unclear to the people living on Bridge Street whether he was adopted or a child from a previous marriage. He called the Mitchells his mother and father, enrolled in the public school for their district, and quietly became a part of their everyday lives.

In fact, Miguel was the true son of Mr. Mitchell, sired unknowingly on a business trip with a Venezuelan prostitute some seven years before. The mother had been killed in a bus accident along with fifty-three other travelers on a road outside of Caracas, and the local police had contacted Mr. Mitchell from a faded company card she had left pressed in her Bible. After a paternity test, the boy arrived at Logan Airport with a worn-out blanket and duffel bag full of chickens (his pets), which were quickly confiscated by customs officials. Mr. Mitchell drove down Route 128 in his station wagon, amazed and panicked at his sudden parenthood, trying to comfort the sobbing boy and wondering how Miguel had managed to keep the birds silent on the plane.

When they pulled into the driveway, Mrs. Mitchell was waiting with a glass of warm milk sweetened with sugar. She was wearing dungarees. She took the boy in her arms and carried him immediately into the bathroom, where she sat him on the counter and washed his face, his hands, his knees, and his feet. Miguel sipped the milk while Mrs. Mitchell gently ran the washcloth behind his ears. When she was finished she tucked him in to their guest bed and read him a stack of Curious George books in Spanish, which she had ordered from their local bookstore. She showed Miguel a picture of the little monkey in the hospital getting a shot from a nurse, and the boy fell asleep, a finger hooked around the belt loop of her jeans. Mrs. Mitchell sat on the bed beside him quietly until he rolled over and let it go.

Mr. Mitchell had met his wife at a gas station in northern California. He had just completed his business degree, and was driving a rented car up the coast to see the Olympic rain forest. She was in a pickup truck with Oregon plates. They both got out and started pumping. Mr. Mitchell finished first, and on his way back to his car after paying, he watched the muscles in her thick arm flexing as she replaced the hose. She glanced up, caught him looking, and smiled. She was not beautiful, but one of her teeth stuck out charmingly sideways. There was a confidence about her, an air of efficiency that made him believe she was the kind of woman who could solve any problem. He started the car, turned out of the station, and glanced into his rearview mirror. He watched the pickup take the opposite road, and as it drove away he felt such a pull that he turned around and followed it for sixty miles.

At the rest stop, he pretended that he was surprised to see her. Later he discovered that many people followed his wife, and that she was used to this, and that it did not seem strange to her. People she had never met came up and began to speak to her in shopping malls, in elevators, in the waiting rooms of doctors, at traffic lights, at concerts, at coffee shops and bistros. An old man took hold of her arm outside of an amusement park and began whispering about his murde̶ woman carrying three children placed her blank̶ top of theirs at the beach, stretched out next to Mrs. Mitch-ell, and began to cry. Even their dog, a stray she fed while camping in Tennessee, came scratching outside their door six weeks later. Mr. Mitchell was jealous and frightened by these strangers, and often used himself as a shield between them and his wife. *What do they want from her?* he found himself thinking. But he also felt, *What will they take from me?*

His wife was a quiet woman, in the way that large rocks just beyond the shore are quiet; the waves rush against them and the seaweed hangs on and the birds gather round on top. Mr. Mitchell was amazed that she had married him. He spent the first few years doing what he could to please her and watched for signs that she was leaving.

Sometimes she got depressed and locked herself in the bathroom. It made him furious. When she came out, tender and pink from washing, she would put her arms around him and tell him that he was a good man. Mr. Mitchell was not sure of this, because sometimes he found himself hating her. He wanted her to know what it felt like to be powerless. He began taking risks.

When he got the call from Venezuela telling him about Miguel, he was terrified that he might lose his wife and also secretly happy to have wounded her. But all of the control he felt as they prepared for his son's arrival slipped away as he watched her take the strange dark boy into her arms and tenderly wash his feet. He realized then that she was capable of taking everything from him.

The three of them formed an awkward family. Mr. Mitch-ell tried to place the boy in a home, but his wife would not let him. He had now been an accidental father for two years.

He took the boy to baseball games and bought him comic books and drove him to school in the mornings. Sometimes Mr. Mitchell enjoyed these things; other times they made him angry. One day he walked in on Miguel talking to his wife in Spanish and the boy immediately stopped. He saw that his son was afraid of him, and he was sure that his wife had done this too. Mr. Mitchell began to resent what had initially drawn him to her, and to offset these feelings he began an affair with their neighbor, Pat.

It did not begin innocently. Pat said hello to Mr. Mitchell at the supermarket, then turned and pressed up against him as someone passed in the aisle. Her behind lingered against his hips, her breasts touched his arm. Mr. Mitchell had never had any conversation with Pat that went beyond the weather or the scheduling of trash, but later that week he walked over to her as she was planting bulbs in her garden and slid his hand into the elastic waistband of her Bermuda shorts. He leaned her up against the fence, underneath a birch tree, right there in the middle of a bright, sunny day where everyone could see. Mr. Mitchell didn't say anything, but he could tell by her breath and the way she rocked on his hand that she wasn't afraid.

He did not know it was in him to do something like this. He had been on his way to the library to return some books. Look, there they were, thrown aside on the grass, wrapped in plastic smeared with age and the fingers of readers who were unknown to him. And here was another person he did not know, panting in his ear, streaking his arms with dirt. Some-one he had seen bent over in the sunlight, a slight glistening of sweat reflecting in the backs of her knees, and for whom he had suddenly felt a hard sense of lonesomeness and longing. A new kind of warmth spread in the palm of his hand and he tried not to think about his wife.

They had hard, raw sex in public places—movie theaters and parks, elevators and playgrounds. After dark, underneath the jungle gym, his knees pressing into the dirt, Mr. Mitchell began to wonder why they hadn't been caught. Once, sitting on a bench near the reservoir, Pat straddling him in a skirt with no underwear, they had actually waved to an elderly couple passing by. The couple continued on as if they hadn't seen them. The experience left the impression that his meetings with Pat were occurring in some kind of alternative reality, a bubble in time that he knew would eventually pop.

Pat told him that Clyde had been impotent since his father died. The old man had been a mechanic, and was working underneath a bulldozer when the lift slipped, crushing him from the chest down. Clyde held his father's hand as he died, and the coldness that came as life left seemed to spread through Clyde's fingers and into his arms, and he stopped using them to reach for his wife. Since the funeral she'd had two lovers. Mr. Mitchell was number three.

There were rumors, later on, that the lift had been tampered with—that Clyde's father had owed someone money. Pat denied it, but Mr. Mitchell remembered driving by the garage and sensing he'd rather buy his gas somewhere else. It seemed like a shady business.

He started arranging meetings with Pat that were closer to home. Mr. Mitchell's desire increased with the risk of discovery, and in his house he began to fantasize about the dining room table, the dryer in the laundry room, the space on the kitchen counter beside the mixer. He touched these places with his fingertips and trembled, thinking of how he would feel later, watching his wife sip her soup, fold sheets, mix batter for cookies in the same places.

On the day Pat was murdered, before she put the roast in

the oven or reminisced about James Dean or thought about the difference between butter and margarine, she was having sex in the vestibule. The coiled inscription of HOME SWEET HOME scratched her behind. Mr. Mitchell had seen Clyde leave for a bowling lesson, and as he waited on the front porch for Pat to open the door, something had made him pick up the welcome mat. Mrs. Mitchell would soon be home with Miguel, and the thought of her so close pricked his ears. When Pat answered he'd thrown the mat down in the hall, then her, then himself, the soles of his shoes knocking over the entry table. Mr. Mitchell brought Pat's knees to his shoulders and listened for the hum of his wife's Reliant.

The following day when Lieutenant Sales climbed the stairs of Pat and Clyde's porch, he did not notice that there was nothing to wipe his feet on. He was an average-looking man: six foot two, 190 pounds, brown hair, brown eyes, brown skin. He had once been a champion deep-sea diver, until a shark attack (which left him with a hole in his side crossed with the pink, puckered scars of new skin) dragged him from the waters with a sense of righteous authority and induced him to join the force. He lived thirty-five minutes away in a basement apartment with a Siamese cat named Frank.

When Sales was a boy he'd had a teacher who smelled like roses. Her name was Mrs. Bosco. She showed him how to blow eggs. Forcing the yolk out of the tiny hole always felt a little disgusting, like blowing a heavy wad of snot from his nose, but when he looked up at Mrs. Bosco's cheeks flushed red with effort, he knew it would be worth it, and it was—the empty shell in his hand like a held breath. Whenever he began an investigation, he'd get the same sensation, and as he stepped into the doorway of Pat and Clyde's house, he felt it rise in his chest and stay.

He interviewed the police who found the bodies first. They were sheepish about their reasons for going into the backyard, but before long they began loudly discussing drywall and Sheetrock and the pros and cons of lancet windows (all of the men, including Lieutenant Sales, carried weekend and part-time jobs in construction). The policeman who had thrown up in the bushes went home early. When Sales spoke to him later, he apologized for contaminating the scene.

Lieutenant Sales found the roast on the counter. He found green beans still on the stove. He found a sour cherry pie nearly burned in the oven. He found the butter and the margarine half-melted on the dining room table. He found that Pat and Clyde used cloth napkins and tiny separate plates for their dinner rolls. The silverware was polished. The edges of the steak knives were turned in.

He found their unpaid bills in a basket by the telephone. He found clean laundry inside the dryer in the basement—towels, sheets, T-shirts, socks, three sets of Fruit of the Loom and one pair of soft pink satin panties, the elastic starting to give, the bottom frayed and thin. He found an unfinished letter Pat had started writing to a friend who had recently moved to Arizona: *What is it like there? How can you stand the heat?* He found Clyde's stamp albums from when he was a boy— tiny spots of brilliant color, etchings of flowers and portraits of kings, painstakingly pasted over the names of countries Lieutenant Sales had never heard of.

He found the bullet that had passed through Pat's body, embedded in the stairs. He found a run in her stocking, starting at the heel and inching its way up the back of her leg. He thought about how Pat had been walking around the day she was going to die not realizing that there was a hole in her panty hose. He found a stain, dark and blooming beneath her shoulders, spreading across the Oriental rug in the foyer and into the hardwood floors, which he noticed, as he got down on his knees for a closer look, still held the scent of Murphy's oil soap. He found a hairpin caught in the carpet fringe. He found a cluster of dandelion seeds, the tiny white filaments coming apart in his fingers. He found a look on Pat's face like a child trying to be brave, lips tightened and thin, forehead just beginning to crease, eyes glazed, dark, and unconvinced. Her body was stiff when they moved her.

There were dog tracks on the back porch. They were the prints of a midsized animal, red and clearly defined as they circled the body in the kitchen, then crisscrossing over themselves and heading out the door, fading down the steps and onto the driveway before disappearing into the yard. Lieutenant Sales sent a man to knock on doors in the neighborhood and find out who let their dogs off the leash. He interviewed Clyde's mother. He went back to the station and checked Pat's and Clyde's records—both clean. When he finally went to sleep that night, the small warmth of his cat tucked next to his shoulder, Lieutenant Sales thought about the feel of satin panties, missing slippers, stolen welcome mats, dandelion seeds from a yard with no dandelions, and the kind of killer who shuts off the oven.

A month before Pat and Clyde were murdered, Mrs. Mitchell was fixing the toilet. Her husband passed by on his way to the kitchen, paused at the door, shook his head, and told her that she was too good for him. The heavy porcelain top was off, her arms elbow deep in rusty water. The man she had married was standing at the entrance to the bathroom and speaking, but Mrs. Mitchell was concentrating on the particular tone in the pipes she was trying to clear, and so she did not respond.

Mr. Mitchell went into the kitchen and began popping popcorn. The kernels cracked against the insides of the kettle as his words settled into her, and when, with a twist of the coat hanger in her hand beneath the water, she stopped the ringing of the pipes, Mrs. Mitchell sensed in the quiet that came next that her husband had done something wrong. She had known in this same way before he told her about Miguel. A breeze came through the window and made the hair on her wet arms rise. She pulled her hands from the toilet and thought, *I fixed it*.

When Miguel came into their home, she had taken all the sorrow she felt at his existence and turned it into a fierce motherly love. Mrs. Mitchell thought her husband would be grateful; instead he seemed to hold it against her. He became dodgy and spiteful. He blamed her for what he'd done, for being a woman too hard to live up to. It was the closest she ever came to leaving. But she hadn't expected the boy.

Miguel spent the first three months of his life in America asking to go home. When the fourth month came he began to sleepwalk. He wandered downstairs to the kitchen, emptied the garbage can onto the floor, and curled up inside. In the morning Mrs. Mitchell would find him asleep, shoulders in the barrel, feet in the coffee grounds and leftovers. He told her he was looking for his mother's head. She had been decapitated in the bus accident, and now she stepped from the corners of Miguel's dreams at night and beckoned him with her arms, his lost chickens resting on her shoulders, pecking at the empty neck.

Mrs. Mitchell suggested that they make her a new one. She bought materials for papier-mâché. The strips of newspaper felt like bandages as she helped Miguel dip them in glue and smooth them over the surface of the inflated balloon.

They fashioned a nose and lips out of cardboard. Once it was dry, Miguel described his mother's face and they painted the skin brown, added yarn for hair, cut eyelashes out of construction paper. Mrs. Mitchell took a pair of gold earrings, poked them through where they'd drawn the ears and said, heart sinking, *She's beautiful.* Miguel nodded. He smiled. He put his mother's head on top of the bookcase in his room and stopped sleeping in the garbage.

Sometimes when Mrs. Mitchell checked on the boy at night, she'd feel the head looking at her. It was unnerving. She imagined her husband making love to the papier-mâché face and discovered a hate so strong and hard it made her afraid of herself. She considered swiping the head and destroying it, but she remembered how skinny and pitiful the boy's legs had looked against her kitchen floor. Then Miguel began to love her, and she suddenly felt capable of anything. She thumbed her nose at the face in the corner. She held her heart open.

Mrs. Mitchell had been raised by her aunts in a house near the river where her mother had drowned. The aunts were hunters; birds mostly, which they would clean and cook and eat. As a girl Mrs. Mitchell would retrieve the shots. Even on a clear day, the birds always seemed wet. Sometimes they were still alive when she found them—wings thrashing, pieces of their chests torn away. She learned to take hold of their necks and break them quickly.

Mrs. Mitchell kept a picture of her mother next to the mirror in her room, and whenever she checked her reflection, her eyes would naturally turn from her own face to that of the woman who gave birth to her. The photo was black-and-white and creased near the edges; she was fifteen, her hair plaited, the end of one braid pressed between her lips. It made Mrs. Mitchell think of stories she'd heard of women who spent their lives spinning—years of passing flax through their mouths to make thread would leave them disfigured, lower lips drooping off their faces; a permanent look of being beaten.

The aunts built a shooting range on an area of property behind the house. It was Mrs. Mitchell's job to set up the targets and fetch them iced tea and ammo. She kept a glass jar full of shells in the back of her closet, shiny gold casings from her aunts' collection of .22 calibers and .45s. They made a shooting station out of an old shed, two tables set up with sandbags to hold the guns, nestling the shape of heavy metal as the pieces were placed down.

When she was twelve years old the aunts gave her a rifle. She already knew the shooting stances, and she practiced them with her new gun every day after school. She could hit a target while kneeling, crouching, lying down, and standing tall, hips parallel to the barrel and her waist turned, the same way the aunts taught her to pose when a picture was being taken. She picked off tin cans and old metal signs and polka-dotted the paper outlines of men.

Mrs. Mitchell remembered this when she pulled into her driveway, glanced over the fence, and saw her husband having sex in the doorway of their neighbors' house. She turned to Miguel in the passenger seat and told him to close his eyes. The boy covered his face with his hands and sat quietly while she got out of the car. Mrs. Mitchell watched her husband moving back and forth and felt her feet give way from the ground. She had the sensation of being caught in a river, the current pulling her body outward, tugging at her ankles, and she wondered why she wasn't being swept away until she realized that she was holding on to the fence. The wood felt smooth and worn, like the handle of her first gun, and she used it to pull herself back down.

Later she thought of the look on Pat's face. It reminded Mrs. Mitchell of the Tin Woodman from the movie *The Wizard of Oz*—disarmingly lovely and greasy with expectation. In the book version she bought for Miguel she'd read that the Woodman had once been real, but his ax kept slipping and he'd dismembered himself, slowly exchanging his flesh piece by piece for hollow metal. Mrs. Mitchell thought Pat's body would rattle with the same kind of emptiness, but it didn't; it fell with the heavy tone of meat. As she waited for the echo, Mrs. Mitchell heard a small cough from the kitchen, the kind a person does in polite society to remind someone else that they are there. She followed it and found Clyde in his slippers, the knife in the roast.

Hello. I just killed your wife. And when she said it, she knew she'd have to shoot Clyde too. The beans were boiling, the water frothing over the sides of the pan and sizzling into the low flame beneath. Mrs. Mitchell turned off the oven and spun all the burners to zero.

The aunts never married. They still lived in the house where they raised their niece. Occasionally they sent her photographs, recipes, information on the NRA, or obituaries of people she had known clipped from the local newspaper. When a reporter called Mrs. Mitchell, asking questions about Pat and Clyde, she thought back to all the notices her aunts had sent over the years, and said: *They were good neighbors and wonderful people. I don't know who would have done something like this. They will be greatly missed.* The truth was that she felt very little for Pat. It was hard to forgive herself for this, so she didn't try. Instead she did her best to forget how Clyde had looked, the surprise on his face, as if he were about to offer her a drink before he crumpled to the floor.

She waited patiently through the following day for someone to come for her. She watched the police cruisers and the news vans come and go. On Monday morning she woke up and let the dog out. She made a sandwich for Miguel and fit it in his lunch box beside a thermos of milk. She poured juice into a glass and cereal into a bowl. Then she locked herself in the bathroom and watched her hands shake. She remembered that she had wanted to cover Clyde with something. Falling out of the box, the cereal had sounded crisp and new like water on rocks, but it quickly turned into a soggy mess that stayed with her as she left him, stepped over Pat, and picked up the welcome mat with her gloves. She could still see her husband moving back and forth on top of it. She wanted to make HOME SWEET HOME disappear, but the longest she could bring herself to touch it was the end of the driveway, and she left it in a garbage can on the street.

She found that she could not say goodbye. Not when her husband pounded on the door to take a shower and not when Miguel asked if he could brush his teeth. She sat on the toilet and listened to them move about the house and leave. Later, she watched through the window as a man wrapped her neighbors' house in police tape. To double it around a tree in the yard, he circled the trunk with his arms. It was a brief embrace and she thought, *That tree felt nothing.*

In the afternoon, when the sun began to slant, Lieutenant Sales crossed the Mitchells' front yard. He was carrying a chewed-up slipper in a bag, jostling the dandelions, and sending seeds of white fluff adrift. Mrs. Mitchell saw him coming. She turned the key in the lock, and once she was beyond the bathroom, she ran her fingers through her hair, smoothing down the rough spots. The bell rang. The dog barked. She opened the door, and offered him coffee.

* * *

Miguel turned nine that summer. In the past two years he'd spent with the Mitchells, the boy had grown no more than an inch; but with the warm weather that June, he'd suddenly sprouted—his legs stretching like brown sugar taffy tight over his new knobby bones, as if the genes of his American father had been lying dormant, biding their time until the right combination of spring breezes and processed food kissed them awake. He began to trip over himself. On his way home from baseball practice that Monday, he caught one of his newly distended feet on a trash can just outside the line of police tape that closed in Pat and Clyde's yard. Miguel fell to the sidewalk, smacking his hands against the concrete. The barrel toppled over beside him, and out came a welcome mat. HOME SWEET HOME.

Miguel was not the best student, but he had made friends easily once he hit several home runs in gym class. Norman and Greg Kessler, twins and the most popular kids in school, chose him for their team and for their friend. Norman and Greg helped him with his English, defended him against would-be attackers, and told him when they saw his father naked.

Mr. Mitchell had driven past them on the highway, stripped bare from the waist down. From the window of their mother's minivan, Norman and Greg could see a woman leaning over the gearshift. *It's true*, said the twins. Miguel made them swear on the Bible, on a stack of Red Sox cards, and finally on their grandfather's grave, which they did, bikes thrown aside in the grass and sweaty hands pressed on the polished marble of his years. At dinner that night the boy watched his father eating. The angle of his jaw clenched and turned.

Miguel felt a memory push past hot dogs, past English, past Hostess cupcakes and his collection of Spider-Man comic books. He was five years old and asked his mother where his father was. She was making coffee—squeezing the grounds through a sieve made out of cloth and wire. He'd collected eggs from their chickens for breakfast. He was holding them in his hands and they were still warm. His mother took one from him. *This is the world and we are here*, she said, and pointed to the bottom half of the egg. *Your father is there*. She ran her finger up along the edge and tapped the point with a dark red nail. Then she cracked the yolk in a pan and threw the rest of the egg in the garbage. He retrieved it later and pushed his fingertips back and forth across the slippery inner membrane until the shell came apart into pieces.

Miguel picked up the doormat and shook it to get the dust off. It seemed like something Mrs. Mitchell might be fond of. That morning he had kept watch through the bathroom keyhole. She was out of sight, but he could sense her worry.

In Caracas he had gone through the trash regularly, looking for things to play with and at times for something to eat. Ever since he heard about his father being naked on the highway, he had been remembering more about his life there, and even reverting to some of his old habits, as if the non sequitur of his father's nudity had tenderly shaken him awake. He lay in bed at night and looked into the eyes of the papier-mâché head for guidance. He had two lives now, two countries and two mothers. Soon he would find another life without his father, and another when he went away to college, and another life, and another, and another, and another, each of them a thin, fragile casing echoing the hum of what had gone before.

The boy walked into the kitchen and found his American mother sitting with a strange man. They both held steaming mugs of coffee. Buster was under the table, waking from his afternoon nap. He saw Miguel and thumped his tail halfheartedly against the floor. The adults turned. *Now, what have you got there?*

Lieutenant Sales took HOME SWEET HOME in his hands. There was something in the look of the boy and the feel of the rope that held possibility, and the twisted pink skin where the shark had bitten him began to itch. It had been tingling all afternoon. Later, in the lab, the welcome mat would reveal tiny spots of Pat's blood, dog saliva, gunpowder, dead ants, mud, fertilizer, and footprints—but not the impression of Mr. Mitchell's knees, or the hesitation of his jealous wife on the doorstep, or the hunger of his son in the garbage. All of this had been shaken off.

Lieutenant Sales would leave the Mitchells' house that afternoon with the same thrill he'd had when the shark passed and he realized his leg was still there. He was exhilarated and then exhausted, as though his life had been drained, and he knew then that he had gone as far as he could go. There would be no scar and no solution to the murder, just the sense that he had missed something, and the familiar taste of things not done. For now, he reached out with a kind of hope and accepted the welcome mat as a gift.

Mrs. Mitchell put her arm around Miguel's shoulders and waited for Lieutenant Sales to arrest her. She would continue to wait in the weeks ahead as suspects were raised and then dismissed and headlines changed and funerals were planned. The possibilities of these moments passed over her like shadows. When they were gone she was left standing chilled.

Clyde's mother arranged for closed caskets. In the pew Mrs. Mitchell sat quietly. Her husband looked nervous and cracked knuckles. After the service they went home and Mr. Mitchell started to pack. His wife listened to the suitcases being dragged down from the attic, the swing of hangers, zipper teeth, the straps of leather buckles. Mr. Mitchell said he was leaving, and his wife felt her throat clutch. She wanted to ask him where he would go; she wanted to ask him what she had done this for; she wanted to ask him why he no longer loved her, but instead she asked for his son.

She had watched Miguel hand the frayed rope to the detective, and as it passed by her, she felt an ache in the back of her mouth as though she hadn't eaten for days. Lieutenant Sales turned HOME SWEET HOME over in his hands. He placed it carefully on the kitchen table and Mrs. Mitchell saw the word *Sweet*. She remembered the milk she had made for the boy when he arrived, and sensed that this would not be the end of her. She could hear the steady breathing of her sleeping dog. She could smell the coffee. She felt the small frame of Miguel steady beneath her hand. These bones, she thought, were everything. *Hey, sport*, Mrs. Mitchell asked, *is that for me?* The boy nodded, and she held him close.

SURROGATE

BY ROBERT B. PARKER

Watertown

(Originally published in 1982)

Brenda Loring sat in my office with her knees together and her hands clasped in her lap and told me that last night a man had broken into her home and raped her for the second time in two weeks.

With my instinct for the *bon mot*, I said, "Jesus Christ."

"It was the same man as before," she said. Her voice was still and clear and uninflected.

I said, "Last night?"

"About ten hours ago," she said. "I've just now left the police." Her face was blank and, without makeup, it looked unprotected.

"You want to talk about the rapes?" I said.

She shook her head slightly and looked down at her clasped hands.

"That's okay," I said. "I can get it all from the cops. You still living in Cambridge?"

She nodded. "My husband's involved," she said, "my ex-husband."

I said *Jesus Christ* again, but only to myself. I don't like to overwork a phrase. "You want to talk about that?" I said.

She was still looking at her hands, folded motionless in her lap. "The police don't believe me about my husband."

Her stillness was profound. But it was stillness of tension, like a drawn bowstring. I said, "Brenda, whatever this is, I can fix it."

She looked up at me for the first time since she'd started speaking. "Two rapes too late," she said in her lucid monotone.

"Yes," I said.

She looked back down at her hands.

"Tell me a little more about your husband," I said.

"Northrop," she said. "Mrs. Northrop May."

"I was at your wedding," I said.

"The day after I was raped the first time," she said, "Northrop came to see me. He came in and sat down and I gave him a cup of coffee and he said with a . . . not a smile . . . a . . . a smirk," she nodded her head decisively in approval of the word's rightness, "and he said to me, 'So, how's your love life?' and I said, 'My God, don't you know I was raped?' and he said no and asked me about it. And . . ." she thought a minute, concentrating on her hands. "He wanted details: what did he do? what did I do? did he make me undress?" She shivered slightly. "And all the time he had that smirk and he was . . ." Again she paused and looked for the right word. "Avid," she said. "He was avid, listening. And then he said, 'Did you like it?'"

I could feel the muscles across my shoulders bunch a little. She was quiet, still examining her hands.

I said, "Then what?"

"I asked him to leave," she said. She raised her head. "I know he's involved."

"But he didn't do it?"

"No. I saw the man's face. It wasn't Northrop. Besides, this man was able to do it."

"You mean erect?"

She nodded.

"And Northrop couldn't?"

"Not very often and, before the divorce, getting worse," she said.

"You think Northrop knows who did it?" I said.

"As he left last week, he looked at me from the doorway with that hot smirky look on his face and said, 'Maybe he'll be back.'"

"Cops check on him?"

"He was with three other people having late supper at the Ritz Café," she said. "After theater."

"The cops figure you for a vindictive divorcée," I said.

"Probably."

Two stories down on Berkeley Street a car horn honked impatiently. Brenda rummaged in her bag and found a pack of cigarettes. She took one out and lit it and inhaled a long lungful.

"Faulkner," I said. "Novel called *Sanctuary*. You ever read it?"

She shook her head. The long inhale began to seep out.

"Character in there called Popeye," I said. "He was impotent, had other people do it for him."

"Yes," Brenda said. She was looking right at me now and her voice was richer. "That's what I think," she said.

"What time of day did he come around to smirk last time?" I said.

"After lunch."

I looked at my watch. "Let's go over to your place and see if he comes around this time."

"So you'll be there if he comes?"

I nodded. Two spots of color appeared on Brenda's cheekbones. She got abruptly to her feet. "Yes," she said, "let's go."

Brenda lived on the fifth floor of a wedge-shaped brick

building at the Watertown end of Mt. Auburn Street. We were on the second cup of coffee, and almost no conversation, when Northrop May showed up. He rang, Brenda spoke to him on the intercom and buzzed him in. I went into the kitchen. In maybe thirty seconds I heard Brenda open the apartment door.

May said, "How've you been, Brenda?" His voice sounded vaguely British. Half the people in Cambridge sounded vaguely British. The other half sounded like me.

"What do you care?"

"I worry about you, Brenda, you know that. Just because our marriage has ended doesn't mean I no longer care for you. I want to know that you're happy. That you're dating and things."

"I'm fine," Brenda said.

"Good," May said. "Good. How about last night, did you have a good time last night?"

I heard a sudden movement and the sound of a slap and I came around the corner in time to see May holding both Brenda's wrists down. I shifted my weight slightly onto my left foot, did a small pivot and kicked May in the middle of the back with the bottom of my right foot. He let go of Brenda and sprawled forward face first on the floor. When he hit he scrambled on all fours toward the couch and behind it before he used it to help him to his feet. His face was the color of skimmed milk when he looked at me.

"Hiho, Northrop," I said.

"What are you doing?" he said. "She was hitting me. You had no reason to do that. I was just defending myself."

Brenda moved toward May. "You son of a bitch," she said. Her voice hissed between her teeth. "You lousy dickless bastard." He edged away, keeping the couch between him and me. Brenda went after him, swinging at him with both fists closed. He put his arms up and edged away some more. But he was edging toward me and he didn't like that.

"Keep her away," he said. Brenda kicked at his shins.

I reached out and caught Brenda's arm. "Stop a minute," I said. "Let's talk."

Brenda leaned steadily against my restraint. May began edging the other way, toward the door. "I'm not talking," he said. "I'm going to leave right now."

I shook my head, still holding Brenda's steady weight with my left hand. Northrop looked at me. He was about my height but much lighter, angular and narrow with round gold glasses and blond hair combed straight back.

"I'm not going to fight with a pug like you," he said.

"A wise choice," I said. "Sit down. We'll talk."

His face tightened and his eyes moved around the room. I was between him and the only door. He went to the couch and sat down. With his legs crossed and his hands folded precisely in his lap he said, "Very well, what is it? why are you here? why are you detaining me? and why on earth is that woman acting even more insane than usual?"

"Your wife has been raped," I said, "and you're responsible."

He shook his head once, brusquely. "That's absurd," he said. "There are half a dozen people who can testify that I was with them, far from here, both times."

"How do you know it was both?" I said.

"You just . . ."

I shook my head, slowly. May was quiet, and I knew he was running back in his mind what I had said. Then he shrugged impatiently.

"I don't know—once, twice, whatever. I have not raped my wife."

"Ex-wife," Brenda said. "But you had it done." Her voice was clotted with intensity. "You had somebody do it and then you came smirking around afterward like some kind of peeping Tom."

She was arched toward him, her face thrust close to his.

"You can't prove that," he said. His voice was as pale as his face.

"We don't need to prove it," I said. "We only have to know it. We're not the law. We don't have to sweat the rules of evidence, Northrop."

"To do what?" he said. He stayed stiffly in his legs-crossed-I'm-completely-at-my-ease pose.

"I'm perfectly willing to kill you," I said. "I can do it easy and I'd feel no guilt."

He didn't move.

"I have killed people before," I said. "I know how. I could float you out that window like a paper airplane, right now. You deserve to go. Brenda would swear you jumped mad with remorse. That would even the score, Brenda would be safe. I can't see any reason not to do it."

"Do it," Brenda hissed. She went to the window and opened it wide. "Do it."

May's composure went. He looked rapidly around the room. He uncrossed his legs and put both feet on the floor and leaned forward as if to get up. He looked at the door. Looked at me. I could see him give up inside, his body tension changed.

"My God, Spenser," he said. "You . . . my God, you can't . . . Please."

It was late October and rainy. The breeze from the open window was cold.

"Who'd you hire to do it?" I said.

He looked at everything: me, Brenda, the window, a brass candlestick on the end table. He was in way over his head.

And he was caught. He'd thought about staving off the law, and provided means. But he hadn't thought about me. He had no way to stave me off.

"Some things you gotta do yourself, Northrop. You can't hire someone for this."

"I'll hire you," he said. "You're a detective. I'll hire you to investigate, to investigate everything. My family has money. I can pay you very well, a lot."

I took a quick step forward, got him by the shirt front, yanked him off the sofa and spun him toward the window. Then I shifted my grip to the back of his collar and the seat of his pants and ran him toward the window.

His head was out in the rain when he screamed, "Hanson! Richie Hanson!"

I held him there, his head out the window, his feet off the ground.

"Where's he live?" I said.

"South End, Clarendon Street, down by the Ballet." May's voice was thin with panic. I pulled him back in and sat him on the couch. He sat shivering. I always hated to see fear. It made me feel lousy, especially when I'd caused it. "What number Clarendon?" I said.

"Nineteen."

I picked up Brenda's phone and punched out a number. On the second ring a voice said, "Harbor Health Club."

"Henry? Spenser. Hawk there?"

"He don't usually come in this early, kid. You know Hawk, probably having breakfast now."

"Yeah. Get hold of him, Henry, and have him call me." I gave him Brenda's number.

"In a hurry?"

"Yes."

"It'll be quick," Henry said.

We hung up and I went and stood against the door. Probably no need to. May sat on the couch without form, limp against the brocade.

"What are you going to do?" he said.

"I'm going to have Hawk bring Richie Hanson over here."

"No," Brenda said.

"It's a way to clean this up," I said. "Might be good, too, for you to get by facing him."

"I don't want to," Brenda said. "I'm afraid."

"No need," I said.

"I don't know this Hawk," Brenda said. "Can he get Richie whatsis?"

"Hawk will bring you Nama the killer whale if he feels like it," I said. "If we get them together we'll know everything. Maybe even understand some of it."

"I understand it," Brenda said softly. She turned back toward May and the angles of her body sharpened. "I understand that he isn't man enough to do it himself. He isn't man enough to do anything." Her voice was hissing again. "Did you ask this guy what it was like? Did you get it up when he told you? Is that what it takes?"

Northrop's face took on some definition as if hatred had disciplined it. "It takes response," he said. "I can feel passion when it's returned."

"Frigid? You have always tried to say that. That's bullshit. I always liked sex. It was you that turned me off, you creepy bastard." A very nasty smile distorted her mouth. "Ask Spenser. Was I cold when we were together?"

I made a small noncommittal gesture with my head.

"I never understood it," May said. "Before we were married . . ." he shook his head and made a helpless measuring motion with his hands. "And afterward it was gone. Now and then you seemed to like it, but mostly it was gone."

"I never turned you down."

"No, you never did. You lay back and gritted your teeth and did your duty like a soldier." May's voice was full of defeat. It had gotten toneless and small as he talked, as if it came from some small recess inside him, out of the light.

Brenda was walking back and forth in front of him, arching toward him as she spoke. "And you, you weird bastard, you always wanted to hear about who else I'd done it with, and what I'd done, and what I'd let them do. It was creepy."

"I wanted all of you," May said. "I wanted to share everything, to have no secrets. Sure, maybe it turned me on a little. That's human, isn't it? But mostly I just wanted us to be closer, and you kept telling me different things, and not telling me anything, and I just wanted the truth. You kept part of you away from me."

"I'm not a goddamned peep show, North. Part of me is mine."

The nickname had crept in. They weren't victim and violator anymore. They were domestic adversaries again, tripping the same old grim fantastic over the same old painful ground.

"I never knew you," he said.

The phone rang. It was Hawk.

I said, "There's a guy named Richie Hanson, 19 Clarendon Street. I need him here as quick as you can get him." I gave him Brenda's address.

Hawk said, "Okay."

I said, "I don't know this guy. It's possible he's dangerous."

Hawk's laugh was liquid. "Me too, babe. I bring him along."

He hung up. While I'd been on the phone the argument

had paused like a stop-action replay. When I put down the phone they began again as if in mid-sentence.

"There was that central part of you," Northrop said, "that was remote and arrogant." He spoke smoothly, almost as if he were speaking a part he'd rehearsed.

"Don't you understand that it is my pride to keep part of me private? To have a part of me intact? You're weird, North. You're sick."

May's eyes filled and tears came down his face.

"Sick," he said, and his voice, despite the tears, was still atonal and remote. "Why is that sick? All I ever wanted . . ." His voice shook a little. "All I ever, ever wanted was so simple, so ordinary . . . I just wanted affection. I wanted you to act like you loved me . . . that's all I wanted . . . is that sick? Is that some sort of weird thing to want, simply, gestures of affection?"

"Your definitions," Brenda said. They were so caught up in the argument that they might have been alone. I was watching a marriage that had been driven into the corner. Its meanness was being reported. *Hurry up, Hawk.*

"Anyone's definitions," May said. He looked at me, almost startled, realizing suddenly that for the first time in all the times they'd had this argument there was a third opinion handy. "If you're making love, do you want response?" he said. I made my noncommittal head gesture. "Do you like your partner to lie quiet and still?" I varied the previous head motion. "She lie quiet and still with you, Spenser?"

Brenda's voice scraped out between her tightened teeth. "You bet your ass I didn't." I thought about blushing. May put his head in his hands.

"The simplest thing in the world," he murmured. "Just love and get it back. Not sick. Not weird. The simplest thing in the world."

The rain spattered against the window, driven by a shifted wind. Somewhere, probably in the kitchen, I could hear a faucet drip.

"Tell me about Richie Hanson," I said.

"Hanson?"

"Richie Hanson. Is he a hood? How's a Brattle Street smartie like you know someone who'd hire out to rape someone?"

"I met him at Concord Correctional Institute," May said. "Isn't that a joke, Correctional Institute. I was giving a poetry and criticism workshop there, part of the University outreach."

"And Hanson was doing time?"

"Yes, when he got out he got in touch with me. Wanted a letter of recommendation."

"Poetry workshop," Brenda snorted. "What the hell do you know about it? You never published a poem in your life, except those things that are mimeographed in Harvard Square."

"You needn't be a cook to judge a soufflé," he said.

Brenda made a spitting sound. "I've heard you say that so often," she said. "Isn't that typical? Always able to describe it; never able to do it. A legless man that teaches running."

Her voice was low, but easy to hear, articulated by her intensity.

The intercom rang, and I heard Hawk's voice when I picked it up: "Mistah Hanson to see Marse Spensah, bawse."

I said, "Considering the years of practice, that's the worst darkie dialect I've ever heard." I pressed the button to let them in and went to the apartment door. In less than a minute Hanson appeared at the door with Hawk behind him. Hanson was a blocky blond guy with scraggly hair, thin on top and long over the ears. There was a slight rim of blood inside one nostril and a darkening bruise under his right eye. In his neighborhood he was probably tough. Compared to Hawk he was butterscotch candy.

Hawk pushed him gently into the room, shut the door and leaned against it. He was Ralph Lauren western this week, snakeskin boots, jeans, denim shirt, western jacket, big hat. He was the only other guy I knew who had an eighteen-inch neck and looked good in clothes. The angular planes of his face gleamed like carved obsidian when he smiled.

"Afternoon, boss," he said.

"Jesus," I said. "Midnight cowboy. Hanson give you any trouble?"

"Nothing that counts," Hawk said.

"Richie," I said, "you know these folks?"

Hanson looked at Brenda. She was motionless, standing near May, hugging herself without seeming to realize it, rubbing her upper arms as if she were cold. He looked at May sitting on the couch. He looked at me and opened his mouth, then shut it and glanced over his shoulder at Hawk. Hawk smiled his glistening pleasant smile.

"Mr. May here on the couch tells us you raped his wife," I said.

"Ex-wife," Brenda said without affect.

Hanson looked at May again, and, half turning his head, out of the corner of his eye, again at Hawk.

"We'd like to know why you did that," I said.

Hanson said, "I don't know what's going on here. Who the hell are you?"

Hawk leaned effortlessly forward from the door and hit Hanson a six-inch punch over the left kidney. Hanson gasped and went to his knees. Hawk leaned back against the door.

"He paid me," Hanson said. He got slowly to his feet and moved a little away from Hawk. "The professor paid me. He came to my place and give me five C's. Said not to hurt her bad, just do it and I'd get the other five when I give him the pictures."

I said, "Pictures?"

Brenda looked at the floor. I glanced at May. He was staring at the fist his two hands made between his knees.

"He wanted pictures of her . . . ah . . . you know, disrobed. Said it would be proof that I done it."

There was no sound for a moment in the room except that rattle of the fall rain against the window.

"We'll want those," I said.

"I give them all to the professor."

I looked at Hawk. He shook his head. I nodded. "Creep like you would keep a couple," I said. "We'll toss your place later. How about you, Northrop? Where's your copies?"

"I burned them," he said.

Hawk grinned broadly. I nodded again. "Yeah. We'll look through your desk too, Northrop."

Brenda had not changed position. She was still rubbing her upper arms, looking at Hanson the way she had been looking at May.

"How could you do it?" she said.

Hanson looked at her blankly. "Huh?"

"How could you rape someone like that, for money?"

Hanson looked puzzled. "Hey," he said, "you're a nice-looking broad."

Brenda's face was bunched in concentration. "But what about me? What about how I felt? It's like I was a . . . a mechanism and you were a mechanic. Didn't you ever think about how I might feel?"

Hanson looked even more confused. "A grand," he said. "A grand's a lot of dough, lady."

Brenda stared at him. Her breathing was getting more rapid.

Hanson looked at May. "How about you, you pansy bastard, what'd you do, get lovey dovey and feel bad and confess?"

May didn't look up.

"I should never have hooked up with a goddamned pansy like you. You don't know how to act."

Without moving from the door Hawk said, "Shh." Hanson stopped as if a lock had clicked.

"Jail," Brenda said, her breathing heavy, like she'd been running. "You are both going to jail forever, don't you care?"

Neither man looked at her.

"Don't you care? Doesn't either of you care how I felt?"

She looked at me and Hawk, a woman alone in a roomful of men. "How would you like it?" she said. "How would you like this pig to walk into your house and strip you naked and rape you? How would you like to be lying on the floor, the floor for crissake, with his sweat all over you, and have him take your picture?"

Hawk's face was impassive and pleasant. For all you could tell he might have been listening to the beat of a different drummer.

"Doesn't anyone care about that?" Brenda said.

"Hanson can't," I said. "Lot of guys like him in the joint. Sometimes, I suppose, it's the joint makes them like that. Sometimes being like that gets them into the joint in the first place. He doesn't care about you; he doesn't even care about himself. Hell, he doesn't understand the question."

"How about you, North? Do you understand the question?" Brenda had turned, still hugging herself, and leaned toward May again.

May pressed his clasped hands against his forehead, his body bent forward. His voice was very small. "I'm sorry, Brenda. I was crazy. It's just that I wanted so little. It seemed so little to ask. I guess it drove me a little crazy."

"What you wanted, 'North,' was total possession," Brenda said.

He nodded. His face against his hands.

"I couldn't give you that," Brenda said, almost gently.

"I know," May said. "I guess, I loved not wisely but too well."

Tears suddenly appeared in Brenda's eyes.

I said, "May, you're not Othello nor were meant to be. It's not her fault that she got raped."

Brenda straightened, turned away from May and said quite briskly to me, "How long will they be in jail?"

"Hard to say, depends on the sentence, and that depends on judges and lawyers and jurors," I shrugged.

"If they go," Hawk said.

"What's he mean?" Brenda said.

"It's an imperfect system," I said. "Hanson will fall. He's done time. They'll mail him right back, express. But Northrop . . . he's a professor; he's got money. He might not go. If he does he might get out soon."

"You mean he could do this to me and get away with it?"

"Not everyone who's bad gets punished," I said.

"I'm still walking around," Hawk murmured.

Brenda stared at me. "He might not even be punished," she said. She didn't seem to be talking to me. "And they're not even sorry." She didn't seem to be talking to anyone.

"I could whack them out for you, if you'd like," Hawk said.

Brenda looked at him a little startled. She smiled. "No," she said. "No thank you."

The room was quiet again. Brenda closed her eyes, put her palms together, and placed the tips of her pressed fingers against her lips. She stood that way for maybe twenty seconds. Then she went to the sideboard and took a small silver automatic pistol from her purse. Holding the gun in both hands as I'd taught her to a long time ago, she began to shoot. The first two rounds got Northrop in the face. The third shattered the lamp behind him on the end table. The fourth thudded into a big gold pillow in the wing chair, and the fifth, after she steadied and aimed, drilled Richie Hanson through the upper lip just below his left nostril. The .25-caliber Colt had made small snapping noises as she fired, like an angry poodle. But in the silence that settled behind the shots, May and Hanson were exactly as dead as if she'd used a bazooka.

Hawk was still leaning against the door. "Dyn-o-mite," he said.

Brenda put the gun down on the sideboard, got a package of Merit cigarettes out of her purse, lit one with a butane lighter, and dragged a third of it in. She looked at the just-created corpses and let the smoke drift slowly out through barely parted lips.

"If they had been sorry," she said.

I looked at Hawk. "Yeah," he said. "I can take care of it."

"Good," I said. "Come on, babe, we're going to go visit Susan Silverman."

Brenda frowned. She spoke slowly now, tiredly: "We're going to . . . cover this up?"

"Yes."

"But what will you do with . . ." She gestured at the dead men.

Hawk said, "I know a man with a salvage yard."

"You came to me for protection," I said. "Directly from the

cops this morning. We went straight to Susan's and have been there ever since. It'll be a few days before they even know Northrop's gone. Nobody'll look for Hanson."

Brenda looked at the apartment.

"Brenda, one of the things Hawk is best at in all the world is covering up a death. You wish you hadn't shot them?"

"No," she said. Her voice was very firm.

I picked up the small silver gun and slipped it in my pocket. I offered her my arm. She took it and we left. As I closed the door behind us I could hear Hawk whistling softly to himself, "Moody's Mood for Love," as he punched out a number on the phone.

In a half an hour we were in Smithfield, and Susan was helping Brenda feel better. Me too.

PART II

CRIMINAL MINDS

MUSHROOMS

BY DENNIS LEHANE

Dorchester

(Originally published in 2006)

Her boyfriend, KL, is driving, and she and Sylvester are packed beside him in the front seat of the Escalade, sucking down Lites as they drive through the rain from Dorchester, Massachusetts, to Hampton Beach, New Hampshire. Every twenty miles or so, KL reaches over her shoulder and taps Sylvester's neck and says, "Sylvester, you know my girlfriend, right?" until Sylvester finally says, "Hey, KL. Okay. We've met."

She and KL dropped two hits of GHB just before they picked Sylvester up, and she thinks it's starting to show. She keeps touching her face with sweaty hands and giggling because they've forgotten the bullets and it's been a long time since she's seen the ocean and here it is raining and because KL keeps flinching every time a puddle explodes against his silver rims.

"KL," Sylvester says, "this girl is fucked up."

She says, "Sylvester, your nose is weird. Anyone ever tell you that? One nostril is tiny. And the other is, like, jet-engine size." She tries to touch his nose.

"Serious, KL," Sylvester says. "Fucked up."

KL says to him, "Relax. Find something on the radio, look at the scenery, do some fucking thing."

Sylvester rests the side of his forehead against the window

and stares out at the rain snapping off the highway, boiling in puddles.

When they reach the beach, it's empty, even the boardwalk, just like KL figured. They sit on the seawall and KL gives her his pissed-off glare. She can't tell if he's pissed off because she left the bullets in her other jacket or if he's still part-pissed about the whole situation in general. Eventually, he gives her a smile when she raises her right eyebrow. He kisses her and his tongue tastes like metal because of the GHB and then he says, "Sylvester, come smoke this with me." He and Sylvester walk down the beach in the rain and she sits on the wall in the cold and watches while they walk into the ocean and KL holds Sylvester under the water until he drowns.

He hands her the gun when he gets back, tells her to hold on to it.

She says, "That's kind of risky, don't you think?"

He puts his thumbs under her eyelids and pulls them down, looks into her eyes. "Drugs making you paranoid. That's a good gun."

They walk the beach for a bit as KL tells her how he did it, how he bluffed with the gun, put it against Sylvester's head and forced him down into the water. "I tell him I'm just going to teach him a lesson, hold him down for a minute because he fucked up with Whitehall and that Rory thing too."

"He believe you?"

KL smiles, kind of surprised himself. "For a few seconds, yeah. After that, it didn't much matter."

She watches the water to see if Sylvester pops up anywhere, but the waves are cold and gray and high, like whales, and KL tells her there was a pretty strong undertow out there too. Clams, a few inches below the wet sand, spit on her feet as she stares at the sea and KL wraps his arms around her from behind. She leans back into his chest, the heat of it, and KL says, "I had a dream about killing him last night. How it would feel."

"And?"

He shrugs. "Wasn't much different."

She wasn't always old.

Not long ago she was a girl, a girl without breasts, with a little boy's body really. She walked back from school one day in a skirt she hated—an itchy, woolen thing with pleats, black-and-gray plaid, a chafing thing. She walked alone—usually she was alone—and the streets she followed home were tired, like they'd had a flu too long, the buildings leaning forward as if they'd topple onto her braided hair, her nose, her little boy's body.

She cut through a playground, and there was a man sitting on the jungle gym, drinking a tall can of beer. He wore an army uniform that had sharp creases in the pants even though the shirt was wrinkled. He stood and blocked her path. She met his eyes and saw that there was a kindness hiding in them behind the rest of what lived there, which was good, because the rest of what lived there was hopeless, as if all the light had been vacuumed out. She never knew how long they stared at each other—a day maybe, an hour, a year—but everything changed. Her little boy's body disappeared forever, sucked into those blasted eyes, replaced with a new body, a body that ached, that tingled as he watched her, a body covered with skin so new and thin it felt raw.

He said, "Fuck you waiting for, little girl? A hall pass?" And he bowed and held out his arm and she saw light fill his eyes for an instant, a moment in which she saw how beautiful they could be, powder blue and soft, love living there like a morning prayer. When he caressed her ass as she passed, she resisted the urge to lean into his hand.

When she got home, she saw his eyes in the mirror. She ran a hand over her new body, over the sudden nubs of her breasts, and she knew for the first time why her father some-times seemed afraid and ashamed when he looked at her. She knew, looking in the mirror, that she was not of him; she was of her mother; she felt buried with her in the dark earth.

The next day, when she walked through the playground, he was waiting. He was smiling, and his shirt had been ironed.

What happened to Sylvester was all Rory's fault, really, part of the stupid shit that went on in their neighborhood so much that to keep up with the whos and the whys you'd need a damn scorecard.

Rory stole some guy's Zoom LeBrons one night while ev-eryone was goofing in the hydrant spray. When the guy asked around, one of Rory's girlfriends, Lorraine, told the guy it was Rory. Lorraine hated Rory because he'd saddled her with a baby who shit and cried all night and kept her from her friends. So the guy kicked Rory's ass and took his LeBrons back, and one night Rory and his buddy Pearl took Lorraine up to Pope's Hill and caved in her head with a tree branch. Once she was dead, they did some other things too so the police would think it was some psycho and not a neighborhood thing.

Rory told some friends, though; said it was like fucking a fish on ice. And Sylvester heard about it. Sylvester was Lor-raine's half brother on the father's side, and one night he and a carload of boys came cruising for Rory.

It was summer and she was sitting on her stoop waiting for KL. Her father was inside snoozing, and her sister, Sonya, was sitting on the big blue mailbox at the head of the alley, saying she was going to tell their father she was seeing KL again, catch her another beating. Sonya was singing it: "I'm a tell Dad-ee / You and KL getting bump-ee."

Then Rory came out of his house and she saw the car come up the street with the windows rolling down and the muzzles sticking out and she began to step off the stoop when the noise started and Sonya floated for a second, as if the breeze had puckered up and kissed her. She floated up off the mailbox and then she flipped sideways and hit a trash can a few feet back in the alley.

Rory danced against the wall of the Korean deli, parts of him popping, his arms flapping like a stork's.

When she reached Sonya, her sister was covering her kneecaps with her palms. She brushed her hair back out of her eyes and held her shoulders until her teeth stopped chattering, until the tiny whistle-noise coming from her chest stopped all at once, just whistled back into itself and went to sleep.

KL calls them mushrooms. It's like that old Centipede game, KL says, where you have to shoot the centipede but those mushrooms keep falling, getting in the way.

Sometimes, KL says, you're aiming for the centipede, but you hit the mushroom.

KL found out the Whitehall crew from Franklin Park was looking for Sylvester because he owed them big and hadn't been making payments. When KL told them he knew firsthand that Sylvester had been borrowing elsewhere, Whitehall agreed to his offer. Just do it out of state, they told him. Too many people hoping to tie us to shit.

So KL waited until October and they ended up driving to Hampton Beach with Sylvester, kept going even after she realized she'd forgotten the bullets. Sylvester, leaning his head against the window, so stupid he doesn't even know KL's girlfriend is the sister of the girl on the mailbox. So stupid he thinks KL's suddenly his best friend, taking him out for a Sunday drive. So stupid.

Period.

On the beach, she asks KL if he looked into Sylvester's eyes before he made him kneel in the ocean, if maybe he saw anything there.

"Come on," KL says, "just, fuck, shut up, you know?"

She's been out to the ocean once before. Not long after KL got back from Afghanistan and she met up with him, he scored off this cop who'd been part of the Lafayette Raiders bust. This cop had known someone who'd served over there with KL, someone who hadn't made it back, and he sold the shit to KL for 40 percent of the street value, called it his "yellow ribbon" price, supporting the troops and shit. KL turned that package over in one night, and the next day they took the ferry to Provincetown.

They walked the dunes and they felt like silk underfoot, large spilling drifts of white silk. They ate lobster and watched the sky darken and become striped with pale pink ribbons. On the ferry back, she could smell the sun in KL's fingers as they played with her hair. She could smell the dunes and the silk sand and the butter that had dripped off the lobster meat. And as the city appeared, all silver glitter and white and yellow light, she could feel the hum and hulk of it wash the smells away. She pressed her palm against KL's hard stomach, felt the cables of muscle under the flesh, and she wished she could still smell it all baked into his skin.

She walks up the wet beach with him now and they cross the boardwalk and she thinks of Sonya floating off that mailbox and floating, right now, somewhere beyond this world, looking down, and she feels that her baby sister has grown older too, older than herself, that she has run far ahead of time and its laws. She is wrinkled now and wiser and she does not approve of what they have done.

What they have done needed to be done. She feels sure of that. Someone had to pay, a message had to be sent. Can't have some fool traveling free through life like he got an all-day bus pass. You got to pay the freight. Everyone. Got to.

But still she can feel her sister, looking down on her with a grim set to her mouth, thinking: Stupid. Stupid.

She and KL reach the Escalade and he opens the hatch and she places the gun in there under the mat and the tire iron and the donut spare.

"Never want to hear his name aloud," KL says. "Never again. We clear?"

She nods and they stand there in the sweeping rain.

"What now?" she says.

"Huh?"

"What now?" she repeats, because suddenly she has to know. She has to.

"We go home."

"And then?"

He shrugs. "No then."

"There's gotta be then. There's gotta be something next."

Another shrug. "There ain't."

In the Escalade, KL driving, the rain still coming down,

she thinks about going back to school, finishing. She imagines herself in a nurse's uniform, living someplace beyond the neighborhood. She worries she's getting ahead of herself. Don't look so far into the future. Look into the next minute. See it. See that next minute pressing against your face. What can you do with it? With that time? What?

She closes her eyes. She tries to see it. She tries to make it her own. She tries and tries.

LUCKY PENNY

BY LINDA BARNES

Beacon Hill

(Originally published in 1985)

Lieutenant Mooney made me dish it all out for the record. He's a good cop, if such an animal exists. We used
to work the same shift before I decided—wrongly—
that there was room for a lady PI in this town. Who knows?
With this case under my belt, maybe business'll take a
180-degree spin, and I can quit driving a hack.

See, I've already written the official report for Mooney
and the cops, but the kind of stuff they wanted—date,
place, and time, cold as ice and submitted in triplicate—
doesn't even start to tell the tale. So I'm doing it over again,
my way.

Don't worry, Mooney. I'm not gonna file this one.

The Thayler case was still splattered across the front page of
the *Boston Globe*. I'd soaked it up with my midnight coffee and
was puzzling it out—my cab on automatic pilot, my mind on
crime—when the mad tea party began.

"Take your next right, sister. Then pull over, and douse
the lights. Quick!"

I heard the bastard all right, but it must have taken me
thirty seconds or so to react. Something hard rapped on the
cab's dividing shield. I didn't bother turning around. I hate
staring down gun barrels.

I said, "Jimmy Cagney, right? No, your voice is too high. Let me guess, don't tell me—"

"Shut up!"

"*Kill* the lights, *turn off* the lights, okay. But *douse* the lights? You've been tuning in too many old gangster flicks."

"I hate a mouthy broad," the guy snarled. I kid you not.

"*Broad*," I said. "Christ! *Broad*? You trying to grow hair on your balls?"

"Look, I mean it, lady!"

"*Lady's* better. Now you wanna vacate my cab and go rob a phone booth?" My heart was beating like a tin drum, but I didn't let my voice shake, and all the time I was gabbing at him, I kept trying to catch his face in the mirror. He must have been crouching way back on the passenger side. I couldn't see a damn thing.

"I want all your dough," he said.

Who can you trust? This guy was a spiffy dresser: charcoal-gray three-piece suit and rep tie, no less. And picked up in front of the swank Copley Plaza. *I* looked like I needed the bucks more than he did, and I'm no charity case. A woman can make good tips driving a hack in Boston. Oh, she's gotta take precautions, all right. When you can't smell a disaster fare from thirty feet, it's time to quit. I pride myself on my judgment. I'm careful. I always know where the police check-points are, so I can roll my cab past and flash the old lights if a guy starts acting up. This dude fooled me cold.

I was ripped. Not only had I been conned, I had a consid-erable wad to give away. It was near the end of my shift, and like I said, I do all right. I've got a lot of regulars. Once you see me, you don't forget me—or my cab.

It's gorgeous. Part of my inheritance. A '59 Chevy, shiny as new, kept on blocks in a heated garage by the proverbial dotty old lady. It's the pits of the design world. Glossy blue with those giant chromium fins. Restrained decor: just the phone number and a few gilt curlicues on the door. I was afraid all my old pals at the police department would pull me over for minor traffic violations if I went whole hog and painted "Carlotta's Cab" in ornate script on the hood. Some do it anyway.

So where the hell were all the cops now? Where are they when you need 'em?

He told me to shove the cash through that little hole they leave for the passenger to pass the fare forward. I told him he had it backwards. He didn't laugh. I shoved bills.

"Now the change," the guy said. Can you imagine the nerve?

I must have cast my eyes up to heaven. I do that a lot these days.

"I mean it." He rapped the plastic shield with the shiny barrel of his gun. I checked it out this time. Funny how big a little .22 looks when it's pointed just right.

I fished in my pockets for change, emptied them.

"Is that all?"

"You want the gold cap on my left front molar?" I said.

"Turn around," the guy barked. "Keep both hands on the steering wheel. High."

I heard jingling, then a quick intake of breath.

"Okay," the crook said, sounding happy as a clam, "I'm gonna take my leave—"

"Good. Don't call this cab again."

"Listen!" The gun tapped. "You cool it here for ten minutes. And I mean frozen. Don't twitch. Don't blow your nose. Then take off."

"Gee, thanks."

"Thank *you*," he said politely. The door slammed.

At times like that, you just feel ridiculous. You *know* the guy isn't going to hang around, waiting to see whether you're big on insubordination. *But*, he might. And who wants to tangle with a .22 slug? I rate pretty high on insubordination. That's why I messed up as a cop. I figured I'd give him two minutes to get lost. Meantime I listened.

Not much traffic goes by those little streets on Beacon Hill at one o'clock on a Wednesday morn. Too residential. So I could hear the guy's footsteps tap along the pavement. About ten steps back, he stopped. Was he the one in a million who'd wait to see if I turned around? I heard a funny kind of *whooshing* noise. Not loud enough to make me jump, and anything much louder than the ticking of my watch would have put me through the roof. Then the footsteps patted on, straight back and out of hearing.

One minute more. The only saving grace of the situation was the location: District One. That's Mooney's district. Nice guy to talk to.

I took a deep breath, hoping it would have an encore, and pivoted quickly, keeping my head low. Makes you feel stupid when you do that and there's no one around.

I got out and strolled to the corner, stuck my head around a building kind of cautiously. Nothing, of course.

I backtracked. Ten steps, then *whoosh*. Along the sidewalk stood one of those new "Keep Beacon Hill Beautiful" trash cans, the kind with the swinging lid. I gave it a shove as I passed. I could just as easily have kicked it; I was in that kind of funk.

Whoosh, it said, just as pretty as could be.

Breaking into one of those trash cans is probably tougher than busting into your local bank vault. Since I didn't even have a dime left to fiddle the screws on the lid, I was forced to deface city property. I got the damn thing open and dumped the contents on somebody's front lawn, smack in the middle of a circle of light from one of those snooty Beacon Hill gas streetlamps.

Halfway through the whiskey bottles, wadded napkins, and beer cans, I made my discovery. I was doing a thorough search. If you're going to stink like garbage anyway, why leave anything untouched, right? So I was opening all the brown bags—you know, the good old brown lunch-and-bottle bags—looking for a clue. My most valuable find so far had been the moldy rind of a bologna sandwich. Then I hit it big: one neatly creased bag stuffed full of cash.

To say I was stunned is to entirely underestimate how I felt as I crouched there, knee-deep in garbage, my jaw hanging wide. I don't know what I'd expected to find. Maybe the guy's gloves. Or his hat, if he'd wanted to get rid of it fast in order to melt back into anonymity. I pawed through the rest of the debris. My change was gone.

I was so befuddled I left the trash right on the front lawn. There's probably still a warrant out for my arrest.

District One headquarters is off the beaten path, over on New Sudbury Street. I would have called first, if I'd had a dime.

One of the few things I'd enjoyed about being a cop was gabbing with Mooney. I like driving a cab better, but, face it, most of my fares aren't scintillating conversationalists. The Red Sox and the weather usually covers it. Talking to Mooney was so much fun, I wouldn't even consider dating him. Lots of guys are good at sex, but conversation—now there's an art form.

Mooney, all six-feet-four, 240 linebacker pounds of him, gave me the glad eye when I waltzed in. He hasn't given up trying. Keeps telling me he talks even better in bed.

"Nice hat," was all he said, his big fingers pecking at the typewriter keys.

I took it off and shook out my hair. I wear an old slouch cap when I drive to keep people from saying the inevitable. One jerk even misquoted Yeats at me: "Only God, my dear, could love you for yourself alone and not your long red hair." Since I'm seated when I drive, he missed the chance to ask me how the weather is up here. I'm six-one in my stocking feet and skinny enough to make every inch count twice. I've got a wide forehead, green eyes, and a pointy chin. If you want to be nice about my nose, you say it's got character.

Thirty's still hovering in my future. It's part of Mooney's past.

I told him I had a robbery to report and his dark eyes steered me to a chair. He leaned back and took a puff of one of his low-tar cigarettes. He can't quite give 'em up, but he feels guilty as hell about 'em.

When I got to the part about the bag in the trash, Mooney lost his sense of humor. He crushed a half-smoked butt in a crowded ashtray.

"Know why you never made it as a cop?" he said.

"Didn't brown-nose enough."

"You got no sense of proportion! Always going after crackpot stuff!"

"Christ, Mooney, aren't you interested? Some guy heists a cab, at gunpoint, then tosses the money. Aren't you the least bit *intrigued*?"

"I'm a cop, Ms. Carlyle. I've got to be more than intrigued. I've got murders, bank robberies, assaults—"

"Well, excuse me. I'm just a poor citizen reporting a crime. Trying to help—"

"Want to help, Carlotta? Go away." He stared at the sheet of paper in the typewriter and lit another cigarette. "Or dig me up something on the Thayler case."

"You working that sucker?"

"Wish to hell I wasn't."

I could see his point. It's tough enough trying to solve any murder, but when your victim is *the* Jennifer (Mrs. Justin) Thayler, wife of the famed Harvard Law prof, and the society reporters are breathing down your neck along with the usual crime-beat scribblers, you got a special kind of problem.

"So who did it?" I asked.

Mooney put his size twelves up on his desk. "Colonel Mustard in the library with the candlestick! How the hell do I know? Some scumbag housebreaker. The lady of the house interrupted his haul. Probably didn't mean to hit her that hard. He must have freaked when he saw all the blood, 'cause he left some of the ritziest stereo equipment this side of heaven, plus enough silverware to blind your average hophead. He snatched most of old man Thayler's goddamn idiot artworks, collections, collectibles—whatever the hell you call 'em— which ought to set him up for the next few hundred years, if he's smart enough to get rid of them."

"Alarm system?"

"Yeah, they had one. Looks like Mrs. Thayler forgot to turn it on. According to the maid, she had a habit of forgetting just about anything after a martini or three."

"Think the maid's in on it?"

"Christ, Carlotta. There you go again. No witnesses. No fingerprints. Servants asleep. Husband asleep. We've got word out to all the fences here and in New York that we want this guy. The pawnbrokers know the stuff's hot. We're checking out known art thieves and shady museums—"

"Well, don't let me keep you from your serious business," I said, getting up to go. "I'll give you the collar when I find out who robbed my cab."

"Sure," he said. His fingers started playing with the type-writer again.

"Wanna bet on it?" Betting's an old custom with Mooney and me.

"I'm not gonna take the few piddling bucks you earn with that ridiculous car."

"Right you are, boy. I'm gonna take the money the city pays you to be unimaginative! Fifty bucks I nail him within the week."

Mooney hates to be called "boy." He hates to be called "unimaginative." I hate to hear my car called "ridiculous." We shook hands on the deal. Hard.

Chinatown's about the only chunk of Boston that's alive after midnight. I headed over to Yee Hong's for a bowl of won-ton soup.

The service was the usual low-key, slow-motion routine. I used a newspaper as a shield; if you're really involved in the *Wall Street Journal*, the casual male may think twice before deciding he's the answer to your prayers. But I didn't read a single stock quote. I tugged at strands of my hair, a bad habit of mine. Why would somebody rob me and then toss the money away?

Solution Number One: He didn't. The trash bin was some mob drop, and the money I'd found in the trash had absolutely nothing to do with the money filched from my cab. Except that it was the same amount—and that was too big a coincidence for me to swallow.

Two: The cash I'd found was counterfeit and this was a clever way of getting it into circulation. Nah. Too baroque entirely. How the hell would the guy know I was the pawing-through-the-trash type?

Three: It was a training session. Some fool had used me to perfect his robbery technique. Couldn't he learn from TV like the rest of the crooks?

Four: It was a frat hazing. Robbing a hack at gunpoint isn't exactly in the same league as swallowing goldfish.

I closed my eyes.

My face came to a fortunate halt about an inch above a bowl of steaming broth. That's when I decided to pack it in and head for home. Wonton soup is lousy for the complexion.

I checked out the log I keep in the Chevy, totaled my fares: $4.82 missing, all in change. A very reasonable robbery.

By the time I got home, the sleepiness had passed. You know how it is: one moment you're yawning, the next your eyes won't close. Usually happens when my head hits the pillow; this time I didn't even make it that far. What woke me up was the idea that my robber hadn't meant to steal a thing. Maybe he'd left me something instead. You know, something hot, cleverly concealed. Something he could pick up in a few weeks, after things cooled off.

I went over that backseat with a vengeance, but I didn't find anything besides old Kleenex and bent paperclips. My brainstorm wasn't too clever after all. I mean, if the guy wanted to use my cab as a hiding place, why advertise by pulling a five-and-dime robbery?

I sat in the driver's seat, tugged my hair, and stewed. What did I have to go on? The memory of a nervous thief who talked like a B movie and stole only change. Maybe a mad toll-booth collector.

I live in a Cambridge dump. In any other city, I couldn't sell the damned thing if I wanted to. Here, I turn real estate agents away daily. The key to my home's value is the fact that I can hoof it to Harvard Square in five minutes. It's a seller's market for tar-paper shacks within walking distance of the Square. Under a hundred thou only if the plumbing's outside.

It took me awhile to get in the door. I've got about five locks on it. Neighborhood's popular with thieves as well as gentry. I'm neither. I inherited the house from my weird Aunt Bea, all paid for. I consider the property taxes my rent, and the rent's getting steeper all the time.

I slammed my log down on the dining room table. I've got rooms galore in that old house, rent a couple of them to Harvard students. I've got my own office on the second floor, but I do most of my work at the dining room table. I like the view of the refrigerator.

I started over from square one. I called Gloria. She's the late-night dispatcher for the Independent Taxi Owners Association. I've never seen her, but her voice is as smooth as mink oil and I'll bet we get a lot of calls from guys who just want to hear her say she'll pick 'em up in five minutes.

"Gloria, it's Carlotta."

"Hi, babe. You been pretty popular today."

"Was I popular at one thirty-five this morning?"

"Huh?"

"I picked up a fare in front of the Copley Plaza at one thirty-five. Did you hand that one out to all comers or did you give it to me solo?"

"Just a sec." I could hear her charming the pants off some caller in the background. Then she got back to me.

"I just gave him to you, babe. He asked for the lady in the '59 Chevy. Not a lot of those on the road."

"Thanks, Gloria."

"Trouble?" she asked.

"Is mah middle name," I twanged. We both laughed and I hung up before she got a chance to cross-examine me.

So. The robber wanted my cab. I wished I'd concentrated on his face instead of his snazzy clothes. Maybe it was somebody I knew, some jokester in mid-prank. I killed that idea; I don't know anybody who'd pull a stunt like that, at gunpoint and all. I don't want to know anybody like that.

Why rob my cab, then toss the dough?

I pondered sudden religious conversion. Discarded it. Maybe some robber was some perpetual screwup who'd ditched the cash by mistake.

Or . . . Maybe he got exactly what he wanted. Maybe he desperately desired my change.

Why?

Because my change was special, valuable beyond its $4.82 replacement cost.

So how would somebody know my change was valuable?

Because he'd given it to me himself, earlier in the day.

"Not bad," I said out loud. "Not bad." It was the kind of reasoning they'd bounced me off the police force for, what my so-called superiors termed the "fevered product of an over-imaginative mind." I leapt at it because it was the only explanation I could think of. I do like life to make some sort of sense.

I pored over my log. I keep pretty good notes: where I pick up a fare, where I drop him, whether he's a hailer or a radio call.

First, I ruled out all the women. That made the task slightly less impossible: sixteen suspects down from thirty-five. Then I yanked my hair and stared at the blank white porcelain of the refrigerator door. Got up and made myself a sandwich: ham, Swiss cheese, salami, lettuce, and tomato, on rye.

Ate it. Stared at the porcelain some more until the suspects started coming into focus.

Five of the guys were just plain fat and one was decidedly on the hefty side; I'd felt like telling them all to walk. Might do them some good, might bring on a heart attack. I crossed them all out. Making a thin person look plump is hard enough; it's damn near impossible to make a fatty look thin.

Then I considered my regulars: Jonah Ashley, a tiny blond Southern gent; muscle-bound "just-call-me-Harold" at Longfellow Place; Dr. Homewood getting his daily ferry from Beth Israel to MGH; Marvin of the gay bars; and Professor Dickerman, Harvard's answer to Berkeley's sixties radicals.

I crossed them all off. I could see Dickerman holding up the First Filthy Capitalist Bank, or disobeying civilly at Seabrook, even blowing up an oil company or two. But my mind boggled at the thought of the great liberal Dickerman robbing some poor cabbie. It would be like Robin Hood joining the sheriff of Nottingham on some particularly rotten peasant swindle. Then they'd both rape Maid Marian and go off pals together.

Dickerman *was* a lousy tipper. That ought to be a crime.

So what did I leave? Eleven out of sixteen guys cleared without leaving my chair. Me and Sherlock Holmes, the famous armchair detectives.

I'm stubborn; that was one of my good cop traits. I stared at that log till my eyes bugged out. I remembered two of the five pretty easily; they were handsome and I'm far from blind. The first had one of those elegant bony faces and far-apart eyes. He was taller than my bandit. I'd ceased eyeballing him when I noticed the ring on his left hand; I never fuss with the married kind. The other one was built, a weight lifter. Not an Arnold Schwarzenegger extremist, but built. I think I'd have noticed that bod on my bandit. Like I said, I'm not blind.

That left three.

Okay. I closed my eyes. Who had I picked up at the Hyatt on Memorial Drive? Yeah, that was the salesman guy, the one who looked so uncomfortable that I'd figured he'd been hoping to ask his cabbie for a few pointers concerning the best skirt-chasing areas in our fair city. Too low a voice. Too broad in the beam.

The log said I'd picked up a hailer at Kenmore Square when I'd let out the salesman. Ah, yes, a talker. The weather, mostly. Don't you think it's dangerous for you to be driving a cab? Yeah, I remembered him all right: a fatherly type, clasping a briefcase, heading to the financial district. Too old.

Down to one. I was exhausted but not the least bit sleepy. All I had to do was remember who I'd picked up on Beacon near Charles. A hailer. Before five o'clock, which was fine by me because I wanted to be long gone before rush hour gridlocked the city. I'd gotten onto Storrow and taken him along the river into Newton Center. Dropped him off at the Bay Bank Middlesex, right before closing time. It was coming back. Little nervous guy. Pegged him as an accountant when I'd let him out at the bank. Measly, undernourished soul. Skinny as a rail, stooped, with pits left from teenage acne.

Shit. I let my head sink down onto the dining room table when I realized what I'd done. I'd ruled them all out, every one. So much for my brilliant deductive powers.

I retired to my bedroom, disgusted. Not only had I lost $4.82 in assorted alloy metals, I was going to lose fifty dollars to Mooney. I stared at myself in the mirror, but what I was really seeing was the round hole at the end of a .22, held in a neat, gloved hand.

Somehow, the gloves made me feel better. I'd remembered

another detail about my piggy-bank robber. I consulted the mirror and kept the recall going. A hat. The guy wore a hat. Not like my cap, but like a hat out of a forties gangster flick. I had one of those: I'm a sucker for hats. I plunked it on my head, jamming my hair up underneath—and I drew in my breath sharply.

A shoulder-padded jacket, a slim build, a low slouched hat. Gloves. Boots with enough heel to click as he walked away. Voice? High. Breathy, almost whispered. Not unpleasant. Accentless. No Boston *r*.

I had a man's jacket and a couple of ties in my closet. Don't ask. They may have dated from as far back as my ex-husband, but not necessarily so. I slipped into the jacket, knotted the tie, tilted the hat down over one eye.

I'd have trouble pulling it off. I'm skinny, but my build is decidedly female. Still, I wondered—enough to traipse back downstairs, pull a chicken leg out of the fridge, go back to the log, and review the feminine possibilities. Good thing I did.

Everything clicked. One lady fit the bill exactly: mannish walk and clothes, tall for a woman. And I was in luck. While I'd picked her up in Harvard Square, I'd dropped her at a real address, a house in Brookline: 782 Mason Terrace, at the top of Corey Hill.

JoJo's garage opens at seven. That gave me a big two hours to sleep.

I took my beloved car in for some repair work it really didn't need yet and sweet-talked JoJo into giving me a loaner. I needed a hack, but not mine. Only trouble with that Chevy is it's too damn conspicuous.

I figured I'd lose way more than fifty bucks staking out Mason Terrace. I also figured it would be worth it to see old Mooney's face.

She was regular as clockwork, a dream to tail. Eight thirty-seven every morning, she got a ride to the Square with a next-door neighbor. Took a cab home at five fifteen. A working woman. Well, she couldn't make much of a living from robbing hacks and dumping the loot in the garbage.

I was damn curious by now. I knew as soon as I looked her over that she was the one, but she seemed so blah, so *normal*. She must have been five-seven or -eight, but the way she stooped, she didn't look tall. Her hair was long and brown with a lot of blond in it, the kind of hair that would have been terrific loose and wild, like a horse's mane. She tied it back with a scarf. A brown scarf. She wore suits. Brown suits. She had a tiny nose, brown eyes under pale eyebrows, a sharp chin. I never saw her smile. Maybe what she needed was a shrink, not a session with Mooney. Maybe she'd done it for the excitement. God knows, if I had her routine, her job, I'd probaby be dressing up like King Kong and assaulting skyscrapers.

See, I followed her to work. It wasn't even tricky. She trudged the same path, went in the same entrance to Harvard Yard, probably walked the same number of steps every morning. Her name was Marcia Heidegger and she was a secretary in the admissions office of the college of fine arts.

I got friendly with one of her coworkers.

There was this guy typing away like mad at a desk in her office. I could just see him from the side window. He had grad student written all over his face. Longish wispy hair. Gold-rimmed glasses. Serious. Given to deep sighs and bright velour V necks. Probably writing his thesis on "Courtly Love and the Theories of Chrétien de Troyes."

I latched onto him at Bailey's the day after I'd tracked Lady Heidegger to her Harvard lair.

Too bad Roger was so short. Most short guys find it hard

to believe that I'm really trying to pick them up. They look for ulterior motives. Not the Napoleon type of short guy; he assumes I've been waiting years for a chance to dance with a guy who doesn't have to bend to stare down my cleavage. But Roger was no Napoleon. So I had to engineer things a little.

I got into line ahead of him and ordered, after long deliberation, a BLT on toast. While the guy made it up and shoved it on a plate with three measly potato chips and a sliver of pickle you could barely see, I searched through my wallet, opened my change purse, counted out silver, got to $1.60 on the last five pennies. The counterman sang out, "That'll be a buck eighty-five." I pawed through my pockets, found a nickel, two pennies. The line was growing restive. I concentrated on looking like a damsel in need of a knight, a tough task for a woman over six feet.

Roger (I didn't know he was Roger then) smiled ruefully and passed over a quarter. I was effusive in my thanks. I sat at a table for two, and when he'd gotten his tray (ham-and-cheese and a strawberry ice cream soda), I motioned him into my extra chair.

He was a sweetie. Sitting down, he forgot the difference in our height, and decided I might be someone he could talk to. I encouraged him. I hung shamelessly on his every word. A Harvard man, imagine that. We got around slowly, ever so slowly, to his work at the admissions office. He wanted to duck it and talk about more important issues, but I persisted. I'd been thinking about getting a job at Harvard, possibly in admissions. What kind of people did he work with? Were they congenial? What was the atmosphere like? Was it a big office? How many people? Men? Women? Any soulmates? Readers? Or just, you know, office people?

According to him, every soul he worked with was brain

dead. I interrupted a stream of complaint with "Gee, I know somebody who works for Harvard. I wonder if you know her."

"It's a big place," he said, hoping to avoid the whole endless business.

"I met her at a party. Always meant to look her up." I searched through my bag, found a scrap of paper and pretended to read Marcia Heidegger's name off it.

"Marcia? Geez, I work with Marcia. Same office."

"Do you think she likes her work? I mean, I got some strange vibes from her," I said. I actually said "strange vibes" and he didn't laugh his head off. People in the Square say things like that and other people take them seriously.

His face got conspiratorial, of all things, and he leaned closer to me.

"You want it, I bet you could get Marcia's job."

"You mean it?" What a compliment—a place for me among the brain dead.

"She's gonna get fired if she doesn't snap out of it."

"Snap out of what?"

"It was bad enough working with her when she first came over. She's one of those crazy neat people, can't stand to see papers lying on a desktop, you know? She almost threw out the first chapter of my thesis!"

I made a suitably horrified noise and he went on.

"Well, you know, about Marcia, it's kind of tragic. She doesn't talk about it."

But he was dying to.

"Yes?" I said, as if he needed egging on.

He lowered his voice. "She used to work for Justin Thayler over at the law school, that guy in the news, whose wife got killed. You know, her work hasn't been worth shit since it happened. She's always on the phone, talking real soft, hanging up if anybody comes in the room. I mean, you'd think she was in love with the guy or something, the way she . . ."

I don't remember what I said. For all I know, I may have volunteered to type his thesis. But I got rid of him somehow and then I scooted around the corner of Church Street and found a pay phone and dialed Mooney.

"Don't tell me," he said. "Somebody mugged you, but they only took your trading stamps."

"I have just one question for you, Moon."

"I accept. A June wedding, but I'll have to break it to Mother gently."

"Tell me what kind of junk Justin Thayler collected."

I could hear him breathing into the phone.

"Just tell me," I said, "for curiosity's sake."

"You onto something, Carlotta?"

"I'm curious, Mooney. And you're not the only source of information in the world."

"Thayler collected Roman stuff. Antiques. And I mean old. Artifacts, statues—"

"Coins?"

"Whole mess of them."

"Thanks."

"Carlotta—"

I never did find out what he was about to say because I hung up. Rude, I know. But I had things to do. And it was better Mooney shouldn't know what they were, because they came under the heading of illegal activities.

When I knocked at the front door of the Mason Terrace house at ten a.m. the next day, I was dressed in dark slacks, a white blouse, and my old police department hat. I looked very much like the guy who reads your gas meter. I've never heard of anyone being arrested for impersonating the gasman.

I've never heard of anyone really giving the gasman a second look. He fades into the background and that's exactly what I wanted to do.

I knew Marcia Heidegger wouldn't be home for hours. Old reliable had left for the Square at her usual time, precise to the minute. But I wasn't 100 percent sure Marcia lived alone. Hence the gasman. I could knock on the door and check it out.

Those Brookline neighborhoods kill me. Act sneaky and the neighbors call the cops in twenty seconds, but walk right up to the front door, knock, talk to yourself while you're sticking a shim in the crack of the door, let yourself in, and nobody does a thing. Boldness is all.

The place wasn't bad. Three rooms, kitchen and bath, light and airy. Marcia was incredibly organized, obsessively neat, which meant I had to keep track of where everything was and put it back just so. There was no clutter in the woman's life. The smell of coffee and toast lingered, but if she'd eaten breakfast, she'd already washed, dried, and put away the dishes. The morning paper had been read and tossed in the trash. The mail was sorted in one of those plastic accordion files. I mean, she folded her underwear like origami.

Now coins are hard to look for. They're small; you can hide 'em anywhere. So this search took me one hell of a long time. Nine out of ten women hide things that are dear to them in the bedroom. They keep their finest jewelry closest to the bed, sometimes in the nightstand, sometimes right under the mattress. That's where I started.

Marcia had a jewelry box on top of her dresser. I felt like hiding it for her. She had some nice stuff and a burglar could have made quite a haul with no effort.

The next favorite place for women to stash valuables is

the kitchen. I sifted through her flour. I removed every Kellogg's Rice Krispy from the giant economy-sized box—and returned it. I went through her place like no burglar ever will. When I say thorough, I mean thorough.

I found four odd things. A neatly squared pile of clippings from the *Globe* and the *Herald*, all the articles about the Thayler killing. A manila envelope containing five different safe deposit box keys. A Tupperware container full of superstitious junk, good luck charms mostly, the kind of stuff I'd never have associated with a straight-arrow like Marcia: rabbits' feet galore, a little leather bag on a string that looked like some kind of voodoo charm, a pendant in the shape of a cross surmounted by a hook, and, I swear to God, a pack of worn tarot cards. Oh, yes, and a .22 automatic, looking a lot less threatening stuck in an ice cube tray. I took the bullets; the loaded gun threatened a defenseless box of Breyers mint chocolate-chip ice cream.

I left everything else just the way I'd found it and went home. And tugged my hair. And stewed. And brooded. And ate half the stuff in the refrigerator. I kid you not.

At about one in the morning, it all made blinding, crystal-clear sense.

The next afternoon, at five fifteen, I made sure I was the cabbie who picked up Marcia Heidegger in Harvard Square. Now cabstands have the most rigid protocol since Queen Victoria; you do not grab a fare out of turn or your fellow cabbies are definitely not amused. There was nothing for it but bribing the ranks. This bet with Mooney was costing me plenty.

I got her. She swung open the door and gave the Mason Terrace number. I grunted, kept my face turned front, and took off.

Some people really watch where you're going in a cab,

scared to death you'll take them a block out of their way and squeeze them for an extra nickel. Others just lean back and dream. She was a dreamer, thank God. I was almost at District One headquarters before she woke up.

"Excuse me," she said, polite as ever, "that's Mason Terrace in *Brookline.*"

"Take the next right, pull over, and douse your lights," I said in a low Bogart voice. My imitation was not that good, but it got the point across. Her eyes widened and she made an instinctive grab for the door handle.

"Don't try it, lady," I Bogied on. "You think I'm dumb enough to take you in alone? There's a cop car behind us, just waiting for you to make a move."

Her hand froze. She was a sap for movie dialogue.

"Where's the cop?" was all she said on the way up to Mooney's office.

"What cop?"

"The one following us."

"You have touching faith in our law-enforcement system," I said.

She tried to bolt, I kid you not. I've had experience with runners a lot trickier than Marcia. I grabbed her in approved cop hold number three and marched her into Mooney's office.

He actually stopped typing and raised an eyebrow, an expression of great shock for Mooney.

"Citizen's arrest," I said.

"Charges?"

"Petty theft. Commission of a felony using a firearm." I rattled off a few more charges, using the numbers I remembered from cop school.

"This woman is crazy," Marcia Heidegger said with all the dignity she could muster.

"Search her," I said. "Get a matron in here. I want my $4.82 back."

Mooney looked like he agreed with Marcia's opinion of my mental state. He said, "Wait up, Carlotta. You'd have to be able to identify that $4.82 as yours. Can you do that? Quarters are quarters. Dimes are dimes."

"One of the coins she took was quite unusual," I said. "I'm sure I'd be able to identify it."

"Do you have any objection to displaying the change in your purse?" Mooney said to Marcia. He got me mad the way he said it, like he was humoring an idiot.

"Of course not," old Marcia said, cool as a frozen daiquiri.

"That's because she's stashed it somewhere else, Mooney," I said patiently. "She used to keep it in her purse, see. But then she goofed. She handed it over to a cabbie in her change. She should have just let it go, but she panicked because it was worth a pile and she was just babysitting it for someone else. So when she got it back, she hid it somewhere. Like in her shoe. Didn't you ever carry your lucky penny in your shoe?"

"No," Mooney said. "Now, Miss—"

"Heidegger," I said clearly. "Marcia Heidegger. She used to work at Harvard Law School." I wanted to see if Mooney picked up on it, but he didn't. He went on: "This can be taken care of with a minimum of fuss. If you'll agree to be searched by—"

"I want to see my lawyer," she said.

"For $4.82?" he said. "It'll cost you more than that to get your lawyers up here."

"Do I get my phone call or not?"

Mooney shrugged wearily and wrote up the charge sheet. Called a cop to take her to the phone.

He got JoAnn, which was good. Under cover of our old-friend-long-time-no-see greetings, I whispered in her ear.

"You'll find it fifty well spent," I said to Mooney when we were alone.

JoAnn came back, shoving Marcia slightly ahead of her. She plunked her prisoner down in one of Mooney's hard wooden chairs and turned to me, grinning from ear to ear.

"Got it?" I said. "Good for you."

"What's going on?" Mooney said.

"She got real clumsy on the way to the pay phone," JoAnn said. "Practically fell on the floor. Got up with her right hand clenched tight. When we got to the phone, I offered to drop her dime for her. She wanted to do it herself. I insisted and she got clumsy again. Somehow this coin got kicked clear across the floor."

She held it up. The coin could have been a dime, except the color was off: warm, rosy gold instead of dead silver. How I missed it the first time around I'll never know.

"What the hell is that?" Mooney said.

"What kind of coins were in Justin Thayler's collection?" I asked. "Roman?"

Marcia jumped out of the chair, snapped her bag open, and drew out her little .22. I kid you not. She was closest to Mooney and she just stepped up to him and rested it above his left ear. He swallowed, didn't say a word. I never realized how prominent his Adam's apple was. JoAnn froze, hand on her holster.

Good old reliable, methodical Marcia. Why, I said to myself, *why* pick today of all days to trot your gun out of the freezer? Did you read bad luck in your tarot cards? Then I had a truly rotten thought. What if she had two guns? What if the disarmed .22 was still staring down the mint chocolate-chip ice cream?

"Give it back," Marcia said. She held out one hand, made an impatient waving motion.

"Hey, you don't need it, Marcia," I said. "You've got plenty more. In all those safe deposit boxes."

"I'm going to count to five—" she began.

"Were you in on the murder from day one? You know, from the planning stages?" I asked. I kept my voice low, but it echoed off the walls of Mooney's tiny office. The hum of everyday activity kept going in the main room. Nobody noticed the little gun in the well-dressed lady's hand. "Or did you just do your beau a favor and hide the loot after he iced his wife? In order to back up his burglary tale? I mean, if Justin Thayler really wanted to marry you, there is such a thing as divorce. Or was old Jennifer the one with the bucks?"

"I want that coin," she said softly. "Then I want the two of you"—she motioned to JoAnn and me—"to sit down facing that wall. If you yell, or do anything before I'm out of the building, I'll shoot this gentleman. He's coming with me."

"Come on, Marcia," I said, "put it down. I mean, look at you. A week ago you just wanted Thayler's coin back. You didn't want to rob my cab, right? You just didn't know how else to get your good luck charm back with no questions asked. You didn't do it for the money, right? You did it for love. You were so straight you threw away the cash. Now here you are with a gun pointed at a cop—"

"Shut up!"

I took a deep breath and said, "You haven't got the style, Marcia. Your gun's not even loaded."

Mooney didn't relax a hair. Sometimes I think the guy hasn't ever believed a word I've said to him. But Marcia got shook. She pulled the barrel away from Mooney's skull and peered at it with a puzzled frown. JoAnn and I both tackled her before she got a chance to pull the trigger. I twisted the gun out of her hand. I was almost afraid to look inside. Mooney stared at me and I felt my mouth go dry and a trickle of sweat worm its way down my back.

I looked.

No bullets. My heart stopped fibrillating, and Mooney actually cracked a smile in my direction.

So that's all. I sure hope Mooney will spread the word around that I helped him nail Thayler. And I think he will; he's a fair kind of guy. Maybe it'll get me a case or two. Driving a cab is hard on the backside, you know?

BLANCHE CLEANS UP (EXCERPT)

BY BARBARA NEELY

Brookline

(Originally published in 1998)

C uriosity—disguised as helping Carrie hand around the canapés—carried Blanche into the library where the guests had gathered for drinks before lunch.

Blanche was generally delighted to come across a group of black people, but her stomach dropped when she saw that the *They* Brindle had referred to were what she called The Down-town Leadership—the black men who the big downtown white folks talked to when they needed blacks with positions and titles to support the latest cut in programs for the poor, or to amen some closet racist like Brindle. Do the Brindles of the world really think we're all stupid enough to believe that shit is sunshine because the idiot who says so is black?

She recognized Ralph Gordon, the new head of the Rox-bury Outpatient Care Center. His face had been all over the papers a couple of months ago when the powers that be hired him after firing the woman who'd directed the health center for years. Her mistake had been complaining about cuts in her budget to the newspapers. Gordon was talking to James McGovern, the head of the Association of Afro Execs. He kept himself in the news by complaining about affirmative ac-tion and lying about black women taking jobs away from black men. Jonathan Carstairs, a lawyer who'd run for city coun-cillor from Roxbury, was guzzling something from a highball glass. His campaign platform had included arresting welfare mothers if their kids got into trouble. Naturally, he'd lost the election. Blanche thought of him as a prime example of how racism made black people crazy. A tall, paunchy man Blanche thought was a high muckety-muck at one of the banks and a couple of men she didn't recognize were hovering around Felicia Brindle.

She watched Allister Brindle work the room, shaking hands and slapping backs. Was it phoniness that made him look like he was made of cardboard? His guests melted before him like butter under a hot knife. The talk was partly about sports and partly a sermon from Brindle against those homos, welfare mothers, and drug-dealing teenage gangsters who were ruining the Commonwealth and the country. Blanche kept waiting for one of the guests to take exception. None did.

Blanche wasn't at all surprised that nobody from what she considered the helpful groups in the community was there. It wasn't likely any of them would be hanging out with someone as far right as Allister Brindle. Like Allister had said, this was a paying gig. Every one of these suckers expected something in return for their sellout—a slot on some board of directors, some photos of them with the governor to hang in their offices and homes as a sign that they were somebody, or a reference to them in the newspaper as black leaders, which was important because they were leaders nobody followed.

Except for one of them.

Why was Maurice Samuelson hanging around Brindle? The Reverend Maurice Samuelson, founder of the Temple of the Divine Enlightenment. He certainly wasn't a leader without followers. She'd walked by Samuelson's temple a couple of times just before services began, and there'd been so many people, mostly women, trying to get in, she'd had to cross the street. He was also probably the only one of these boys who actually lived in Roxbury, where most blacks in Boston lived. There were signs all over Roxbury about the temple and its programs for elders and young people. He was the best-known outside of Boston, too. There'd been a story about Samuelson in *Jet* magazine. The article said his temple was a new kind of African-American religion where Christian, Jewish, and Muslim holy books and beliefs were mixed together. She watched him as she offered the tray around the room.

He was a short man who tried to make himself look taller by walking with his shoulders up to his ears and wearing thick-heeled shoes, both of which Blanche thought made him look like an old-time gangster. He slicked his long hair down with pomade heavy enough to turn his kinks into waves that curled at the top of his collar in the back. His dark-blue suit fit as though he and Allister Brindle had the same tailor. His blue-and-cream-polka-dot bow tie and cream silk shirt were a perfect match. Of course, it wouldn't matter to her how he looked. She was suspicious of anyone who was pushing not one, not two, but three boy-led religions rolled into one.

And was Samuelson the only minister here? In this town, white politicians and black ministers seemed to go together like tears and tissues. At election time, the pols got religion and came looking for the blessings of black ministers as a way to get black votes without providing the kinds of services to black communities that they at least promised to East Boston and Charlestown and the other mostly white Boston neighborhoods.

"I wouldn't raise a dog in Roxbury," she heard someone say, but turned too late to see which man had spoken. She wished a pox on the speaker and all the listeners, too, since not one had disagreed.

Brindle clamped his hand on Maurice Samuelson's shoulder and steered him toward an empty corner. They looked like bad boys up to something nasty. Blanche worked her way close enough to hear what they were talking about.

Brindle set his glass on the mantle over the fireplace. "Now, about the election." He gave Samuelson's shoulder a little shake. "I really need your help in Roxbury, Maurice."

"Not to worry, not to worry," Samuelson assured him. "Aunt Jemima and Uncle Ben know which side their bread is buttered on. And if they don't, it's my job to tell them."

Both men laughed.

Flames engulfed Blanche's brain. She'd never before heard a black person promise to keep the Darkies in line for Massa. A tremble went up her arms as she fought the urge to smash Samuelson over the head with the tray of hors d'oeuvres, an urge so strong she could see bits of smoked salmon in his hair. She told herself to breathe deeply, to stay calm, to simply ease away. But before she could stop herself, she turned abruptly and jabbed a sharp elbow into Samuelson's lower spine, knocking him off balance and splashing whatever he was drinking onto his shirt. Uncle Ben and Aunt Jemima that, you butt-sucking maggot!

Samuelson staggered a step or two before he recovered his balance. He whipped out a handkerchief and dabbed at the stain.

"Oh, so sorry, excuse me." Blanche turned her head so that Samuelson, but not Brindle, could see that her apology was just words. She was pleased by the momentary flicker of uncertainty in Samuelson's eyes. Was he wondering if she'd bumped him on purpose? She certainly hoped so.

Samuelson hardly missed a beat. "No harm done, sister. No harm done." He reached out to pat her arm.

Blanche stepped back. If he touched her, she'd break his face in four places, and she let her eyes tell him so. He pulled his hand back.

"Everything all right?" Felicia Brindle made hostess sounds at Samuelson, but her eyes were on Blanche, who felt a sudden chill.

Two other men gushed up to Brindle, and he began telling them a joke about a Jew, a gay man, and an old black woman stuck in an elevator together as he led them toward the dining room. Blanche hurried off. Her blood was already sizzling. One more insult and she was likely to really go off in here.

She threw herself onto a kitchen chair, as startled by what she'd just done as Samuelson had been. What had possessed her? She'd been riled before. Worse than this. Once in a while she'd been messed with so badly, she'd had to let her finger slip into somebody's drink, put too much salt or hot pepper in the eggs rancheros, or add a couple tablespoons of cat food to the beef bourguignonne. But never anything like this.

Of course, she wasn't about to deny the wave of pleasure she'd felt when her elbow found Samuelson's spine. He'd deserved it, no doubt about it.

Still, what she'd done was unprofessional behavior of the worst kind—the kind that made you lose your job—and this job wasn't even hers to lose. So why had she acted like it was? Had she passed her sell-by date? Had she lost the looseness needed to roll with the kind of blows that came with this work? Or maybe she was just sick to death of nigger-minded dickbrains like Samuelson making pacts with the devil in the name of black folks.

"Spiritual leader, my foot!" She fiddled and fumed, moving pots from the sink to the dishwasher, emptying the kettle, wiping the counter, anything to keep moving, to help her fidget away the last of her outrage. At the same time, she was depressed by the knowledge that there was really nothing surprising about what Samuelson had done. She knew that all these years of being hated for no reason beyond color had convinced some black people that the racists must be right. Did Samuelson hate himself as much as he did the people he called Aunt Jemima and Uncle Ben? Or did being a man of the cloth make him an honorary white in his own eyes?

She didn't go into the dining room, but she listened at the door to Brindle announcing his run for governor. He also thanked his guests, men he knew would help him "convince your people that old-style liberalism must give way to new-style pragmatism," which Blanche understood to mean that the few crumbs being passed down to poor black people would be taken back if Brindle were elected—for their own good, of course. Brindle spoke in a kind of imitation Martin Luther King singsong she'd once heard Ted Kennedy use while talking to a group of blacks on TV. She liked to think some black consultant with a wicked sense of humor had suggested this black-speak strategy. When Brindle was done, his guests all clapped. Blanche went back to the kitchen, wondering what their mothers and children would think of them.

Voices in the hall told her when the guests were leaving. Felicia lurched into the kitchen like someone struggling to remember how her legs worked. She stood in the doorway staring in Blanche's direction but looking at something only she could see.

"Can I help you, ma'am?" Blanche watched Felicia pull herself back from wherever she was.

"We'll be back for drinks and out for dinner," she said.

Blanche could have driven a car through the spaces between Felicia's words, as if she had to search for each one and figure out how to say it before she spoke. Blanche wondered what had happened to curl those sharp edges she'd sensed earlier. Something surely had. Felicia had the slack-faced look of someone who'd just had a serious shock. Blanche's curiosity pushed her to ask Felicia what was wrong, but her mother wit wouldn't have it. As far as she knew, she wasn't being paid extra for hand-holding.

She helped Carrie put the library back in order and load the dishwasher.

"So, no more nice Saxe what's-his-name until Saturday," Blanche teased Carrie.

Carrie sniffed and tossed her head. "Don't mean nothin' to me who comes and goes in this here house, not even that one who does the massage. She'll be stompin' in here tomorrow right on time. She don't miss a day. She—"

"Why you call her 'that one who does the massage,' like she ain't got a name?"

"'Cause God don't mean for women to do what she do."

"A lesbian, hunh?"

Had Carrie been a few shades lighter, Blanche was sure she'd have seen blood rush to the woman's face.

"It's against God. It says so in the Bible."

"But what's it got to do with you?"

"Ain't none of my business. But my pastor say it ain't natural. It's ungodly!" Carrie hissed.

"I don't get it," Blanche said. "You Christians say God made everything and everybody, which has gotta include lesbians. But then you say lesbians are ungodly. Seems to me that you, your pastor, or your God is very confused, honey."

Carrie looked at her as though Blanche had just grown horns. "I'm gonna put you in my prayers." She hurried away to the laundry room and closed the door firmly behind her.

Blanche could hear her shrieking some hymn about being delivered from the heathen. It was so tuneless and off-key, Blanche suspected Carrie had made it up for her benefit.

Wanda came down the back stairs lugging the tools of her trade. She hauled the vacuum, bucket, mop, sprays, and sponges into the maintenance closet and took out her tote bag and sweaters.

"Well, darlin', it's been more than a pleasure. I'm lookin' forward to our next meetin', I am." And she was off.

Blanche sat down at the kitchen table, thinking about her best friend, Ardell, down in North Carolina, and what she'd say about the Samuelson thing. She also thought about going to the Y for a sit in the sauna, about calling home to check on the kids, but right now she didn't have the energy to move. Her eyelids lowered; her neck and shoulder muscles relaxed; her hands folded over her belly. She was a breath away from sleep.

Then she was wide awake. Why? She straightened up and looked around. Carrie was still in the laundry room, Wanda and the Brindles had gone, and there was no one else in the house. She walked through to the front hall. But there *was* someone else in the house. Someone who'd just been in the front hall, judging by the whiff of soap or deodorant she caught. She didn't even think about going upstairs. If there was somebody up there stealing the Brindles' shit, she wasn't about to put her life in the way. But she didn't need to go up. The person upstairs was just coming down.

"What are you doing here?" Blanche and Ray-Ray asked each other at the same time.

From this angle, Miz Inez's overgrown son looked even more like a chocolate-covered tank than usual. Blanche didn't care for overmuscled men; she always suspected those extra muscle bulges were substitutes for a pea brain or a pencil-stub penis and not enough sexual imagination to make up for it. Ray-Ray was an exception. When they'd first met, Blanche had found it hard to believe that anyone could be so in love with himself, so sure that whatever was good in life was his by right. Then she'd thought about it. Who needed more self-love and confidence than a black man in America? He was smart too and usually found a way to make her laugh or otherwise get on her good side. But there were limits.

"I'm where I'm supposed to be," she told him. "You ain't. What you doing in these people's upstairs?"

"Oh, that's right. This is the week Mama's away. I was upstairs stealing from your white folks, of course," he teased.

"You must mean your mama's white folks."

"Touché, Miz Blanche, touché." Ray-Ray bounced down the last of the stairs and gave her a peck on the cheek. As usual, he managed to move in ways that showed off his muscles.

"What *were* you doin' up there, Ray-Ray?"

"Getting my shirt." He held it out to her. "I left it here when I fixed the window on the third floor. See? My initials." Ray-Ray headed for the front door.

Blanche stepped in front of him. "How'd you get in here?"

"Through the front door, like everybody else." He gave her an amused look. "You're not pissed because I use the front door, are you? I always use the front. I used to play in this house. And ain't no white man gonna make me use the back door. Not ever."

Blanche wished him luck, but given the many shapes and forms the back door could take, she was pretty sure he'd already been through a couple of them, whether he knew it or not. Was it even possible to grow up a poor black man in America and avoid the back door?

"Honey, I don't care what door you use; I just wanna know how you got in here."

Ray-Ray held up a key. "From the usual place under the mat," he said. "I'll put it back on my way out."

"Well, I'll tell the Brindles you came to call."

Ray-Ray spun around. "You don't have to. They might not like the idea of you letting me in their upstairs when they're not home. Let's just pretend you never saw me." He gave her a full-faced grin.

"Ray-Ray, I don't want no mess from these people about the missing gold cuff links or—"

"Don't worry, Blanche," Ray-Ray told her. "You'll be glad I came, trust me." He opened the door and slipped out.

Oh shit. "Ray-Ray!"

He was gone.

Blanche hurried upstairs. She could feel he'd been in Allister's rooms, but didn't know if anything had been moved. She checked Felicia's rooms. She couldn't tell if Ray-Ray had been in there because the rooms reeked of that moist, bleachy smell of clean-body sweat, vaginal juices, and sperm. Saxe might tease the help with his sex appeal, but he was obviously delivering more than just promises to his client. She wondered if Allister knew, and why Felicia had sounded so down after having just had one of the world's greatest mood lighteners.

She went back to the kitchen and brought out the food she'd held back from the buffet for her and Carrie's lunch, and tapped on the laundry room door.

"Ungodliness can seep through wood, honey, so you might as well come on out here and help me eat this food."

Blanche didn't want to tell Carrie about Ray-Ray's unexpected visit, but she couldn't shut him out of her mind.

"Do you know Ray-Ray, Inez's son?" she asked Carrie when they'd settled at the table.

Carrie filled her plate. "Um-hum. Useta do odd jobs around here."

"How come he left?"

Carrie shook her head and forked some potato salad into her mouth.

"What happened?" Blanche asked her.

Carrie kept chewing. Her eyes strayed to the platter in the middle of the table.

"Try some of this ham. It's good." Blanche eased a large slice onto Carrie's plate.

"He useta be around here all the time, working and not working."

"You want that last piece of roast beef?" Blanche pushed the platter closer to Carrie. "What was he doing here if he wasn't working?" she asked as Carrie speared the meat.

"Come to visit Mr. Marc. Mr. Brindle useta take them both to ball games, stuff like that when they was boys."

The kind white folks thing, Blanche thought. Proving your decency through the help. But she was surprised Allister went in for it. Wanda said he came from old money. They didn't usually go in for touchy-feely with the help. It didn't fit with their deep belief that they deserved what they had and the poor deserved to be poor.

"It's a shame to waste the rest of this food," Blanche said. "I couldn't convince you to take it along home, could I?"

The first big smile Blanche had seen lit up Carrie's face as she bobbed her head up and down.

Blanche got some plastic bags and aluminum foil to wrap the food. "So, why did Ray-Ray stop working here?" she asked.

Carrie cut her roast beef into bite-sized pieces. "Seems like him and Mr. B had some kinda fallin' out."

Oh shit! Ray-Ray coulda been upstairs cutting up all of Allister's clothes. Blanche leaned forward. "What kind of falling out?"

Carrie shrugged. "Don't know. Happened on my day off. Inez just said they had a fallin' out and Ray-Ray wasn't working here no more."

"When was this?"

Carrie wiped her mouth. "Year or so, I guess." She folded her napkin and laid it beside her plate. "Well, better git back to work."

She left Blanche sitting at the kitchen table, glad it was the Brindles' and not her own food she'd used to pay for that paltry bit of information.

"I'll get it!" Carrie shouted almost before the front door-bell stopped ringing.

She was wearing her sparkly eyes when she came back a few minutes later.

"It was Mr. Saxe."

Men running in and of here like it's a cathouse, Blanche thought. "What'd he want?"

"He was looking for his pictures."

"What pictures?"

"Ones I put on Miss Felicia's dresser, I guess," Carrie said.

"What kind of pictures?"

Carrie shrugged. "One of them envelopes you git pictures in from the drugstore."

"Where'd you get it?"

"Found it on the floor in the hall. Outside Miss Felicia's room."

"So you figured they were hers?"

Carrie nodded. "Put 'em on her dresser."

"Did Saxe get them?"

"He went up to get them, but he said they weren't there no more. Miss Felicia musta moved 'em."

Or somebody else moved them, Blanche thought. Somebody who claimed to have been getting his shirt. But why?

"Pictures of what?"

"Don't know."

"You mean you didn't look at them?"

Carrie adjusted her hair net. "Weren't none of mine. I didn't have no business to look at . . ."

Blanche tried to imagine herself a person who could find an envelope full of pictures and not look at them. She thought Carrie would be better off if she was lying about looking in the envelope, but given what she'd seen of Carrie, Blanche was surprised she'd even picked it up from the floor. She shook her head in wonder and went to the library to set up for drinks.

Inez's note said Allister liked a frozen daiquiri in the afternoon and Felicia took an olive and an onion in her martini.

Allister looked tired but upbeat when he and Felicia got home. "It all went very well, don't you think?" he asked.

Felicia shrugged as if she couldn't care less.

Blanche gave her a closer look. Felicia's hair and clothes were clean and in order, but there was something smudged about her, as though she'd been flattened against a windowpane and smeared like a bug. Felicia ran her hands over her hair. It didn't help. It's them eyes she needs to do something about, Blanche thought.

"Where'd you disappear to?" Allister asked Felicia.

"What?"

"At the reception. I looked around and you were nowhere to be seen."

"You're running for office, Allister, not me. I don't have to be ever-present." Felicia's hand shook when she took her drink from the tray Blanche held. She looked up at Blanche and quickly away.

"A candidate's wife can be more important than his platform. You know that. You promised you would . . ."

Felicia rose with the martini glass still in her hand.

"Blanche, please send the shaker upstairs," she said, and walked out of the room and up the stairs as though Allister didn't exist.

Allister closed his eyes and laid his head against the back of his armchair and sighed a sigh that was almost a moan. Then he, too, rose and left the room.

Blanche was expecting Felicia to send for her and ask what had happened to Saxe's pictures. She was relieved when it didn't happen. Maybe she was wrong about those pictures. Maybe Ray-Ray had taken something of Allister's, as she'd first thought.

Allister was in the breakfast room when Blanche passed by on her way to the kitchen. She waited half a minute before she strolled past the breakfast room again. Allister was now in the sunroom leaning over the stand of African violets. She couldn't see his face, but she watched his hands as he slowly, gently removed browning leaves, moved pots from one spot to another, and brushed his fingers lightly against the blossoms. His body looked softer, more round, as if he'd been stiffening his spine and sucking in his gut until this moment when he thought he was alone. Like everybody else, Allister had more than one side, but she didn't think it mattered. Was a rattlesnake sunning itself all that much less dangerous than one on the hunt?

When Allister finally went upstairs to dress for dinner, Blanche waited again for shouts of "I've been robbed!" but all was quiet. Either Ray-Ray had pinched something of Allister's that wasn't obvious, or she'd been right the first time and it was Saxe's pictures he'd taken and Felicia just hadn't missed them yet.

The wind had died down by the time Blanche left work. The air was still on the cold side, but she could feel spring just waiting to burst out. She climbed the driveway and walked up Cottage Street—really a one-lane, one-way road.

This was the greenest part of the city she'd seen outside of Boston Common and the gardens downtown. It looked like country around here. Just like the Brindles' place, the few other houses along the road were all down in a kind of valley tucked away out of sight behind stone or wooden fences. Following Inez's directions, Blanche turned left at the top of the hill and followed a two-lane road until it turned into Perkins Street, where she saw the lake she'd noticed on the way in. The sign she passed said BROOKLINE, and she realized the Brindle house was about three blocks outside the city of Boston.

But she'd crossed the line and was back in Boston now. Another sign announced that the lake was called Jamaica Pond, which told her she must be in the Jamaica Plain section of Boston.

Her regular jobs took her into the South End, Back Bay, and Beacon Hill, but she'd never been here before or to other neighborhoods like East Boston, Charlestown, South Boston, or the North End. Somebody had told her that some of these places had once been separate towns, but that was a long time ago. From what she heard and read, the major use of these neighborhood names now seemed to be to keep people apart and suspicious of one another. And she knew there were Boston communities unfriendly to folks from outside, particularly black, brown, and yellow folks.

From where she now stood, she couldn't see the other side of the pond. Canada geese and ducks skimmed along its surface. People strolled, jogged, and pushed strollers on the path beside the pond. Blanche stretched out her arms to the greening trees and blue water. She missed all of this over in the part of Roxbury where she lived. There were some trees on its streets, but if there were any bodies of water in the neighborhood, besides public pools and mud puddles, she'd never heard about them.

She'd been in Boston nearly three years, but having to build up her clientele and take care of the kids and the house, along with winters that demanded she stay indoors as much as possible, had reduced her learn-about-Boston time down to about six months. Still, she hadn't even done six months worth of exploring. Maybe it was because she hadn't had much choice about moving here. It was not so much her idea as her only alternative: she'd needed to get out of Farleigh in a hurry, and Cousin Charlotte had been able and willing to help her out. Blanche would have left Boston by now if it weren't for Taifa and Malik. They'd been in three different school systems in as many years. It didn't feel right to ask them to move again.

She waited for the light to change at Jamaica Way and Perkins Street, where the traffic was moving at expressway speed. She looked down Jamaica Way with its huge houses on one side and the pond on the other. Nice. When the light changed, she hurried across and walked on toward Centre Street, where she'd get the bus. It was a longish walk. Miz Inez had offered her banged-up car, but Blanche had seen enough of Boston driving to know she didn't want to be on the road unless she had to. Anyway, her fast-approaching-fifty-year-old body could use the exercise.

She walked up Perkins Street, past big old houses that were now apartments, and over to Centre Street, where the store signs and street language were in Spanish, past the Bromley-Heath projects to the Jackson Square bus depot next door. She was on the tip of Roxbury now. She got the number 44 bus and let her mind slip back to the other events of her first day on Miz Inez's job.

Lord! Had she really poked that man? She had a feeling she'd be hearing about *that*. Shit! And didn't Ray-Ray have a nerve, which was probably one of the reasons she liked him in spite of herself. A poor black person without nerve was a dead person. But that didn't mean she approved of his sneaking onto his mother's job to steal something, which was the only reason she could think of for him sneaking around upstairs. From what Carrie said, he was definitely no stranger to the house, but if he hadn't worked for the Brindles for at least a year, why hadn't Carrie or Wanda found his shirt and given it to Miz Inez to take home, and what did Ray-Ray mean when he said she'd be glad he came? She still didn't know what he'd been doing in the Brindle house, but she knew his shirt didn't have doodly-squat to do with it. Maybe Saxe's pictures did, although it was hard to figure out how Ray-Ray would know Saxe had left them there. But she definitely intended to ask Ray-Ray about those pictures the next time she saw him. And that Carrie! Her and her pastor and her thing for "Mr. Saxe!" Lord! did she have stories to tell Ardell. Blanche got off the bus on Humboldt and walked up the street to Rudigere Homes, eager to be on her own turf.

THE BALANCE OF THE DAY

BY GEORGE V. HIGGINS

Roxbury

(Originally published in 1985)

J ohn Lynch turned left off Washington Street onto Boswell and found number 27 among the neat three-deckers by driving slowly between the parked cars until he saw the '51 Ford coupe, black, listing to port on a flat rear tire next to the pillared porch. There were two faded bumper stickers plastered to the trunk, one on either side of the lock, each reading: "Support the Blanket Men." Lynch without stopping continued on up the street toward where it intersects with Centre, turned right, and headed east toward Jamaica Plain. He angle-parked the lime-green '85 Ford sedan at the curb in front of a block of stores next to a Getty station, about a mile from Boswell, and shut the engine off. In the rearview mirror, he could see another block of stores across the street.

There was a small variety store directly in front of him. A man about seventy, carrying a newspaper and a cardboard container of coffee, came out into the spring morning onto the sidewalk. He glanced casually at Lynch's car, and headed west on foot. When he reached the lunchroom at the end of the block, he went inside.

Lynch sighed and switched his gaze back to the window of the variety store. In approximately forty seconds, a man about fifty in a white shirt open at the collar peered through the plate glass at Lynch's car. He scowled. He came out onto the sidewalk and looked up at the sky like an air raid warden. Then he looked directly at Lynch through the windshield of the Ford and scowled again. He went back into the store. A few more seconds passed and Lynch saw him come to the window. He had a telephone in his left hand, the coiled cord stretching out behind him. He spoke with vehemence that Lynch could not hear, nodding vigorously. When the conversation was evidently complete, he lowered the phone and stood staring at Lynch. He pantomimed spitting. Then he disappeared into the deeper gloom of the store.

After about five more minutes a blue '84 Ford sedan carrying three men came up Centre Street, heading west, and pulled into a parking place on the opposite side of the road. Lynch through his rearview mirror watched the brake lights go off. He waited thirty seconds. No other cars passed on Centre Street. He leaned over the passenger seat, opened the glove box, took out the microphone, pressed the transmitting button, sighed again, grimaced, and put the mike back, shutting the box as he straightened up.

Lynch got out of the green Ford, locked it, hitched up his pants, buttoned his blazer, and after looking both ways crossed Centre Street to the blue Ford. He got into the backseat on the right and closed the door behind him.

The driver met his gaze in the rearview mirror. The front-seat passenger turned so that his left elbow rested on the back of the seat and he could look at Lynch directly. He had a trace of a smile on his face. "Now are you impressed?" he said.

"I certainly am," Lynch said. "I realize those guys've been at it for a long time now. But after all, they're getting old. You'd think they'd've slowed down a little by now. What are they, crowding eighty?"

The other man in the backseat snickered. "How you think

they got to *be* eighty, John?" he said. "Not by being careless."
He was about fifty-five. He had iron-gray hair and he looked
resigned.

"Besides seeing them make you in record time, John," the
front passenger said, "what else did you see? Get anything?"

Lynch shrugged. "Nothing the Judge'd turn cartwheels to
read. The old car's in the driveway, with the stickers on it.
Looks like it hasn't been driven for years, but that's probably a
decoy. Old Sean's probably got a bulletproof Cad in the barn
with a couple of Sidewinder pods, case he feels like going out."

"Unlikely," the front passenger said.

"Yeah," the man in the backseat said. "Sean's legs're giving out. He doesn't go out much alone. Needs someone to
steady him."

"Well," Lynch said, "why's he need to, now I think of it?
Network he's got working, what's the point of going out? Just
stay inside, give orders, monitor the street, make sure nobody
does nothing he doesn't know about. He's got the scanner, by
the way. You can only see a little bit of the lead coming out of
the window in the front room on the third floor, and most of
it's hidden behind the shutter until it gets to where they had
to cross it over and hide it behind the drainspout before they
could drill a hole through the eaves and get it back into the
attic. But it's there all right. Wonder how many crystals he's
got for that thing. Hundred be a good guess?"

"Nah, way too high," the man in the backseat said. "Why'd
he need that many? One for Boston, one for State, one for us,
one for MDC that he probably doesn't use. Say, a half a dozen
spares, plus a couple or three old ones that he took out a year
ago, when we changed frequencies. I'll bet old Sean hasn't
got more than a dozen of the things." He snickered again.
"Old bastards weren't so damned and determined to spend

everything they get on guns and ammunition, he'd be computerized. Except probably not, now I think about it. For that he probably is too old. Doesn't trust anything invented since gelignite."

"Don't be too sure of that, Nick," the driver said, craning his neck to see the man in the back through the mirror. "Last shipment had ten Redeyes in it. BOAC isn't nervous because these guys use bows and arrows, you know. They're sophisticated."

"Your thoughts, John," the front passenger said.

"We know what Sean is doing," Lynch said. "We know he's some sort of guru to the money-raisers. We know the money-raisers are raising money. We know they're bringing it to him. We know the old bombthrower's sitting there and ordering the ordinance."

"Ordnance," Nick said absently.

"Huh?" Lynch said.

"Ordnance," Nick said. "I assume you mean: cannons and rockets and rifles and sidearms, and the ammunition for those things. 'Ordnance.' 'Ordinance' is different. Says you can't leave your dog run loose. City ordinance: 'Leash your mangy dog.' Army ordnance: 'Bazookas.' Not the same thing at all."

"Whatever," Lynch said impatiently.

"Right," Nick said.

"We get into that house," Lynch said, "we have got a pretty decent chance of intercepting either a whole bunch of money or a whole bunch of weapons that're headed for some-place that the Judge doesn't want them going."

"We get into heaven," the driver said, "we don't have to worry about any of this crap anymore. We can all retire to Florida where it's warm all the time, and play a little golf."

"I don't see what that's got to do with anything," Lynch said.

The front passenger sighed. "Your thoughts, John," he said again.

"The people on the first floor work," Lynch said. "Both of them work days. Cornelius Finn and his child bride, the lovely Mary Anne. Connie's down at Sawyer Steel. She's at Mass. Rehab. We have a little weight with Connie—least I think we do. Brother Andrew's on parole. He's working nights at Daley's and he's seeing the wrong guys. I could tell Connie, as a favor, 'Baby brother's gonna fall, you don't do me a favor.'"

"And what might this favor be?" Nick in the backseat said. "You think if you can't drive by the house once without getting spotted, you can sneak into the place and set up shop? Sean'd have you made in ten seconds. The last time somebody sneaked onto Sean Geogan's turf without getting made was in 1916, before the moon rose. And what'd you do once you got in there? Hold a housewarming and invite him? Say you're the new boyo in town, want to get acquainted?"

"Well," Lynch said, "we have got the junction box in the basement under the pantry floor, you know. Get one of Lester Daley's magicians in there with a spool of wire and a bitstock, might be able to pick up some interesting stuff on the phone."

"Won't work," the front passenger said. "One thing they have got for modern improvements is state-of-the-art sweepers. He'd pick up the drain on the first call he made."

Nick snorted in the backseat. "No, he wouldn't, Ernie," he said. "There wouldn't be any first call on that phone after the wire went on. The *last* call on that line would've been made fifteen seconds after John got finished putting the hammer on Connie down at Sawyer Steel. Sean's friends'd spend the next afternoon and evening bringing in carrier pigeons and putting them in the attic next to the scanner antenna. You'll get more out of wiring a rock'n you will out of tapping Sean's phone."

Lynch sighed again and squared his shoulders. "*Oh*-kay," he said. "The second floor. The second floor occupants are Tom and Kathy Dolan and their two lovely children, Brian and Kate. Tom I sort of know. He was two years ahead of me in school. He's got a department-head job in the schools. He's got something to lose. Assistant superintendency, I hear, may be coming up. Kathy? Same sort of thing. Very hardworking lady. Busts her hump down at the Brigham, working Night Emergency. Those people've got something at stake, that old Bolshevik gets busted or bombed out on the top floor of their house."

"How do you know Kathy?" Nick said, looking interested and skeptical at the same time.

"Well," Lynch said, "I don't. Not personally, at least. But I ran her through the computer, you know, and I got all this stuff, and I know her type. I know what she'll do."

"Right," Nick said. He put his left hand under his chin and cupped his fingers over his mouth.

"You think I'm wrong?" Lynch said. "You think I don't know what I'm talking about?"

Nick removed his hand from his face. "Frankly," he said, "yes."

"Nick," Lynch said, "all right? Have you ever seen Sean Geogan? Have you ever laid eyes on the man? Personally?"

Nick shook his head. "Nope," he said. "I know what he looks like. I have seen his picture and he looks like Captain Kangaroo, only smaller and without the hair. But personally? No, I have not."

"That's what I thought," Lynch said smugly.

"It's no disgrace, John," Nick said. "Thousands of British soldiers have never laid eyes on Sean Geogan, and they've been trying for more than sixty years. Very hard, too. Very hard. I've just never felt the need that bad."

"Well," Lynch said, "I have."

"And you're going to again, too," Nick said.

"I hope so," Lynch said.

"Bank on it," Nick said.

"The way I look at this approach," Lynch said, speaking earnestly to the front passenger, "and not that it's basically different from the idea I had with the Finns, but we just sort of approach them and tell them, you know, this is how it's going to be. And these people are not gunmen. I mean, it's one thing you've got this old revolutionary living on the top floor of your house and all, and maybe you think that's amusing. But people are dying in Ireland today because of him and his kind, and we want to stop it. And we're *going* to stop it. 'And if you, Kathy Dolan, and you, Thomas Dolan, don't cooperate with us in this, we're going to cause you come inconvenience.'" He turned toward Nick. "And like I say, Nick, I know these people. I know what they will do."

"I think you're wrong," Nick said. "I don't think Kathy Dolan will do what you expect. Not if she is the Kathy Dolan that I think she is. Which is the former Kathy Brennan, daughter of State Representative Edmund and his lovely wife, Rosemary, both of them deceased. Tragic highway accident in Saugus, back in 1969, if I recall. Edmund was shitfaced. Both under forty, too, I think. Really a tragic thing. Leaving a little babe like that, almost alone in the world."

"I guess that's right," Lynch said, perplexed. "I didn't look it up, of course, but that does sound right."

"Take his word for it, John," the front passenger said firmly. "Nick has blown his share of details, but never one like this."

"Thank you, Ernie," Nick said. "Always like a word of praise. Rosemary Brennan, John, Kathy Brennan's mother, had a maiden name of Keating. Father's name was Ted, I think—his brother's name was John.

"John and Ted came here from Galway back in 1921. It's reported that they traveled across the pond in crates shipped as cargo in the hold of a tramp freighter out of Liverpool—no passengers on her manifest. Their law-abiding friends assure us that the Keatings traveled in those spartan accommodations because they were poor farm lads who had no money for their passage to the promised land. Their detractors have more exciting explanations which describe bridges blowing up and similar events that attracted the attention of the soldiers of the Crown. Who became so anxious to talk to the Keatings that they thought they'd better leave.

"Wherever the truth lies," Nick continued, slouching down in the seat and rubbing his left eye with the knuckle of his left forefinger, "John and Ted once on these shores proved to be industrious greenhorns who found gainful employment and worked diligently at it. And, when Prohibition ended, they were made law-abiding in their chosen trade. By then, of course, they were fairly prosperous, and had been able to send for their loved ones back in Galway. John sent for his sweetheart, Mary Shea, and married her, but for some reason or another they never had any children. Unkind persons said that this was because Mary failed to conceive on John's first night of conjugal bliss, and that because John on that occasion was so rough with her, he never got another crack at her. Mary ran that roost.

"The result was that John Keating after Mary's death had no children of his own to whom to leave his fine three-decker he had worked so hard to build at 27 Boswell Street. Therefore he left it to his only and beloved grandniece, Kathy. Who is the daughter of the daughter that Ted Keating and his bride conceived soon after she came from Ireland after Ted got prosperous. Which was Rosemary.

"Soon after that conception, Ted Keating died. Peacefully in bed, for which the Lord be praised, but still a young man, as they say. Made a good living while he lasted, but died before he really managed to pile up much of an estate. His widow, Annie, went to work, and John of course helped out. But then she died when Rosemary was about sixteen. The girl moved in with her uncle, John, and his good wife, Mary. So naturally, when she got married, she got the second floor for herself and her new husband, the up-and-coming young State Rep, Edmund Brennan. And they had Kathy. Then they got killed. So it was only natural, when old John died, Kathy got the house. He had nobody else. And the house came complete, course, with the vacant owner's apartment on the third floor, where old Sean lives today.

"Ted Keating's bride was Annie Geogan. She was Kathy's grandmother. Annie Geogan was Sean Geogan's sister. Him you know about. Sean was on his uppers back on the old sod, too old to fight much more. Kathy brought him over here, about nine years ago.

"Now, let me ask you this, John," Nick said, grinning at him. "What you think your chances are, of putting this together using Kathy Dolan's help?"

"Not too good," Lynch said. "Not too good at all."

"That's what I think, too," Ernie said meditatively, staring past Lynch's right shoulder through the back window. Lynch wrenched his body around so that he could rest his left arm on the top of the backseat and look back across the street.

He saw an old black Oldsmobile sedan pull slowly into the space next to his green Ford. A man about forty, wearing a black suit coat and trousers and a white shirt with no tie, got out of the driver's side and opened the left rear passenger door, carefully preventing it from touching the flank of the Ford. Lynch saw a man's right hand emerge from the backseat and grasp the top of the door. Then the left hand and the left leg emerged, the hand grasping a blackthorn walking stick and the foot in a black shoe groping for the pavement. The head came next, a few white hairs trailing over the mottled scalp, and then the short and frail torso in the dull green suit. Lynch saw several decorations pinned to the left lapel of the coat. "Son of a bitch," he said.

"The very same," Nick said. He was opening the car door.

"Where the hell're you going?" Lynch said, as the old man headed lamely toward the door of the variety store.

"Well," Nick said, "we started this. Man has to finish it. Finish what he starts. I'm going to buy a paper and I'm going to say hello."

"You want me to come with you?" Lynch said.

"I think you should," Nick said.

"What do you think he'll say to us?" Lynch said, leaving the car.

"He'll say," Nick said, "'Top of the morning.' That's what I would say."

"And what do we say back to him?" Lynch said across the car.

"The same thing he'd say back to us, if he came on our turf, and we had caught him there. 'And the balance of the day to yourself, sir.' A man should show some class."

BAIT (EXCERPT)

BY KENNETH ABEL

South Boston

(Originally published in 1994)

From his office window, Johnny D'Angelo looks down upon the back lot of South Boston Auto Repair, James P. Gallo, Prop., a business in which he has no documented interest. At one end of the lot, a row of crumpled cars stands behind a wall of melting snow. During the last year, each car has been sold at least four times, the names on the transfers drawn from residents of nursing homes in the western part of the state. Only days after each sale, accident reports are submitted to the insurance companies, with damage listed a few hundred dollars below the car's value. It is a very profitable business, which, by virtue of its three employees' vast appetites, deposits a large percentage of its income at the end of each week into the cash registers of its neighbor, D'Angelo's Pizza.

Johnny D'Angelo shakes his head.

Stupid, he thinks. *They should push that snow out of the way. Some insurance guy has a slow afternoon, comes down here to look at the car. Maybe he remembers there hasn't been any snow in the last three weeks, starts thinking about how that car could get wrecked when it hasn't moved.*

He swivels his chair to face his desk. Across from him, Jackie Mullen from the South End leans forward, tapping one finger on the desk as he talks. Johnny shifts in his chair, not looking at him. *Fat Jackie. Like a meatball in that cheap suit.*

"This guy, he's into me for thirty-two hundred this month alone. Over fifteen thousand for the year. I got two guys in the hospital. He tried to run 'em down with a fuckin' Buick."

Fat Jackie settles back in his chair, one hand raised like he's trying to stop a bus.

"You and me, we've had our problems over the years. But we always worked it out. But this guy, he's way outta line. I'm supporting him and his whole family here. Don't get me wrong, it's not the money, Johnny. I got money. You hear what I say? Fuck the money. It's the lack of respect. I'm supposed to let him walk away from this, just 'cause he's gonna marry your daughter? I ask you."

He spends too much time staring out the window lately, his stomach twisted with pain. *Jimmy's a good guy. He doesn't think, is all. Lets things slide, I gotta send someone down there to get him to move that snow. Can't figure it out for himself.*

And yet, as he reaches for the phone, raising one finger to silence Fat Jackie, he knows it isn't the snow that bothers him. Nor the letter dangling from the sign for the last three weeks. (*Sout Boston Auto Repair, just like you say it,* Jimmy'd said, trying to get him to laugh.)

Even Russo can figure it out, standing with Jimmy while a kid drags a shovel out of the garage.

"You gotta think," he tells Jimmy. "He sits up there staring at that oil spot on the pavement over by the fence. Only he doesn't want to look at it, so he looks at the sign, or the snow, or whatever." He shakes his head. "It's gonna take him awhile, Jimmy. He's gonna be on you about something until then."

And as he says it, they can see him in the window, one hand smoothing his tie with a practiced gesture, silver hair combed straight back, his face expressionless. Russo lets a hand fall on Jimmy's shoulder, gives it a shake.

"You want my advice, Jimmy?" Russo sweeps his arm across the parking lot. "You get some black paint, get a truck in here during the night to move the cars for a couple hours, and do the whole lot. He doesn't see the oil every day, maybe it won't bother him so much."

"I don't know, Tommy. Used to be, he had a gripe 'bout me, he told me. I didn't have to hear it from you."

"What d'ya want, Jimmy? It's like when we gotta go up to the North End, up by where Vinnie got killed. He makes me drive all the way down Hanover through all the traffic, so we don't have to pass the street. He doesn't want to see it, you know? We get where we're going, he's in a bad mood. Tells me the shocks need work. Or he's in a restaurant, I can see him through the window yelling at the waiter. Poor guy didn't do nothing, but he's angry. Like with you."

"You think he's angry at me?"

Russo shrugs, tugs his collar up against the wind. *Not my problem*, he thinks. *Some guy over at the police yard wants the car off his lot, has it towed over to Jimmy's, dumps it in the back. And Jimmy, he gets shook at the police truck pulling up in back, so he lets 'em. Leaves it sitting out there, what, six weeks? He's looking at it every day, seeing Vinnie's face like he was on the table, bits of glass in a little dish next to his head.*

When he glances back at the window, it is empty.

As Johnny settles into his chair, Fat Jackie leans forward once more. He doesn't like waiting, staring at D'Angelo's back while he watches some fucking kid shovel snow. He can feel the anger on his face, his skin hot. But he holds his temper, knowing if he walks out he'll get no satisfaction. He plays along with it, waiting his chance. Now, as Johnny's eyes meet his own, he leans into him, keeps his voice quiet, takes his best shot.

"He's not your kid, Johnny. I known him since he was stealing cigarettes out of the machine down at the Trailways. He's a punk, and he's done violence to my people."

He raises one finger, same as Johnny did, holds it there for a moment to make the point.

"Where I come from," he says, his voice almost a whisper, "we don't let that slide."

Johnny looks at him, his eyes tired. "I'll take care of it," he says.

According to papers filed with a grand jury convened by the United States Attorney for the District of Massachusetts, D'Angelo's Pizza, Inc. employs thirty-two people at six retail outlets, another twelve at a central warehouse, and an administrative staff of seven, including its president and sole stockholder, John Anthony D'Angelo. The company employs an additional seven people at two subsidiaries, D'Angelo Restaurant Supply and DRS Farms, Inc.

After an evening slogging through the financial records, Haggerty had to admit she was impressed. The restaurants offered a documented cash source, with register receipts to support the entire operation. The trick was that some of the sales were legitimate—a fact, Haggerty saw from the file, that had sunk Riccioli's last indictment. The restaurants sold pizza (*By the Slice! By the Pie!*) from an outlet two blocks from the federal courthouse. Haggerty smiled, shook her head. Try telling a juror the place is a front when he's just eaten lunch there.

Yet, a former employee had testified—reluctantly, Haggerty noted—to false receipts, a night manager who kept the cash registers chattering until dawn, recording sales that never took place. *A good system,* Haggerty thought. *No way to prove the money's dirty.* On the other end, the company bought all its supplies—flour, tomato sauce, cheese, kitchen equipment—from the two subsidiaries, leaving a hazy trail of invoices and checks that hid the fact that no money was spent. *From one pocket to the other,* Haggerty thought. *Lots of cash comes in, but nothing going out.* Pure profit.

The way Riccioli figured it, the money—from drugs, truck hijacking, insurance fraud, kickbacks—was laundered through local banks as receipts from the pizza joints. For decades, criminal prosecutions had failed as witnesses, under the stares of mob lawyers, grew forgetful. In recent years, the prosecutors had turned to accountants where the police had failed. The guys on the federal organized crime task force had a joke: *The mob has a retirement plan, death and taxes.* By selling a few pizzas, D'Angelo could avoid the tax weasels. Haggerty had heard that during the last audit the IRS boys had come away shaking their heads, claiming that the restaurants showed a documented profit. On the books, the income from the six pizza joints scattered across the city was larger than the combined sales of the two largest burger chains, statewide. A lot of pizzas.

Haggerty pushed the records aside, stretched. She needed a run, a shower, more sleep. Too many hours in the office, chasing leads that had been checked dozens of times. For over a year, the D'Angelo file had remained in her files, unopened. A week of surveillance during the funeral of D'Angelo's son had produced nothing, and Riccioli had abruptly pulled her from the case. As a last gesture, to satisfy her own mania for order, she had scribbled a note to a file clerk she was cultivating at the Department of Corrections, requesting—along with the name of her hair stylist—notice of the disposition of the charges against the police officer, sentence imposed, and estimated date of release. The clerk's note returned a few days later, and she dropped it into the file and forgot it.

When, almost a year later, she found on her desk a Notice of Release for "Walsh, John D., Vehicular Homicide," it took her a moment to make the connection. She set her briefcase on the floor, slipped off her shoes, and slumped into her chair. It was late, and she was tired. The streetlights shimmered through a thin rain beyond the window. The tiny office was strewn with files, stacks of papers, exhibit boxes. The ancient leather chair was cracked, the stuffing spilling out in several places. She had draped it with a Navajo shawl, held in place by strips of masking tape. At idle moments, her fingers sought the fringes taped to the base of the chair, twirling them into elaborate knots. She picked up the paper, tapped it with one finger. Footsteps receded down the dark hall. *The cop!*

She pushed back from the desk with one foot, tugging at a heavy file drawer. The folder was covered with a thin layer of dust. At the back of the file, she found three sheets, captioned in boldface, "Update to Main File," that Janice, her secretary, had slipped into the folder when she was out. The sheets were dated in the last four months.

Someone's been working the file, Haggerty thought. *Funny no one mentioned it.*

She shrugged. It wasn't her case. If Riccioli wanted to re-assign it, that was his business. She had too much work as it was, too little time off, no life beyond the walls of this tiny office.

She stuffed the release form into the file, and shoved it into the drawer. She hooked the edge of the metal drawer with her toes to shove it closed, then paused. If the file was active, she should keep up with it. Riccioli knew she had done the background; if he assigned it to her, there would be no time to catch up. She sighed, lifted the file back onto her lap.

The tax reports took hours. When she found her mind drifting, she got up, switched off the office light. In the darkness, she fumbled for the desk lamp, feeling her senses grow alert. She bent the lamp down, so the only light in the room was the glare that reflected off the pages. An old law school trick: eliminate the distractions.

Confused by the details of corporate structure, she sketched a series of boxes on a legal pad, marking one "Pizzas," the next "Supplier," which she linked by a dotted line to "Farms." Below that, she drew a series of arrows, charting the flow of money from the restaurants to the subsidiary companies, and, by a complicated series of transfers, back into the main company. *A very clever boy, our Johnny.*

When she felt that she had glimpsed the faint trail of money from the cash registers in the restaurants to the private accounts at the bank, she stuffed the reports back into the file. Again, as she slid the thick folder into the drawer, she hesitated. The updates. She pushed the chair back to her desk, noted the dates from the forms on her legal pad. She bit her lip for a moment, then retrieved the release form on the cop.

All right, maybe it means nothing. Maybe you're obsessive. Disappointed it never came to anything. That's what Riccioli will think. Still, it can't hurt to get it in the file.

She gathered her papers, glancing at her watch. Nine fifty. The file room closed at ten o'clock. She would have to sign the file out and get it back first thing in the morning. Another late night.

When she got home, she spread the file on her couch, flicked on the television to chase the silence from the tiny apartment. The furniture—a battered couch, an oak coffee table painted an unspeakable brown, and her father's old leather recliner—had emerged from her parents' attic when she left for college, following her to law school. She kicked off her shoes, scratched the soles of her feet on the edge of the table. One day . . .

Taking up the file, she added the release notice to the jumble of papers at the back of the file and initialed the change on the file log, alerting the file clerk to send out update notices. Next, she flipped through her own reports on the surveillance two years before, looking for comments in Riccioli's cramped hand. A red marker had noted D'Angelo's spotting the surveillance van, an exclamation mark in the margin. *So do it better, asshole.*

She flipped to the back of the file. There were only two new entries. She consulted the dates on her legal pad, confirmed that a third update notice had gone out only three weeks before. She sorted through the clipped pages more slowly, found nothing more recent than January.

"Well, shit." She would have to ask the file clerk, a silent woman who loathed disorder in her files. Haggerty could imagine her scowling, glaring at her with suspicion. She shrugged. "Not my fault."

She set the file aside, stretched out on the couch with the new entries—a recent IRS report concluding that there was insufficient evidence for prosecution on tax fraud charges, and, stapled to a blank sheet of paper, an embossed wedding invitation, folded once, addressed to Thomas Riccioli, United States Attorney. Inside, in a flowing script:

Mr. and Mrs. John A. D'Angelo
request the pleasure of your company
at the wedding of their daughter

Maria D'Angelo
and
Francis Anthony Defeo
Sunday, February 10, 1991
at 2:00 p.m.
St. Vincent's Church, Boston

"That's balls!" she laughed. "Good for you, Johnny."

Attached to the sheet was a news clipping, "Assault Charges Dropped," and a photograph of a young man pushing through a crowd of reporters. Beside the photograph, Riccioli had scrawled, "Frankie Defeo meets the press." She glanced at the clipping, a fight in a bar in Revere spilled out into the parking lot. Frankie had taken an axe handle from his car and broken three ribs on some kid from Saugus. The kid filed charges, then refused to testify when the case came to trial. *Little league stuff,* Haggerty thought. *Must be ambitious, though, marrying Johnny's girl.* She remembered a photograph of the daughter from the cop's sentencing, clutching her mother's arm, shouting at the press. Pretty girl, small, with angry eyes, a cascade of black hair across her shoulders.

Haggerty tried to imagine the girl's life—the little girl visiting her father in prison, the police cars in the driveway after school, urgent phone calls in the middle of the night, her mother dragging her from bed to hide with a neighbor. And in high school, the boys watching her from a distance, leaning against the fence at the convent school as she walked past, their eyes following her to the car, where Tommy Russo chewed his cigar.

Haggerty smiled. She knew these boys, had met them at the fence when the afternoon bell rang. The nuns watched from the windows, taking notes on which girls tugged their skirts up at the afternoon bell, accepted drags on a boy's cigarettes, or, shielded by a crowd of boys, slipped into a car for the ride home. But Kate Haggerty, a lawyer's daughter, had gotten grades and gotten out. If she smiled at the memory of the boys at the fence, it was because distance is kind to such boys, smoothing their rough edges, giving their crude jokes, their dangling cigarettes, their battered cars the innocence of a life that holds no claim anymore. *And if you can't get out?* Haggerty wondered. *If you're marked by the rumor of violence, the need for silence? If the boys at the fence watch you with wary eyes, what then?*

"You marry one," she murmured. "The first one who has the courage to ask you."

She turned back to the news clipping, the photograph of Defeo pushing his way through the crowd, his eyes empty. A small guy, but wiry. His face was pale, the dark hair combed back. He had a weak mouth, curled up at one edge in a sarcastic grin.

A boy who wants that life, who watches with envy as the car drives you away.

"This wedding thing, it's gonna kill me."

Russo could see him in the rearview, flicking the ash from his cigar through a crack in the window.

"Angela, she's got this list. The fucking florist, the photographer, the band. It's three feet long, Tommy."

He leaned forward, peering through the windshield. A block away, a car pulled into the parking lot of the International House of Pancakes, stopping in the pale light of the streetlamp. A Chevy, blue. He settled back in his seat.

"You think I'm kidding? She calls 'em all at least twice a week. The colors are wrong. The song list is too short, some fucking thing."

"Keeps her busy."

"Am I complaining?"

"Yeah, Johnny."

"All right. Give me a break here, Tommy. It's making me crazy, that's all I'm saying. Like we're launching a ship here, or something."

His cigar glowed in the darkness.

"She's busy, she's happy," Russo said. "Got no time to think, you know?"

"Maria came to me; I figured, you know, it's too soon. I told her, 'Your mother, she's not ready for this. She's still thinking about Vinnie, right?' I mean, Tommy, I'd wake up in the middle of the night, and she's crying. Every night this happened. I get up in the morning, she's got the covers up over her head. I come back a couple hours later, she's still there. How's she gonna make a wedding?"

The cigar glowed. *Like it was his fault,* Russo thought. *Angie screaming at him. What's he gonna do about it? Doesn't he care? And him just sitting there, listening to it. Asks me one day, can we get a guy inside the prison? I told him, we got a dozen guys in there. They can't get at this guy. Sleeps with the guards, for Christ's sake. Just wait, I told him. He's gonna get out of there one day.*

Tell her, he says, shaking his head. *Tell her.*

"Maria, she wants to go right in there, give her the news. What am I gonna say, no? So next thing I know, Angie's outta bed, she's in the kitchen on the phone to Mr. Charles, making an appointment to get her hair done. Telling me she's gotta start looking for a dress, for Christ's sake."

He flicked at his lip with one finger.

"I'll tell you, though, I gotta get outta there, she starts with that list."

"Here he comes," Russo said.

A second car turned into the restaurant lot—a Lincoln, the leather roof shining under the lights.

"Look at him in that car."

"He's got an account down at the Soft-Wipe. You can see him over there every morning."

Johnny grunted. He pressed a button, and the window rolled down. He leaned forward.

The Lincoln parked in front of the entrance. As the head-lights died, the Chevy pulled out, tires squealing. It swung past the Lincoln, came to a sudden stop. A man leaped out of the passenger side, approached the car. Even from their distance, they could see the driver look up, surprised, raising one fat arm as the man yanked the door open, lifted the gun . . .

Jackie Mullen felt the door jerked from his grasp. He looked up, saw the gun reflected in the window, raised one hand. The gun swatted his hand aside, nestled in the hollow of his ear.

"Wait," he whispered.

Three faint pops, echoing along the wet street. Jackie slumped across the front seat. The gunman trotted back to the Chevy. It pulled out with a screech, bumped over a curb in a shower of sparks. Headlights flaring, it rounded the corner and pulled to a stop beside them.

Johnny nodded to the driver, looked past him at the gunman.

"All right, Frankie," he said. "Angie said to remind you 'bout the fitting tomorrow. Mr. Tux, on Washington."

The passenger nodded, a flash of teeth, and the Chevy roared off. Johnny settled back in his seat, the cigar glowing.

"Okay, Tommy. Let's go."

PART III

VOYEURS & OUTSIDERS

TOWNIES

BY ANDRE DUBUS

Merrimack River

(Originally Published in 1980)

T he campus security guard found her. She wore a parka
and she lay on the footbridge over the pond. Her left
cheek lay on the frozen snow. The college was a small
one, he was the only guard on duty, and in winter he made
his rounds in the car. But partly because he was sleepy in the
heated car, and mostly because he wanted to get out of the
car and walk in the cold dry air, wanted a pleasurable solitude
within the imposed solitude of his job, he had gone to the
bridge.

He was sixty-one years old, a tall broad man, his shoulders
slumped, and he was wide in the hips and he walked with his
toes pointed outward, with a long stride which appeared slow.
His body, whether at rest or in motion, seemed the result of
sixty-one years of erosion, as though all his life he had been
acted upon and, with just enough struggle to keep going, he
had conceded; fifty years earlier he would have sat quietly at
the rear of a classroom, scraped dirt with his shoe on the periphery of a playground. In a way, he was the best man to find
her. He was not excitable, he was not given to anger, he was
not a man of action: when he realized the girl was dead he did
not think immediately of what he ought to do, of what acts
and words his uniform and wages required of him. He did not
think of phoning the police. He knelt on the snow, so close

to her that his knee touched her shoulder, and he stroked her cold cheek, her cold blonde hair.

He did not know her name. He had seen her about the campus. He believed she had died of an overdose of drugs or a mixture of drugs and liquor. This deepened his sorrow. Often when he thought of what young people were doing to themselves, he felt confused and sad, as though in the country he loved there was a civil war whose causes baffled him, whose victims seemed wounded and dead without reason. Especially the girls, and especially these girls. He had lived all his life in this town, a small city in northeastern Massachusetts; once there had been a shoe industry. Now that was over, only three factories were open, and the others sat empty along the bank of the Merrimack. Their closed windows and the dark empty rooms beyond them stared at the street, like the faces of the old and poor who on summer Sundays sat on the stoops of the old houses farther upriver and stared at the street, the river, the air before their eyes. He had worked in a factory, as a stitcher. When the factory closed he got a job driving a truck, delivering fresh loaves of bread to families in time for their breakfast. Then people stopped having their bread delivered. It was a change he did not understand. He had loved the smell of bread in the morning and its warmth in his hands. He did not know why the people he had delivered to would choose to buy bread in a supermarket. He did not believe that the pennies and nickels saved on one expense ever showed up in your pocket.

When they stopped eating fresh bread in the morning he was out of work for a while, but his children were grown and his wife did not worry, and then he got his last and strangest job. He was not an authorized constable, he carried no weapons, and he needed only one qualification other than the usual ones of punctuality and subservience: a willingness to work for very little money. He was so accustomed to all three that none of them required an act of will, not even a moment's pause while he made the decision to take and do the job. When he worked a daylight shift he spent some time ordering possible vandals off the campus: they were usually children on bicycles; sometimes they made him chase them away, and he did this in his long stride, watching the distance lengthen between him and the children, the bicycles. Mostly during the day he chatted with the maintenance men and students and some of the teachers; and he walked the campus, which was contained by an iron fence and four streets, and he looked at the trees. There were trees he recognized, and more that he did not. One of the maintenance men had told him that every kind of New England tree grew here. There was one with thick, low, spreading branches and, in the fall, dark red leaves; sometimes students sat on the branches.

The time he saw three girls in the tree he was fooled: they were pretty and they wore sweaters in the warm autumn afternoon. They looked like the girls he had grown up knowing about: the rich girls who came from all parts of the country to the school, and who were rarely seen in town. From time to time some of them walked the three blocks from the campus to the first row of stores where the commercial part of the town began. But most of them only walked the one block, to the corner where they waited for the bus to Boston. He had smelled them once, as a young man. It was a winter day. When he saw them waiting for the bus he crossed the street so he could walk near them. There were perhaps six of them. As he approached, he looked at their faces, their hair. They did not look at him. He walked by them. He could smell them and he could feel their eyes seeing him and not seeing him. Their smells were of perfume, cold fur, leather gloves, leather suitcases. Their voices had no accents he could recognize. They seemed the voices of mansions, resorts, travel. He was too conscious of himself to hear what they were saying. He knew it was idle talk; but its tone seemed peremptory; he would not have been surprised if one of them had suddenly given him a command. Then he was away from them. He smelled only the cold air now; he longed for their smells again: erotic, unattainable, a world that would never be open to him. But he did not think about its availability, any more than he would wish for an African safari. He knew people who hated them because they were rich. But he did not. In the late sixties more of them began appearing in town and they wore blue jeans and smoked on the street. In the early seventies, when the drinking age was lowered, he heard they were going to the bars at night, and some of them got into trouble with the local boys. Also, the college started accepting boys, and they lived in the dormitories with the girls. He wished all this were not so; but by then he wished much that was happening was not so.

When he saw the three girls in the tree with low spreading branches and red leaves, he stopped and looked across the lawn at them, stood for a moment that was redolent of his past, of the way he had always seen the college girls, and still tried to see them: lovely and nubile, existing in an ambience of benign royalty. Their sweaters and hair seemed bright as the autumn sky. He walked toward them, his hands in his back pockets. They watched him. Then he stood under the tree, his eyes level with their legs. They were all biting silenced giggles. He said it was a pretty day. Then the giggles came, shrill and relentless; they could have been monkeys in the tree. There was an impunity about the giggling that was different from the other graceful impunity they carried with them as they carried the checkbooks that were its source. He was accustomed to that. He looked at their faces, at their vacant eyes and flushed cheeks; then his own cheeks flushed with shame. It was marijuana. He lifted a hand in goodbye.

He was not angry. He walked with lowered eyes away from the giggling tree, walked impuissant and slow across the lawn and around the snack bar, toward the library; then he shifted direction and with raised eyes went toward the ginkgo tree near the chapel. There was no one around. He stood looking at the yellow leaves, then he moved around the tree and stopped to read again the bronze plaque he had first read and marveled at his second day on the job. It said the tree was a gift of the class of 1941. He stood now as he had stood on that first day, in a reverie which refreshed his bruised heart, then healed it. He imagined the girls of 1941 standing in a circle as one of the maintenance men dug a hole and planted the small tree. The girls were pretty and hopeful and had sweethearts. He thought of them later in that year, in winter; perhaps skiing while the *Arizona* took the bombs. He was certain that some of them lost sweethearts in that war, which at first he had followed in the newspapers as he now followed the Red Sox and Patriots and Celtics and Bruins. Then he was drafted. They made him a truck driver and he saw England while the war was still on, and France when it was over. He was glad that he missed combat and when he returned he did not pretend to his wife and family and friends that he wished he had been shot at. Going over, he had worried about submarines; other than that, he had enjoyed his friends and England and France, and he had saved money. He still remembered it as a pleasurable interlude in his life. Looking at the ginkgo tree and the plaque he happily felt their presence like remembered music: the girls then, standing in a circle around the small tree on that spring day in 1941; those who were in love and would grieve; and he stood in the warmth of the afternoon staring at the yellow leaves strewn on the ground like deciduous sunshine.

So this last one was his strangest job: he was finally among them, not quite their servant like the cleaning women and not their protector either: an unarmed watchman and patrolman whose job consisted mostly of being present, of strolling and chatting in daylight and, when he drew the night shift, of driving or walking, depending on the weather, and of daydreaming and remembering and talking to himself. He enjoyed the job. He would not call it work, but that did not bother him. He had long ago ceased believing in work: the word and its connotation of fulfillment as a man. Life was cluttered with these ideas which he neither believed nor disputed. He merely ignored them. He liked wandering about in this job, as he had liked delivering bread and had liked the army; only the stitching had been tedious. He liked coming home and drinking coffee in the kitchen with his wife: the daily chatting which seemed eternal. He liked his children and his grandchildren. He accepted the rest of his life as a different man might accept commuting: a tolerable inconvenience. He knew he was not lazy. That was another word he did not believe in.

He kneeled on the snow and with his ungloved hand he touched her cold blonde hair. In sorrow his flesh mingled like death-ash with the pierced serenity of the night air and the trees on the banks of the pond and the stars. He felt her spirit everywhere, fog-like across the pond and the bridge, spreading and rising in silent weeping above him into the black visible night and the invisible space beyond his ken and the cold silver truth of the stars.

* * *

On the bridge Mike slipped and cursed, catching himself on the wooden guardrail, but still she did not look back. He was about to speak her name but he did not: he knew if his voice was angry she would not stop and if his voice was pleading she might stop and even turn to wait for him but he could not bear to plead. He walked faster. He had the singular focus that came from being drunk and sad at the same time: he saw nothing but her parka and blonde hair. All evening, as they drank, he had been waiting to lie with her in her bright clean room. Now there would be no room. He caught up with her and grabbed her arm and spun her around; both her feet slipped but he held her up.

"You asshole," she said, and he struck her with his fist, saw the surprise and pain in her eyes, and she started to speak but he struck her before she could; and when now she only moaned he swung again and again, holding her up with his left hand, her parka bunched and twisted in his grip; when he released her she fell forward. He kicked her side. He knew he should stop but he could not. Kicking, he saw her naked in the bed in her room. She was slender. She moaned and gasped while they made love; sometimes she came so hard she cried. He stopped kicking. He knew she had died while he was kicking her. Something about the silence of the night, and the way her body yielded to his boot.

He looked around him: the frozen pond, the tall trees, the darkened library. He squatted down and looked at her red-splotched cheek. He lifted her head and turned it and lowered it to the snow. Her right cheek was untouched; now she looked asleep. In the mornings he usually woke first, hung over and hard, listening to students passing in the halls. Now on the snow she looked like that: in bed, on her pillow. Under the blanket he took her hand and put it around him and he woke and they smoked a joint; then she kneeled between his legs and he watched her hair going up and down.

He stood and walked off the bridge and around the library. His body was weak and sober and it weaved; he did not feel part of it, and he felt no need to hurry away from the campus and the bridge and Robin. What waited for him was home, and a two-mile walk to get there: the room he hated though he tried to believe he did not. For he lived there, his clothes hung there, most of all he slept there, the old vulnerable breathing of night and dreams; and if he allowed himself to hate it then he would have to hate his life too, and himself.

He walked without stealth across the campus, then up the road to town. He passed Timmy's, where he and Robin had drunk and where now the girls who would send him to prison were probably still drinking. He and Robin had sat in a booth on the restaurant side. She drank tequila sunrises and paid for those and for his Comfort and ginger, and she told him that all day she had been talking to people, and now she had to talk to him, her mind was blown, her father called her about her grades and he called the dean too so she had to go to the counselor's office and she was in there three hours, they talked about everything, they even got back to the year she was fifteen and she told the counselor she didn't remember much of it, that was her year on acid, and she had done a lot of balling, and she said she had never talked like that with anybody before, had never just sat down and *list*ed what she had done for the last four years, and the counselor told her in all that time she had never felt what she was doing or done what she felt. She was talking gently to Mike, but in her eyes she was already gone: back in her room; home in Darien; Bermuda at Easter; the year in Europe she had talked about before, the year her father would give her when she got out of school. He could not remember her loins, and he felt he could not remember himself either, that his life had begun a few minutes earlier in this booth. He watched her hands as she stirred her tequila sunrise and the grenadine rose from the bottom in a menstrual cloud, and she said the counselor had gotten her an appointment in town with a psychiatrist tomorrow, a woman psychiatrist, and she wanted to go, she wanted to talk again, because now she had admitted it, that she wasn't happy, hadn't been happy, had figured nobody ever could be.

Then he looked at her eyes. She liked to watch him when they made love, and sometimes he opened his eyes and saw on her face that eerie look of a woman making love: as if her eyes, while watching him, were turned inward as well, were indeed watching his thrusting from within her womb. Her eyes now were of the counselor's office, the psychiatrist's office tomorrow, they held no light for him; and in his mind, as she told him she had to stop dope and alcohol and balling, he saw the school: the old brick and the iron fence with its points like spears and the serene trees. All his life this town had been dying. His father had died with it, killing himself with one of the last things he owned: they did not have a garage so he drove the car into the woods and used the vacuum cleaner hose. She said she had never come, not with anybody all these years, she had always faked it; he finished his drink in a swallow and immediately wished he had not, for he wanted another but she didn't offer him one and he only had three dollars which he knew now he would need for the rest of the night; then he refused to imagine the rest of the night. He smiled.

"Only with my finger," she said.

"I hope it falls off."

She slid out of the booth; his hand started to reach for

her but he stopped it; she was saying something that didn't matter now, that he could not feel: her eyes were suddenly damp as standing she put on her parka, saying she had wanted to talk to him, she thought at least they could talk; then she walked out. He drank her tequila sunrise as he was getting out of the booth. Outside, he stood looking up the street; she was a block away, almost at the drugstore. Then she was gone around the bend in the street. He started after her, watching his boots on the shoveled sidewalk.

Now he walked on the bridge over the river and thought of her lying on the small one over the pond. The wind came blowing down freezing over the Merrimack; his moustache stiffened, and he lowered his head. But he did not hurry. Seeing Robin on the bridge over the pond he saw the dormitory beyond it, just a dormitory for them, rooms which they crowded with their things, but the best place he had ever slept in. The things that crowded their rooms were more than he had ever owned, yet he knew for the girls these were only selected and favorite or what they thought necessary things, only a transportable bit of what filled large rooms of huge houses at home. For four or five years now he had made his way into the dormitory; he met them at Timmy's and they took him back to the dormitory to drink and smoke dope and when the party dissolved one of them usually took him to bed.

One night in the fall before Robin he was at a party there and toward three in the morning nearly all the girls were gone and no one had given him a sign and there were only two girls left and the one college fag, a smooth-shaven, razor-cut boy who dressed better than the girls, went to Timmy's, and even to the bar side of it, the long, narrow room without booths or bar stools where only men drank; he wore a variety of costumes: heels and yellow and rust and gold and red, and drank sloe gin fizzes and smoked like a girl. And Mike, who rarely thought one way or another about fags but disliked them on sight, liked this one because he went into town like that and once a man poured a beer over his head, but he kept going and joking, his necklaces tapping on his chest as he swayed back and forth laughing. That night he came over and sat beside Mike just at the right time, when Mike had understood that the two remaining girls not only weren't interested in him, but they despised him, and he was thinking of the walk home to his room when the fag said he had some Colombian and Mike nodded and rose and left with him. In the room the fag touched him and Mike said twenty-five bucks and put it in his pocket, then removed the fag's fingers from his belt buckle and turned away and undressed. He would not let the fag kiss him but the rest was all right, a mouth was a mouth, except when he woke sober in the morning, woke early, earlier than he ever woke when he slept there with a girl. A presence woke him as though a large bird had flown inches above his chest. He got up quickly and glanced at the sleeping fag, lying on his back, his bare, smooth shoulders and slender arms above the blanket, his face turned toward Mike, the mouth open, and Mike wanted to kill him or himself or both of them, looking away from the mouth which had consumed forever part of his soul, and with his back turned he dressed. Then quietly opening the door he was aware of his height and broad shoulders and he squared them as glaring he stepped into the corridor; but it was empty, and he got out of the dormitory without anyone seeing him and ate breakfast in town and at ten o'clock went to the employment office for his check.

Through the years he had stolen from them: usually cash from the girls he slept with, taking just enough so they would believe or make themselves believe that while they were drunk at Timmy's they had spent it. Twice he had stolen with the collusion of girls. One had gone ahead of him in the corridor, then down the stairs, as he rolled and carried a ten-speed bicycle. He rode it home and the next day sold it to three young men who rented a house down the street; they sold dope, and things other people stole, mostly things that kids stole, and Mike felt like a kid when he went to them and said he had a ten-speed. A year later, when a second girl helped him steal a stereo, he sold it at the same house. The girl was drunk and she went with him into the room one of her friends had left unlocked, and in the dark she got the speakers and asked if he wanted any records while he hushed her and took the amplifier and turntable. They carried everything out to her Volvo. In the car he was relieved but only for a moment, only until she started the engine, then he thought of the street and the building where he lived, and by the time she turned on the heater he was trying to think of a way to keep her from taking him home.

All the time she was talking. It was the first time she had stolen anything. Or anything worth a lot of money. He made himself smile by thinking of selling her to the men in the house; he thought of her sitting amid the stereos and television sets and bicycles. Then he heard her say something. She had asked if he was going to sell his old set so he could get some bucks out of the night too. He said he'd give the old one to a friend, and when she asked for directions he pointed ahead in despair. He meant to get out at the corner but when she said Here? and slowed for the turn he was awash in the loss of control which he fought so often and overcame so little, though he knew most people couldn't tell by looking at him or even talking to him. She turned and climbed up the street, talking all the time, not about the street, the buildings, but about the stereo: or the stealing of it, and he knew from her voice she was repeating herself so she would not have to talk about what she saw. Or he felt she was. But that was not the worst. The worst was that he was so humiliated he could not trust what he felt, could not know if this dumb rich girl was even aware of the street, and he knew there was no way out of this except to sleep and wake tomorrow in the bed that held his scent. He had been too long in that room (this was his third year), too long in the building: there were six apartments; families lived in the five larger ones; one family had a man: a pumper of gasoline, checker of oil and water, wiper of windshields. Mike thought of his apartment as a room, although there was a kitchen he rarely used, a bathroom, and a second room that for weeks at a time he did not enter. Some mornings when he woke he felt he had lived too long in his body. He smoked a joint in bed and showered and shaved and left the room, the building, the street of these buildings. Once free of the street he felt better: he liked feeling and smelling clean; he walked into town. The girl stopped the Volvo at another of his sighed directions and touched his thigh and said she would help him bring the stuff in. He said no and loaded everything in his arms and left her.

Robin had wanted to go to his room too and he had never let her and now for the first time grieving for her lost flesh, he wished he had taken her there. Saw her there at nights and on the weekends, the room—rooms: he saw even the second room—smelling of paint; saw buckets and brushes on newspaper awaiting her night and weekend hand, his hand too: the two of them painting while music played not from his tinny-sounding transistor but a stereo that was simply there in his apartment with the certainty of something casually purchased with cash neither from the employment office nor his

occasional and tense forays into the world of jobs: dishwash-
ing at Timmy's, the quick and harried waitresses bringing the
trays of plates which he scraped and racked and hosed and
slid into the washer, hot water in the hot kitchen wetting his
clothes; he scrubbed the pots by hand and at the night's end
he mopped the floor and the bartender sent him a bottle of
beer; but he only worked there in summers, when the students
were gone. He saw Robin painting the walls beside him, their
brushstrokes as uniform as the beating of their hearts. He was
approaching the bar next to the bus station. He did not like
it because the band was too loud, and the people were losers, but he often went there anyway, because he could sit and
drink and watch the losers dancing without having to make
one gesture he had to think about, the way he did at Timmy's
when he sat with the girls and was conscious of his shoulders
and arms and hands, of his eyes and mouth as if he could
see them, so that he smiled—and coolly, he knew—when girl
after girl year after year touched his flesh and sometimes his
heart and told him he was cool.

He went into the bar, feeling the bass drum beat as though
it came from the floor and walls, and took the one untaken
stool and ordered a shot of Comfort, out of habit checking his
pocket although he knew he had three ones and some change.
Everyone he saw was drunk, and the bartender was drinking. Vic was at the end of the bar; Mike nodded at him. He
drank the shot and pushed the glass toward the bartender. His
fingers trembled. He sipped the Comfort and lit a cigarette,
cold sweat on his brow, and he thought he would have to go
outside into the cold air or vomit.

He finished the shot then moved through the crow to Vic
and spoke close to his ear and the gold earring. "I need some
downs." Vic wanted a dollar apiece. "Come on," Mike said.

"Two." Vic's arm left the bar and he put two in Mike's hand; Mike gave him the dollar and left, out onto the cold street, heading uphill, swallowing, but his throat was dry and the second one lodged; he took a handful of snow from a mound at the base of a parking meter and ate it. He walked on the lee side of the buildings now. He was dead with her. He lay on the bridge, his arm around her, his face in her hair. At the dormitory the night shift detectives would talk to the girls inside, out of the cold; they would sit in the big glassed-in room downstairs where drunk one night he had pissed on the carpet while Robin laughed before they went up to her room. The girls would speak his name. His name was in that room, back there in the dormitory; it was not walking up the hill in his clothing. He had two joints in his room and he would smoke those while he waited, lying dressed on his bed. When he heard their footsteps in the hall he would put on his jacket and open the door before they knocked and walk with them to the cruiser. He walked faster up the hill.

DRIVING THE HEART

BY JASON BROWN

Boston General Hospital

(Originally published in 1999)

Traveling between Danvers and Natick yesterday I saw a man in a flower truck drive by at 80 m.p.h. with his eyes closed. I turned to Dale, a guy the hospital hired for me to train, and said, "Nothing, not even someone's liver, is that important." He put his hand on top of the metal case marked *Liver* and nodded.

We drive the no-rush jobs, eyeballs, livers, morphine, or kidneys, through the day traffic to or from the airport. Sometimes when a patient decides to die at home and runs out of painkillers, we will bring extra morphine out to them at night. Tonight we are driving way out to Lebanon Springs, to the town where I was born, with a heart for a woman about to die from some accident or some disease. Hearts travel at night.

Dale sits next to me holding the metal box marked *Heart*. His eyes droop. His head leans to the right. Next thing he'll be sleeping, dreaming down the highway. I know what it's like.

When the weather is foul like tonight and the airplane can't make it, they send us. We're the only choice they have of reaching such a small town in such an out-of-the-way place. Cellular phone service is out and in many places the power is out, but most of the regular pay phones still work. We stop every hour at designated places and call the hospital to make sure the patient in Lebanon is still alive. The hospital is in contact with Lebanon. We are not allowed to stop for food or drink and, if we can help it, even to urinate on this six-hour journey. We make the call and if she's still alive we rush on. If not then we can pause briefly for food and bathroom before we turn around and drive without stopping for Worcester, where a plane will take the heart to some other person in a city with a major airport. This heart, however, is getting old. There probably won't be time to take it anywhere after Lebanon.

Hearts are packed in ice. But even a frozen heart will only last for twenty-four hours on the outside, unofficially. That's why if we have to take it to Worcester, there will only be time to fly the heart to a major airport, then rush it from there by helicopter to a hospital in the same city. There is always a patient. Driving to Lebanon, we shoot for six or seven hours at the most. Tonight we have to hurry through the high winds and beating rain, in order not to waste this heart.

I stop the car and have Dale run out through the rain to the pay phone with the number I gave him.

"What's her name?" he asks.

"You won't be talking to her," I say, "and it doesn't matter. Just give the hospital the job number. They'll say drive on if she's still alive, or turn around."

A few minutes later he comes running back, gets in the car, brushes the rain off his sleeves, and nods his head. After a few more minutes he says, "I'm hungry," even though I've already explained the rules.

Hospital delivery often attracts people like myself, who have cared very deeply about the wrong things. Who, in less than half an average life span, have been born, born again, arrested for armed robbery, and born once more. A person can only be born so many times before even the Christians don't want to take you seriously. The second time I was born I was twenty years old and lying in a donated suit on the floor of a jail in Sturgis, Michigan. I remember one of the officers brought me a bowl of stew and suggested I eat something before going into court, but I shook my head. I was being charged with driving under the influence and assaulting a police officer, although I didn't remember doing those things. The judge informed me that I had drunk ten ounces of 151 in a few hours. He lowered his head after this announcement, not because I was a startling case, but because I was the same kind of case he saw day after day and he was tired. I asked what I could do to show him that I had finally gotten the picture, that all I wanted was one more chance. He looked at me and laughed, which was to say: that's what everybody says. He didn't know that I was reborn, that over in Grass Lake, where I wanted to go after I was released, people believed.

We drive all over New England, sometimes to New York, but mostly we stay around the Boston area. If you know the Wenham-Woburn-Needham-Braintree route, then you know that the places to live are Belmont, Weston, Concord, or beyond but not so far out as Lowell. All the names up and down the coast, Weekapaug, Quonochontaug, Naquit, Teaticket, Menauhaunt, and Falmouth Heights, remind me of the life I could have had if things had been different. I have a friend living that life over in Sakonnet right now. I go over and visit him once in a while—from his second-floor bathroom window a sliver of ocean can be seen.

Dale reaches over and turns the radio up; he leans on his right elbow against the window. He slumps in his seat. I turn the radio back down. No amount of training will make a kid like this understand his job. Even as the passenger you should sit alert. Someone else's life sits in your hands. His head nods against the passenger window as I flick the radio off. "No more radio," I say. That wakes him up. Dale straightens himself and asks what happened to the woman who needs the heart, but I can tell by the way he fiddles with the buttons on his coat that he doesn't really care. I tell him I don't know, that the woman could be thirty, could be seventy. Could be heart disease, could be anything, they never tell me. Usually they take the heart from someone who is alive but brain-dead and transport it to someone whose thoughts are clear but whose heart is dead. And in truth, I explain, they usually give preference to the young. The moment the heart leaves the body of the donor, it is cross-clamped and the clock starts ticking. In the Lebanon hospital they are standing there in the operating room right now, smocked and ready, waiting for us. Dale nods and we drive on in silence.

I roll the window down for a moment to let in some air and then roll it back up again. I turn to Dale: "A man in Abilene, Texas, gets drunk and drives his car through a 7-Eleven. Three hours later his heart travels on a plane bound for Logan Airport. Six hours later his heart sits next to you in a large silver case marked *Heart*, and we are driving down the highway at the speed limit toward some supine client in a hospital room asleep or possibly in a coma who will not live another day without this heart. This," I say to Dale, "is the importance of your job." He nods, furrowing his brow. No matter how many times I explain, I don't think he will understand.

"What if something goes wrong?" he asks.

"Nothing will go wrong if you don't get any ideas. Now go make the call," I say, pointing at the variety store.

I live in a so-so neighborhood. The people there smell and never take out the trash. I look out my window at a funeral home. For four months each year the sun rarely shines in this part of the country. Some mornings I consider the consequences of quitting my job and doing nothing for the rest of my life. People will still get their organs and their drugs, driven here and there by someone like myself. A replacement. The hospital has them. The only thing that will happen differently in the world if I quit my job is that I will not be able to eat.

I ask Dale if he has ever donated an organ. He shakes his head, looks at me in silence, and then we sit there, ahead of schedule, thinking. I feel like telling him to keep his eyes open.

I've seen some strange things. A woman from Nova Scotia once came into the hospital and offered to sell two kidneys. She said she had four. The doctor on duty said he was interested in such a claim, but that it was the hospital's policy, the law in fact, not to accept such offers.

I know what it's like to want things. I've always wanted to travel the world but probably never will. I've seen pictures. I've always wanted to date a very beautiful woman.

Only once have I flown in an airplane, crossing the water to London with a case of hospital files to be signed by a man there. Somewhere out over Labrador the pregnant woman across the aisle started to scream. The husband started running up and down the aisle while his wife was pulling on her seat and pushing with her knees against the people in front, her stomach seizing with contractions. The man suddenly whipped around, focused on me, and yelled, "I need a doctor! Is anyone a doctor?" A woman sitting in back came forward saying she used to be a nurse. The man stepped aside, pointing at his wife in her light cotton floral dress, the makeup washing down onto her neck. "She's only seven months—not even," the husband said. When he stepped aside a little more to allow the nurse to move in, I could see liquid from between the pregnant woman's legs pouring off her seat and onto the floor. The woman who used to be a nurse looked directly away, holding her head with her hand. She was looking at me and through me. "How much time before we land?" the man blurted at the stewardess, who had just arrived. "Too much time," the ex-nurse, looking at me, said.

The most exciting thing that can be said about me is that I delivered pizzas in dangerous neighborhoods when I lived in New York. How I can be both obsessed and relaxed at the same time is a mystery to me, but I consider it one of my greatest accomplishments. I'm not very old, but I would say that so far nothing has gone according to plan, that people have been unpredictable and that's about the extent of it. I would also say that certain ideas seem basically true to me. You cannot serve two masters well. Our thoughts are of little consequence. Live cautiously. You have to in my family. Back when I was twelve, for instance, I was traveling down Capisic Street in Lebanon when a woman traveling thirty, forty miles an hour hit the rear tire of my bike. I rolled over the hood and the roof, bounced off the trunk, and landed standing on my feet. She screeched to a stop and broke out weeping on the steering wheel, afraid to look. I walked up and tapped on her window. Her fingers danced on the dashboard. She looked at me. "Are you all right?" I asked. "I don't believe it," the woman said, resting her head back down on the wheel. "I don't believe it."

The road we're traveling down tonight feels familiar, the rhythm of the bumps and ruts against the tires, but in the dark nothing looks the same. Dale fumbles with the map, turning it toward the window so he can read with the help of an occasional streetlight. "Where is this place we're going to?" he asks.

"Lebanon Springs."

"It's not on the map," Dale says.

"What?" I ask.

"Lebanon."

"Turn it over. It's on the other side." Dale turns the map over and brings it up close to his face. "Find the green line I made. It starts in Boston; follow to where it ends."

"I found it," he says. "It's tiny. There can't be much to this town."

"There's a woman who needs a heart," I say. "That's all you need to know."

Some people say I was thinking too much and some people say I wasn't thinking enough, but I probably just wasn't thinking about the right things. Don't take advice from yourself, don't leave your apartment without a good reason, don't have a telephone, don't own too many things, don't own too few. Live on the first floor. Watch out for people.

Dale lets out a long sigh. He runs his hands through his slicked-back hair, then rubs the back of his neck. Dale is wrong for the job. There's no use even getting to know him because I'll just be training someone new next week and asking all the same questions, explaining all the same rules.

Dale asks if he can look at the heart, to see how it's kept alive. He thinks it might be helpful for the job, but I think otherwise. Does he think I haven't sat alone in this seat next to a case marked *Heart* and not looked inside? There's nothing to look at. It either works or it doesn't.

I turn to Dale: "You've read the manual?"

He nods, but I'm not sure he even knows what manual I'm talking about.

"You get to one of the designated stops only to find that the phone is out. What do you do? Stop at the next phone along the road or drive on? No time to think. Page fifty-two of the manual, right?"

"Stop at the next phone," he says. "The next phone along the road, I mean."

"I know what you mean and you're wrong. You drive on." I let him fiddle with the glove compartment handle and crack his knuckles. "When in doubt," I tell him, "always drive on. Just remember that one thing, all right? All right?"

"All right," he says.

He looks out the window. I look briefly where he's looking, but the shape of the hills on the horizon depends on the phase of the moon. I don't recognize a thing. On a night like tonight when the moon is hidden by the storm, we can only recognize the windshield wipers, the sheets of rain, and the vague shape of the white road sign letters. We could be headed anywhere. The last time I traveled down this road I was hitchhiking home and ended up in a car accident. I told a guy and a girl who picked me up on Route 302 somewhere that I would go as far as they were going. He told me that they were headed for her parents' house in a little town out where 302 turns into 89, called Lebanon Springs. I nodded, and he drove faster than the speed limit. I had been outside in the snow for too long, and my feet were numb. I took off my shoes in the backseat and rubbed each toe, worried that they might not come back. Suddenly there was a thud, breaking glass, and we slid into the guardrail. The head of a large buck had smashed against the windshield, spraying glass shards onto the driver, whose head rested against the steering wheel. I crawled out the back door. The tiny glass fragments melted into the bottoms of my bare feet. The guy's girlfriend had to crawl out her window and over the hood. She walked toward me, swaying her hips like a model, rubbing her head. The deer stood in front of the car watching us. Then he closed his eyes. I never made it back to Lebanon that time.

In the dawn haze I start to recognize sections of forest from the last time I was here, eight years ago. We'll enter from the east side of town, so we won't have to use the Thurman Bridge, where I was born crossing over from Stockton in a Pinto, my father behind the wheel and my mother sprawled out in back. The story goes that my mother said she wasn't going to make it, and my father said she had to wait. She said she couldn't and there was much screaming. She wanted something to kill the pain. He told her just to think about something else and hold it in and then before she knew it they would be there. But all she knew was that she couldn't wait another second, and I was born at 11:42 p.m., before we even crossed the river.

Staring through the rain-splattered windshield into the dark gray forest, I am reminded of the same forest twenty miles from here, where I lived with my parents at the end of a long dirt road. We lived there for five or six years, but one morning it was so cold that the storm pane cracked down the middle and fell into the backyard. I woke up and wandered into my parents' bathroom, waiting for them to wake, stepped up on a stool, opened the medicine cabinet, and pulled down a box of razor blades hidden from me behind the shaving cream. Taking out two, I placed one in the palm of my right hand, then squeezed my fingers shut. With my left hand I ran the other blade lightly, painlessly up and down my arm from the shoulder to the palm. It was so long ago, I don't remember what I was thinking. The little slits remained dry for a second, caught off guard, before red lines appeared and eventually washed together like flooding rivers. I walked into their bedroom, groping my hand along the wall for the light switch. Her head bolted up. Then I found the light switch.

Several years later—I can't remember how many; we must have lived there for more than seven years—I was ten years old standing at the same window, my father having been gone from the house for quite some time, I heard my mother's faltering footsteps climbing the stairs. I locked my bedroom door, pushed one of the chairs up against the knob, and then returned to the window. I heard the floorboards creak as she crept up to the door and carefully, trying not to wake me, turned the doorknob and pushed forward. When the door would not open, she pushed more frantically and cursed under her breath. The rain splashed against the window.

It has stopped raining now and the sky has started to lighten. Dale runs off into Ken's Variety, twenty miles east of our destination, to make our last call. Twenty minutes to go. I decide that when Dale returns I'll ask him some questions about his life, about the letter D sewn onto his high school jacket, about what he wants to do with his life after this. I should try to be nice.

Maybe he wants to live over in Wayland or Lexington and summer down at Marion or Pocasset, slightly off the beaten path, where it's warm and the grass comes right down to the ocean and the beaches keep going. It sounds like a good life to me.

I hear a car engine gearing down behind me and then the grumble of the braking wheels against the gravel of the shoulder. Two guys pull up beside my window in a pickup. The truck weaves a little as it comes to a stop. The driver rolls down his window, spits out some of his chew, and moves his hand in a circle, signaling me to roll my window down. When I do he raises his upper lip and asks me what time it is. I look down at the blank face of my digital watch, tap it a couple times, and tell him my watch is dead. There is a clock on the case, but I would have to get out of the car and walk over to the passenger side to check it. I'm not about to waste time doing that. The guy says he thinks I'm lying about not knowing the time, so I show him the watch. "The watch is dead," I say. Then he asks how much money I have and I tell him. "Nothing." He says he knows I'm lying and I say, "Is that so?"

"We're hungry," he says. "We're driving all the way down from Elmira with no food. We want to buy some food at the store."

His partner raises a shotgun and hands it to the driver, who points it at me. "How much for your life?" he says. He turns back to his buddy, then back to me. "My friend here says ten dollars. Fair price, huh? Ten dollars and your life is yours."

I put my hand over the wallet in my pocket and thumb through the bills inside, thinking about the heart. "I don't have a dime," I say.

"Not a dime," he says.

"Not a cent."

The driver squints and releases the safety on the shotgun. "I know this isn't true," he says, closing one eye and lowering his head down next to the stock. "My friend says shoot you before someone comes along, but I'd rather have the ten dollars, so I'm waiting another couple seconds to see what happens."

I look down the double barrel, stop breathing, and I wait to see what happens. For a long time I listen to the unsteady rumble of their truck's engine like it's my own breath.

Suddenly he opens his eyes wide. "Bang," he says pulling the gun back in but leaving his eyes pointed at me. His lips move up around his teeth. "Guess you're hungrier than we are," he says, and they drive away. I fall against the steering wheel, my chest heaving, my right hand on the silver case.

Dale comes out of Ken's, trips on the steps, picks himself up, and keeps running. He climbs in the car, sucking in a mouthful of air, and says, "I couldn't get through." I throw it into drive and pull forward, knowing perfectly well what the situation is and what we have to do. "The phone lines around here are fine," Dale explains, "but Ken said the storm is worse back in Boston. Maybe the lines are down there."

"No matter," I say.

"Hey," Dale says, sitting up in his seat as if remembering an important message. "When I was on the phone, Ken looked out the window and mumbled something about your being in trouble. Anything happen?"

"It was nothing," I say. "Now in this situation, what do we do?"

"What situation?" Dale says, rubbing his forehead.

"You made the phone call and were not able to get through."

"Oh. We drive on, right?"

"You tell me."

"We drive on," Dale says, and we sit there in silence. After a few minutes a police car approaches from behind and flashes its blue lights. I pull over to the side of the road and roll down my window. The officer parks his car, pulls some papers off the dashboard, opens his door, closes it carefully, and starts walking toward us. He stops halfway, removes his cap, smooths back his gray hairs, and puts the cap back on before continuing forward. Dale looks at the floor.

"How are you this morning?" the old officer says.

"Fine, sir," I answer.

"Glad to hear it," he says. "I stopped you because old Ken gave the dispatch a ring saying you were having some trouble out in front of his store."

"It was nothing," I say.

"Ken said that some guys in a pickup—"

"Officer," I say, "I hate to interrupt, but we are on an urgent job, delivering a heart to the hospital just across town. We're coming all the way from Boston through the storm and every second counts. We have to drive on. After we deliver the package I will be happy to answer any of your questions."

"A heart, you say?" the officer rubs his head. "I've never heard of such a thing."

"Yes, sir."

"Is that what your partner has there in that case?"

"Yes it is."

"And you're taking it over to Community?"

"Yes we are."

"Then I won't hold you up."

"Thank you, officer."

"Well. I won't hold you up," he says again, staring down at me. "But please stop down at the station when you're done. We'd like a description."

"Certainly."

"Thank you," he says and backs away from the car.

I drive on, spinning the wheels a bit in the gravel and holding the pedal all the way down as the speedometer slowly climbs back up to fifty-five. After ten minutes of silence, passing swiftly over Washington Avenue, down Winthrop Street, and across Thorton Ave., we swing up to the hospital and stop outside the electric doors and the lighted sign, EMERGENCY. "Here," I say, grabbing the case. "Follow me." Holding the case in front of me, I head for the doors of the emergency room. Dale takes several leaps to keep up with me. I walk right up to the glass booth where a woman behind a desk is filling out forms. Someone else, an enormous woman, sits in one of the waiting chairs with no obvious injuries. The man next to her holds a rag clamped over his bloody hand. They both stare at the opposite wall.

I tap nervously on the glass. "Can I help you?" the woman says without looking up.

"I'm here with the heart from Boston General. Here are the forms," I say, shoving them in front of her face. She takes the forms but does not look at them.

"A heart?" she says, looking at me and my metal case.

"Yes," I say.

She takes a deep breath and shifts her behind on the swivel chair. "What do you mean, you're here with a heart?"

"Look," I say. "It's an emergency. We've been delayed. There is a woman here who needs this heart. Who knows how long she will last, but I know that this heart will not last much longer." The woman stares at me, looks at the forms. "Didn't anyone tell you?" I ask.

"I just came on," she says. "I haven't heard anything about this."

I set the case down and grab onto the edge of the partition separating this woman from myself. I stare down, fixed on her lower lip. "Look," I say. "The heart is here."

"I'll have to go back and check with one of the doctors," she says, smiling faintly and disappearing down a corridor. I lean against the glass and close my eyes. I can hear the large woman in the chair shift from one hip to another. The man with the injured hand coughs briefly and then starts tapping his foot. He taps it out of boredom, not pain. Once every couple seconds he lets the toe hit the floor. Then he stops and I feel his eyes on me and the silver case. The fluorescent lights lining the ceiling buzz like insects, becoming louder with every moment until in the distance I hear the clicking heels of the receptionist and the squeaks of a doctor's rubber heels coming down the corridor. I turn around suddenly, wondering what has happened to Dale. And just as the doctor comes up behind me, I see Dale appear from around a corner and pause next to a black sign with an arrow that says *Cafeteria*. The doctor puts his hand on my shoulder and rests it there, waiting for me to turn toward him.

"I'm sorry," he says when I don't turn. "Boston General should have told you on the last call."

He removes his hand and waits patiently for me to respond. The receptionist returns to her desk and picks up the next form off the enormous stack. Dale has stopped to unwrap the rest of a sandwich he just bought down the hall. He leans over, allowing the lettuce strands to fall on the floor instead of his jacket, and then continues toward me. A sliced tomato hangs over his bottom lip. He swallows and keeps walking. After a few steps he stops to take another bite, this time scooping up the strands of lettuce with his free hand and pushing them in the corner of his mouth. The doctor picks the case up and, placing it against the wall, says a few words to the receptionist, who opens a drawer and shuffles through a bunch of papers. It is too late for Worcester, I think. When Dale sees that I am staring he stops walking and tries to swallow what's left in his mouth.

The doctor steps up beside me again carrying a clipboard. "We need to have you sign these," he says. I take the clipboard and the pen without looking at him.

"I was hungry," Dale says, shrugging his shoulders. "I figured we were here. I couldn't wait any longer."

"That's no excuse," I say and lower my head to the forms resting in my hands. I sign my name. *Time of arrival*, it says. I turn my wrist and look down at my blank watch. I look at the doctor. "Time?" I say.

He raises his naked wrist. "Forgot to wear it today." He smiles, dark circles under his eyes.

Dale shoves the rest of the sandwich into his pocket. "It's seven o'clock," he says, pursing his lips in an effort to take our job more seriously. He walks over to the silver case and picks it up. "What do we do now? I thought we were here."

I walk over to him, take the case out of his hand, and lay it down next to the wall. "It's too late," I say, but he furrows his brow and stares at the case. It is a good sign when a trainee doesn't understand how a job can fail. I remind him as we head for the door that a heart, once removed from the body, will last only twenty-four hours. There is nowhere left for us to drive. At the door he turns away from me looking for the silver case, which a nurse is carrying down a long yellow hallway. I give just a light tug on his arm, but he won't start walking until the nurse has disappeared down another corridor. I understand that this is the hardest part of the job; there is no way for me to explain how we could have driven all this way with a heart for which, in the end, there is no life.

THE 5:22

BY GEORGE HARRAR

Kendall Square

(Originally published in 1998)

For more than a year Walter Mason and the woman with one ear nodded to each other at 5:22 p.m., or thereabouts, when the Western Local pulled into Lincoln station. As he descended the steep metal steps clutching his briefcase, she would be standing near last in the small line of passengers waiting on the wooden platform to board. If it were lightly raining or snowing, she might hold a newspaper over her head. Sometimes she turned her face to the sky and opened her mouth a little, as if thirsty. In heavy rain she held a small yellow umbrella while the others waited under the eaves of the nearby shops. She always carried an overstuffed white shopping bag, but nothing ever protruded from the top to hint at what was inside.

Her complexion was dark, perhaps Mediterranean or Middle Eastern. But she dressed as any American woman might, in a blouse and skirt, or pants and a sweater. Invariably, though, she wore a colorful scarf around her head, wrapped delicately, it seemed to Walter, as one would a bouquet or live thing.

The scarf covered, of course, the missing right ear, as Walter assumed it was meant to do. He would never have known of the deformity if a gust of wind one afternoon had not whipped the scarf suddenly free of her head. She dropped her purse and shopping bag and fumbled to secure the fine silk under her chin. Then she looked up and saw his rude stare. It was awful of him, he knew that, and he averted his eyes. What had possessed him to gaze at her for those few seconds that the crimson scarf fluttered in the wind, revealing the thick, slashing scars of an ear that wasn't there anymore?

When the woman didn't appear on the platform the following Monday, Walter didn't think much of it. She had missed other days over the last year—he could recall two for sure. But both were during snowstorms, it occurred to him as he crossed the rutted dirt parking lot, not on unusually warm spring days such as this. He opened the door of his Saab to let the day's hot air exhale from the car. Then it came to him: perhaps she had not appeared today because he had noticed her missing ear. It charmed Walter to think of this woman's being so shy. He was shy himself. He hadn't married, even though he was forty-seven and interested—that in itself would demonstrate a lagging sense of forwardness. He did cheerfully submit to the blind dates arranged for him through the unstinting efforts of the married women at the institute. But they remained one-time affairs—or rather more precisely, one-time intersections of two people looking for something other than what they found.

What was he looking for? A certain sweetness of temperament was uppermost on his list, a flexible mind (though not one incapable of holding a firm opinion), and perhaps a sense of mankind's insignificance in the totality of the universe. The ability to apply order to the world would also be handy in a wife. These attributes, which he obligingly scrawled down as an aid to the matchmakers in his department, apparently were no help at all. They wanted to know what he desired in height and weight, profession, previous marital status, and postmarital attachments, such as children. He supposed it was curious that he never thought in those terms, but there it was. He didn't care about shape, occupation, or legal connections, just as he hoped a woman wouldn't care that he was unfit in the athletic sense of the word, underemployed for the number of degrees appended to his name, and suspiciously unattached for all of his adult years. He didn't try to camouflage the gray in his hair or wear the kind of tailored suits that would slim down the excesses of his appetite. Though he was not overly proud of his condition, he was at least comfortable with it. But if he had only one ear, he wondered, what would he do, without a scarf to hide the terrible secret?

When the woman didn't appear on Tuesday, Walter concluded with some certainty that she had begun a week's vacation. Each succeeding day that the train arrived at 5:22 and she was not there only stiffened his reasoning. On Thursday, cold rain draped the region, and Walter found himself lamenting that the woman's time off might be spoiled by inclement weather. Perhaps she was a reader and would be happy enough within doors. When he leafed through the *New York Times Book Review* that Sunday, he imagined her vacation reading list, perhaps a book on exotic foods, such as *Bengali Cooking*, or an intimate collection of short stories, such as *Women in Their Beds*. For a lingering moment, Walter pictured her as the woman on the cover of that book, with her long black hair languishing on the pillow and one breast peeking above the sheet.

It was with some sense of anticipation on the following Monday that Walter rose from his usual seat and hurried along the aisle even before the train began its slow braking into Lincoln. He reached the heavy sliding door just as Mel, the conductor, opened it from the other side and called out, "Next stop, Lincoln. That's Lincoln, next stop."

Walter squeezed past him so he would have a good view out of the open car. "Where's the fire?" Mel asked.

"Oh, no fire, Mel," Walter answered with a little shrug. "I'm just . . . expecting someone."

Mel winked at him, which made Walter feel a bit odd. The train crept past the crossing signal on Concord Road, and he leaned out of the car to scan the small group waiting to get on. The woman with one ear was not among them.

"Mind your step," Mel said as Walter made his way down to the platform, and these words reassured him, as always, that his welfare was being looked after. He walked slowly across the parking lot, glancing over his shoulder to make sure the woman didn't come running late from one of the station stores. In a few moments, the train took off without her.

Why was he so disappointed? It wasn't a sexual attraction, Walter decided, unless one so subtle that he couldn't discern it. Frankly, he didn't find her particularly attractive. He supposed that in another age she would have been considered a handsome woman. But he disliked handsome women—the blocky faces, the large eyes, the broad cheekbones. To another man, he supposed, she might be considered mysterious, and thereby interesting. But Walter disliked mystery. The simple question "What if?" could lead to so many disturbing places.

He was obviously not attracted to this woman sexually, and the evidence was perfectly clear: he had never spoken to her. Surely if he were propelled by a secret fuel of desire he would have managed some small step on the route to intimacy—a brief hello, a smile, perhaps even "Have a good day." No, not that insulting phrase. Who was he to be using the imperative with this woman? "I *hope* you have a very nice day"—that would be perfectly appropriate. And yet, there were only so many words one could say in passing. She might not hear all of them. She might misconstrue. Better not to risk conversation at the station, but rather simply stay on board one day in a seat precisely halfway down the car—her customary spot—where the rows turned from facing backward to facing forward. She would slide into the wide seat without even realizing he was there.

As the second week of the woman's absence stretched on, Walter became worried. His concentration, normally among his strongest attributes at work, failed him several times. At one point, a fellow researcher had the temerity to tap him on the shoulder and ask, "Daydreaming, Walter?" "No," he had replied courteously, "I was thinking." Thinking he certainly was, about why a person would take vacation time at the end of March, of all months, known as mud season in these parts. There were other possibilities, of course. She might have fled to some warm-weather island. Perhaps the woman with one ear had simply returned to wherever she had come from, or moved on to someplace new. Perhaps she would never again take the 5:22.

By Thursday Walter had decided to make inquiries, starting with Mel. The conductor knew something about each of his passengers, and it was his habit to share the news, discreetly, up and down the car. For example, with a nod of his head and a few well-chosen words, Mel let it be known to the single women in the car that James, the investment adviser, had just landed a big promotion and was available. On the other hand, Kelly—the young woman with the sad brown eyes—was definitely "not looking and might never be again." She had recently lost her boyfriend of three years as well as her beloved Honda Civic, events that left her crying some days and required Mel to start carrying tissues.

Walter had overheard himself being referred to in a respectful tone as "the professor . . . MIT—never married." That wasn't strictly true. He had been hired as a senior researcher to conduct experiments in machine vision, his specialty. It suited Walter to labor among just a few other engineers and their support staff. It suited him even more to retreat each evening to his apartment in the suburbs, where he could work uninterrupted on his book of odd designs. He was near finishing his collection of Impossible Objects, such as a teapot with the spout and handle on the same side. It amused him to imagine things that could never work. Often he listened to his shortwave, and the crackling sound of far-off voices seemed to him as if coming from a large immigrant family living on the other side of the thin walls. Sometimes, usually before one of his arranged dates, he imagined a woman in his apartment, a wife. What would she be doing right now, he wondered, what would she do there?

When Walter, with money in hand, looked up from his seat to ask Mel about the missing woman, he was shocked to see another conductor. "Where to?" the man asked. Mel never talked in such a clipped expression. He always asked, "And where would you be heading?" or, "Where can I take you today?"

Walter handed over his three dollars to Edward, as the man's badge read, and said brusquely, "Lincoln."

"Lincoln it is."

"Where's Mel," Walter asked as he peered over the seats, "working up front?"

"Mel? Don't know him."

"He's been the conductor on this line for years."

Edward handed over the ticket. "Well, that explains it then. I've only been the conductor for a day."

"You mean you've replaced Mel?"

Edward shook his head. "I can't say that exactly, not knowing anything about Mel. I guess he was before my time."

Your time? Walter thought. You've only worked this train for one day. You haven't had a "time" yet. Edward moved through the train. Every few rows Walter heard him say, "Where to?"

There were others besides Mel to ask about the woman with one ear. Several people regularly waited with her at the station to board. Perhaps she had spoken to them.

Walter spent the twenty-minute ride to Lincoln plotting what he would say in the brief seconds as he got off and the others got on. "Excuse me," he might begin, "I just wanted to ask—do you happen to know anything about the woman with . . ." He certainly couldn't mention the ear. ". . . the woman in the colorful scarves who used to get on here each day?" Walter practiced his question at different speeds and emphases as the train slowed into Lincoln. As he moved down the aisle toward the door, he noticed that no one else was getting off with him, and no one was waiting to get on either. The Western Local left quickly.

Because March 28 was Good Friday, Walter had no opportunity to continue his inquiry until the following Monday. On that day, he boarded in Cambridge as always, took his seat at the back of the car, and waited for the conductor. This time he would be forceful in inquiring about Mel. Then in Lincoln he would stop in the shops by the station to ask about the woman. Surely she had made some small purchases there—a newspaper or mints, perhaps even medicine at the pharmacy. She would be remembered.

Edward approached, humming. "Where to?" he asked, with not a hint of recognition in his eyes.

"Lincoln," Walter said with a trace in his voice of *You should know that by now. Mel knew the second day.*

"Don't stop at Lincoln," Edward said.

The words and tone confused Walter. Was the conductor offering advice—*Do not stop at Lincoln*—or some new information? "What do you mean?" Walter asked. "The five o'clock out of Cambridge always stops in Lincoln."

"I wouldn't know about always," Edward said. "I only know about today. Today this train doesn't stop at Lincoln— the engineer told me himself. Now where else do you want to go?"

"I don't want to go anywhere else. I live in Lincoln. I've been getting off there for two years."

"I can see your problem," Edward said. "That's why people should always ask when they get on where the train's stopping. Saves a lot of this kind of trouble."

The train pulled into Waverly station, and Edward hurried to attend to the doors. When he returned he said, "Where to?"

Was it some kind of game this strange conductor was playing? Walter wondered. But Edward didn't appear to be a man capable of sustaining a joke this long. He did appear to be a man capable of stupidity, and so Walter said, "I'll prove the train stops in Lincoln. Let me see a schedule."

Edward checked inside his lapel pocket, but his hand came back empty. "Sorry, all out."

Walter had reached that point his mother had customarily

referred to as her "wit's end." He had no wit left, at least to deal with Edward. Walter stood up to appeal to the familiar faces of the Western Local. There were more people than he had ever seen in this car before, but he recognized none of them. Walter sank in his seat. "Just let me off at the next stop—that's still Concord, isn't it?"

"Of course it is," Edward said, taking the three dollars. "That will be another fifty cents."

Walter exited from the train at Concord and stood alone on the platform. His Saab was a couple of miles back in Lincoln. There was no cab in sight. A few cars were going by, but he couldn't imagine standing with his thumb out while dressed in a tie and jacket. He would walk. And since the shortest route between stations was undoubtedly the rail line, he would go by the tracks.

He felt a bit adventuresome as he set out. The dwindling daylight did not bother him. He had never been afraid of the dark. He started off briskly, walking between the rails and stretching his stride to land on every other wooden plank. After a while he broke the monotony by balancing on one rail, and he surprised himself by how far he could do it. He looked back frequently, even though he knew he would hear a train coming well before he would need to step aside. At one point he knelt and pressed his ear to the cold rail to sense the vibration of an approaching train, but he felt nothing.

The woman gone, Mel gone, the Lincoln stop gone—what else might disappear from his life? Walter descended the long stairway to the platform in Cambridge on Tuesday. Perhaps the train itself wouldn't show up today. Then tomorrow, the whole station would vanish. He laughed at these fanciful ideas. They were more appropriate for some giddy science fiction story, not the real life of a mechanical engineer.

The train approached on time. Walter climbed aboard behind a half-dozen strangers. The car was quite full of commuters already. Walter scanned the aisle and finally spotted a vacant seat midway down the car, where the rows turned from facing forward to backward. As he slid into the wide seat, the train pulled away.

"Where can I take you today, my friend?"

Walter practically jumped at the voice. He turned around, and there was Mel at the end of the car punching out tickets. Walter called to him, but the conductor was busy and did not look up. The train sped on from one station to another, and Mel slowly worked his way closer. When he reached Walter he said, "Hey, Professor, how's your book coming?"

"Mel," Walter stammered, "where have you been?"

The old conductor leaned against the seat for a moment. "Oh, just a little safety retraining course they put us through every few years. You know, a train crashes out west and they rush everybody into emergency classes. Why, what did you think?"

"I don't know. You were just suddenly gone."

"That's how the railroad works, they don't give anybody notice." Mel slipped his punch over the green ticket. "Lincoln, I presume."

"Lincoln?" Walter said. "No, I came in from Concord this morning. You don't stop in Lincoln anymore. Didn't they tell you?"

Mel laughed and pulled a paper from his lapel pocket. "Here's the new supply of schedules—just came out today." His big forefinger worked down the row of times and stopped at 5:22. "There it is," he said, "Lincoln."

"But yesterday the train didn't stop there—Edward made me go to Concord."

Mel nodded as if not overly surprised. "We had to drop Lincoln on the earlier run at 4:50 to gain some time going to Springfield. The engineer subbing yesterday must have gotten the stops confused."

The explanation pleased Walter. Edward had been wrong. "Well, today I'll have to go to Concord, where my car is."

"Did you ever notice," Mel said as he processed the ticket, "how people always return to where they come from? Wouldn't it be a more interesting world if people sometimes ended up far away from where they set out?"

Walter shook his head to dismiss the crazy thought. But why did each day have to be a perfect circle? Why couldn't a person take a sidetrack, go a little way, and then come back, if need be?

As the train neared Lincoln, a few people got up, and Walter wondered how they knew it would stop there today when he did not. He watched them crossing the parking lot to their cars. As the train moved on, he sensed a person sitting down at the edge of his seat. When he looked over, he saw the woman with one ear.

"I am sorry to intrude," she said, "but the train is so full today."

"No, it's fine, there's plenty of room," he said, drawing himself closer to the window so she would not be frightened. Walter breathed the intoxicating scent of some delicate perfume. He felt the vinyl seat shift under him as she settled into her place. He said, "It's nice to see you again."

She nodded pleasantly and fixed her large shopping bag on the floor between them. The top fell open and he could see a white uniform inside, the kind a nurse might wear. Then her thin hand reached to the knot beneath her chin and began loosening the bright orange scarf. What could she be doing? Walter looked away so as not to stare at the scar. But as he gazed into the train window he saw the reflection of the silk fall from her head. She folded the scarf neatly on her lap.

He turned to her. There on the right side of her head was a perfectly formed little pink ear. It was smoothly curved at the top and delicately lobed at the bottom. The ear seemed magical to him, as if sewn on by miniature hands.

She tucked a few errant strands of her short black hair behind the ear. He smiled at this gesture, wishing that he had something new and wonderful about himself to show her. She smiled back at him. "Wasn't that your stop?"

He was pleased that she had noticed. He looked through the bleary window at the lights of Lincoln station receding quickly. "No," he said, "I'm going farther today.

INFINITE JEST (EXCERPT)

BY DAVID FOSTER WALLACE

Brighton

(Originally published in 1996)

E n route, R. Lenz's mouth writhes and he scratches at the little rhynophemic rash and sniffs terribly and complains of terrible late-autumn leaf-mold allergies, forgetting that Bruce Green knows all too well what coke-hydrolysis's symptoms are from having done so many lines himself, back when life with M. Bonk was one big party.

Lenz details how the vegetarian new Joel girl's veil is because of this condition people get where she's got only one eye that's right in the middle of her forehead, from birth, like a sea horse, and asks Green not even to think of asking how he knows this fact.

While Green acts as lookout while Lenz relieves himself against a Market St. dumpster, Lenz swears Green to secrecy about how poor old scarred-up diseased Charlotte Treat had sworn him to secrecy about her secret dream in sobriety was to someday get her G.E.D. and become a dental hygienist specializing in educating youngsters pathologically frightened of dental anesthesia, because her dream was to help youngsters, and but how she feared her Virus has placed her secret dream forever out of reach.[1]

---

1. *Because he'd been sworn to secrecy, Green doesn't tell Lenz that Charlotte Treat had shared with Green that her adoptive father had been one-time Chair of the Northeast Regional Board of Dental Anesthesiologists, and had been pretty liberal with the use of*

All the way up the Spur's Harvard St. toward Union Square, in a barely NW vector, Lenz consumes several minutes and less than twenty breaths sharing with Green some painful Family-of-Origin Issues about how Lenz's mother Mrs. Lenz, a thrice-divorcée and Data Processor, was so unspeakably obese she had to make her own mumus out of brocade drapes and cotton tablecloths and never once did come to Parents' Day at Bishop Anthony McDiardama Elementary School in Fall River MA because the parents had to sit in the youngsters' little liftable-desktop desks during the Parents' Day presentations and skits, and the one time Mrs. L. hove her way down to B.A.M.E.S. for Parents' Day and tried to seat herself at little Randall L.'s desk between Mrs. Lamb and Mrs. Leroux she broke the desk into kindling and needed four stocky cranberry-farmer dads and a textbook-dolly to arise back up from the classroom floor, and never went back, fabricating thin excuses of busyness with Data Processing and basic disinterest in Randy L.'s schoolwork. Lenz shares how then in adolescence (his), his mother died because one day she was riding a Greyhound bus from Fall River MA north to Quincy MA to visit her son in a Commonwealth Youth Corrections facility Lenz was doing research for a possible screenplay in, and during the voyage on the bus she had to go potty, and she was in the bus's tiny potty in the rear of the bus going about her private business of going potty, as she later testified, and even though it was the height of winter she had the little window of the potty wide open, for reasons Lenz predicts Green doesn't want to hear about, on the northbound bus, and how this was one of the last years of Unsubsidized ordinational year-dating, and the final fiscal year that actual maintenance-

---

the old N_2O and thiopental sodium around the Treats' Revere MA household, for personal and extremely unsavory reasons.

work had ever been done on the infernous six-lane commuter-ravaged Commonwealth Route 24 from Fall River to Boston's South Shore by the pre-O.N.A.N.ite Governor Claprood's Commonwealth Highway Authority, and the Greyhound bus encountered a poorly marked UNDER CONSTRUCTION area where 24 was all stripped down to the dimpled-iron sheeting below and was tooth-rattlingly striated and chuckholed and torn up and just in general basically a mess, and the poorly marked and unflagmanned debris plus the excessive speed of the northbound bus made it jounce godawfully, the bus, and swerve violently to and forth, fighting to maintain control of what there was of the road, and passengers were hurled violently from their seats while, meanwhile, back in the closet-sized rear potty, Mrs. Lenz, right in the process of going potty, was hurled from the toilet by the first swerve and proceeded to do some high-velocity and human-waste-flinging pinballing back and forth against the potty's plastic walls; and when the bus finally regained total control and resumed course Mrs. Lenz had, freakishly enough, ended up her human pinballing with her bare and unspeakably huge backside wedged tight in the open window of the potty, so forcefully ensconced into the recesstacle that she was unable to extricate, and the bus continued on its northward sojourn the rest of the way up 24 with Mrs. Lenz's bare backside protruding from the ensconcing window, prompting car horns and derisive oratory from other vehicles; and Mrs. Lenz's plaintiff shouts for Help were unavailed by the passengers that were arising back up off the floor and rubbing their sore noggins and hearing Mrs. Lenz's mortified screams from behind the potty's locked reinforced plastic door, but were unable to excretate her because the potty's door locked from the interior by sliding across a deadbolt that made the door's outside say OCCUPIED/OCCUPADO/OCCUPÉ, and the door was locked, and Mrs. Lenz was wedged beyond the reach of arm-length and couldn't reach the deadbolt no matter how plaintiffly she reached out her mammoth fat-wattled arm; and, like fully 88% of all clinically obese Americans, Mrs. Lenz was diagnosed clinically claustrophobic and took prescription medication for anxiety and ensconcement-phobias, and she ended up successfully filing a Seven-Figure suit against Greyhound Lines and the almost-defunct Commonwealth Highway Authority for psychiatric trauma, public mortification, and second-degree frostbite, and received such a morbidly obese settlement from the Dukakis-appointed 18th-Circus Civil Court that when the check arrived, in an extra-long-size envelope to accommodate all the zeroes, Mrs. L. lost all will to Data Process or cook or clean, or nurture, or finally even move, simply reclining in a custom-designed 1.5-meter-wide recliner watching *InterLace Gothic Romances* and consuming mammoth volumes of high-lipid pastry brought on gold trays by a pastry chef she'd had put at her individual 24-hour disposal and outfitted with a cellular beeper, until four months after the huge settlement she ruptured and died, her mouth so crammed with peach cobbler the paramedics were hapless to administer C.P.R., which Lenz says he knows, by the way—C.P.R.

By the time they hit the Spur, their northwest tacking has wheeled broadly right to become more truly north. Their route down here is a Mondrian of alleys narrowed to near-defiles from all the dumpsters. Lenz goes first, blaze-trailing. Lenz gives these sort of smoky looks to every female that passes within eyeshot. Their vector is now mostly N/NW. They stroll through the rich smell of dryer-exhaust from the backside of a laundromat off Dustin and Comm. The city of metro Boston MA at night. The ding and trundle of the B and C Greenie trains heading up Comm. Ave.'s hill, west. Street-drunks sitting with their backs to sooted walls, seeming to study their laps, even the mist of their breath discolored. The complex hiss of bus-brakes. The jagged shadows distending with headlights' passage. Latin music drifting through the Spur's Projects, twined around some 5/4 'shine stuff from a boombox over off Feeny Park, and in between these a haunting plasm of Hawaiian-type music that sounds at once top-volume and far far away. The zithery drifting Polynesian strains make Bruce Green's face spread in a flat mask of psychic pain he doesn't even feel is there, and then the music's gone. Lenz asks Green what it's like to work with ice all day at Leisure Time Ice and then himself theorizes on what it must be like, he'll bet, with your crushed ice and ice cubes in pale-blue plastic bags with a staple for a Twistie and dry ice in wood tubs pouring out white smoke and then your huge blocks of industrial ice packed in fragrant sawdust, the huge blocks of man-sized ice with flaws way inside like trapped white faces, white flames of internal cracks. Your picks and hatchets and really big tongs, red knuckles and rimed windows and thin bitter freezer-smell with runny-nosed Poles in plaid coats and kalpacs, your older ones with a chronic cant to one side from all the time lugging ice.

They crunch through iridescent chunks of what Lenz IDs as a busted windshield. Lenz shares feelings on how between three ex-husbands and feral attorneys and a pastry-chef that used pastry-dependence to warp and twist her into distorting a testament toward the chef and Lenz's being through red-tape still in Quincy's YCA hold and in a weak litigational vantage, the ruptured Mrs. L.'s will had left him out in the cold to self-fend by his urban wits while ex-husbands and patissiers lay on Riviera beach furniture fanning themselves with high-denomination currency, about all which Lenz says he grapples with the Issues of on a like daily basis; leaving Green a gap to make understanding sounds. Green's jacket creaks as he breathes. The windshield-glass is in an alley whose fire escapes are hung with what look like wet frozen tarps. The alley's tight-packed dumpsters and knobless steel doors and the dull black of total grime. The blunt snout of a bus protrudes into the frame of the alley's end, idling.

Dumpsters' garbage doesn't have just one smell, depending. The urban lume makes the urban night only semidark, as in licoricey, a luminescence just under the skin of the dark, and swelling. Green keeps them updated re time. Lenz has begun to refer to Green as "brother." Lenz says he has to piss like a racehorse. He says the nice thing about the urban city is that it's one big commode. The way Lenz pronounces *brother* involves one *r*. Green moves up to stand in the mouth of the alley, facing out, giving Lenz a little privacy several dumpsters behind. Green stands there in the start of the alley's shadow, in the bus's warm backwash, his elbows out and hands in the jacket's little pockets, looking out. It's unclear whether Green knows Lenz is under the influence of Bing. All he feels is a moment of deep wrenching loss, of wishing getting high was still pleasurable for him so he could get high. This feeling comes and goes all day every day, still. Green takes a gasper from behind his ear and lights it and puts a fresh one on-deck behind the ear. Union Square, Allston: Kiss me where it smells, she said, so I took her to Allston, unquote. Union Square's lights throb. Whenever somebody stops blowing their horn somebody else starts blowing their horn. There's three Chinese women waiting at the light across the street from the guy with the lobsters. Each of them's got a shopping bag. An old VW Bug like Doony Glynn's VW Bug idling mufflerless outside Riley's Roast Beef, except Doony's Bug's engine is exposed where the back hood got removed to expose the Bug's guts. It's like impossible to ever spot a Chinese woman on a Boston street that's under sixty or over 1.5 m. or not carrying a shopping bag, except never more than one bag. If you close your eyes on a busy urban sidewalk the sound of everybody's different footwear's footsteps all put together sounds like something getting chewed by something huge and tireless and patient. The searing facts of the case of Bruce Green's natural parents' deaths when he was a toddler are so deeply repressed inside Green that whole strata and substrata of silence and mute dumb animal suffering will have to be strip-mined up and dealt with a Day at a Time in sobriety for Green even to remember how, on his fifth Xmas Eve, in Waltham MA, his Pop had taken the hydrant-sized little Brucie Green aside and given him, to give his beloved Mama for Xmas, a gaily Gauguin-colored can of Polynesian Mauna Loa–brand[2] macadamia nuts, said cylindrical can of nuts then toted upstairs by the child and painstakingly wrapped in so much foil-sheen paper that the final wrapped present looked like an oversized dachshund that had required first bludgeoning and then restraint at both ends with two rolls each of Scotch tape and garish fuchsia ribbon to be subdued and wrapped and placed under the gaily lit pine, and even then the package seemed mushily to struggle as the substrata of paper shifted and settled.

Bruce Green's Pop Mr. Green had at one time been one of New England's most influential aerobics instructors—even costarring once or twice, in the decade before digital dissemination, on the widely rented *Buns of Steel* aerobics home-video series—and had been in high demand and very influential until, to his horror, in his late twenties, the absolute prime of an aerobics instructor's working life, either one of Mr. Green's

---

2. ®*The Mauna Loa Macadamia Nut Corp., Hilo, HI—"A LOW SODIUM FOOD."*

legs began spontaneously to grow or the other leg began spontaneously to retract, because within weeks one leg was all of a sudden nearly six inches longer than the other—Bruce Green's one unrepressed visual memory of the man is of a man who progressively and perilously *leaned* as he hobbled from specialist to specialist—and he had to get outfitted with a specialized orthopedic boot, black as a cauldron, that seemed to be 90% sole and resembled an asphalt-spreader's clunky boot, and weighed several pounds, and looked absurd with Spandex leggings; and the long and short of it was that Brucie Green's Pop was aerobically washed up by the leg and boot, and had to career-change, and went bitterly to work for a Waltham novelty or notions concern, something with 'N in the name, Acme Novelties 'N Notions or some such, where Mr. Green designed sort of sadistic practical-joke supplies, specializing in the Jolly Jolt Hand Buzzer and Blammo Cigar product-lines, with a sideline in entomological ice cubes and artificial dandruff, etc. Demoralizing, sedentary, character-twisting work, is what an older child would have been able to understand, peering from his nightlit doorway at an unshaven man who clunkily paced away the wee hours on a nightly basis down in the living room, his gait like a bosun's in heavy seas, occasionally breaking into a tiny tentative gluteal-thruster squat-and-kick, almost falling, muttering bitterly, carrying a Falstaff tallboy.

Something touching about a gift that a toddler's so awfully overwrapped makes a sickly-pale and neurasthenic but doting Mrs. Green, Bruce's beloved Mama, choose the mugged-dachshund-foil-sheen-cylinder present first, of course, to open, on Xmas morning, as they sit before the crackling fireplace in different chairs by different windows with views of Waltham sleet, with bowls of Xmas snacks and

Acme-'N-logoed mugs of cocoa and hazelnut decaf and watch each other taking turns opening gifts. Brucie's little face aglow in the firelight as the unwrapping of the nuts proceeds through layer and stratum, Mrs. Green a couple times having to use her teeth on the rinds of tape. Finally the last layer is off and the gay-colored can in view. Mauna Loa: Mrs. Green's favorite and most decadent special-treat food. World's highest-calorie food except for like pure suet. Nuts so yummy they should be spelled S-I-N, she says. Brucie excitedly bobbing in his chair, spilling cocoa and Gummi Bears, a loving toddler, more excited about his gift's receipt than what he's going to get himself. His mother's clasped hands before her sunken bosom. Sighs of delight and protest. And an EZ-Open Lid, on the can.

Which the contents of the macadamia-labeled can is really a coiled cloth snake with an ejaculatory spring. The snake sprongs out as Mrs. G. screams, a hand to her throat. Mr. Green howls with bitterly professional practical-gag mirth and clunks over and slaps little Bruce on the back so hard that Brucie expels a lime Gummi Bear he'd been eating—this too a visual memory, contextless and creepy—which arcs across the living room and lands in the fireplace's fire with a little green *siss* of flame. The cloth snake's arc has terminated at the imitation-crystal chandelier overhead, where the snake gets caught and hangs with quivering spring as the chandelier swings and tinkles and Mr. Green's thigh-slapping laughter takes awhile to run down even as Brucie's Mama's hand at her delicate throat becomes claw-shaped and she claws at her throat and gurgles and slumps over to starboard with a fatal cardiac, her cyanotic mouth still open in surprise. For the first couple minutes Mr. Green thinks she's putting them on, and he keeps rating her performance on an Acme interdepartmental 1-8 Gag Scale until he finally gets pissed off and starts saying she's drawing the gag out too long, that she's going to scare their little Brucie who's sitting there under the swinging crystal, wide-eyed and silent.

And Bruce Green uttered not another out-loud word until his last year of grade school, living by then in Winchester with his late mother's sister, a decent but Dustbowly-looking Seventh-Day Adventist who never once pressed Brucie to speak, probably out of sympathy, probably sympathizing with the searing pain the opaque-eyed child must have felt over not only giving his Mama a lethal Xmas present but over then having to watch his widowed asymetrical Pop cave psycho-spiritually in after the wake, watching Mr. Green pace-and-clunk around the living room all night every night after work and an undermicrowaved supper-for-two, in his Frankensteinian boot, clunking around in circles, scratching slowly at his face and arms until he looked less scourged than brambled, and in loosely associated mutters cursing God and himself and Acme Nuts 'N Serpents or whatever, and leaving the fatal snake up hanging from the fake-crystal fixture and the fatal Xmas tree up in its little red metal stand until all the strings of lights went out and the strings of popcorn got dark and hard and the stand's bowl of water evaporated so the tree's needles died and fell brownly off onto the rest of the still-unopened Xmas presents clustered below, one of which was a package of Nebraska corn-fed steaks whose cherub-motif wrapping was beginning ominously to swell . . . ; and then finally the even more searing childhood pain of the public arrest and media-scandal and Sanity Hearing and Midwest trial as it was established after the fact that the post-Xmas Mr. Green—whose one encouraging sign of holding some tattered remnants of himself together after the funeral had been the fact that he still went faithfully every day to work at Acme Inc.—had gone in and packed a totally random case of the company's out-going Blammo Cigars with vengefully lethal tetryl-based high explosives, and a VFW, three Rotarians, and 24 Shriners had been grotesquely decapitated across Southeastern Ohio before the federal ATF traced the grisly forensic fragments back to B. Green Sr.'s Blammo lab, in Waltham; and then the extradition and horribly complex Sanity Hearing and trial and controversial sentencing; and then the appeals and death-watch and Lethal Injection, Bruce Green's aunt handing out poorly reproduced W. Miller tracts to the crowds outside the Ohio prison as the clock ticked down to Injection, little Bruce in tow, blank-faced and watching, the crowd of media and anti-Capital activists and Defarge-like picnickers milling and roiling, many T-shirts for sale, and the red-faced men in sportcoats and fezzes, oh their rage-twisted faces the same red as their fezzes as the men careened this way and that in their little cars, formations of motorized Shriners buzzing the gates of the ODC-Maximum facility and shouting *Burn Baby Burn* or the more timely *Get Lethally Injected Baby Get Lethally Injected*, Bruce Green's aunt with her center-parted hair visibly graying under the pillbox hat and face obscured for three Ohio months behind the black mesh veil that fluttered from the pillbox hat, clutching little Bruce's head to her underwired bosom day after day until his blank face was smooshed in on one side. . . . Green's guilt, pain, fear and self-loathing have over years of unprescribed medication been compressed to the igneous point where he now knows only that he compulsively avoids any product or service with 'N in its name, always checks a palm before a handshake, will go blocks out of his way to avoid any parade involving fezzes in little cars, and has this silent, substratified fascination/horror gestalt about all things even remotely Polynesian. It's probably the distant and attenuated luau-music echoing erratically back and forth through angled blocks of Allston cement that causes Bruce Green to wander as if mesmerized out of Union Square and all the way up Comm. Ave. into Brighton and up to like the corner of Comm. Ave. and Brainerd Rd., the home of The Unexamined Life nightclub with its tilted flickering bottle of blue neon over the entrance, before he realizes that Lenz is no longer beside him asking the time, that Lenz hadn't followed him up the hill even though Green had stood there outside the Union Square alley way longer than anybody could have needed to take a legitimate whiz.

He and Lenz have become separated, he realizes. Now way southwest of Union on Comm., Green looks around at traffic and T-tracks and bar patrons and T.U.L.'s huge bottle's low-neon flutter. He wonders whether he's somehow blown Lenz off or whether Lenz's blown him off, and that's all he wonders, that's the total complexity the speculation assumes, that's his thought for the minute. It's like the whole nut-can-and-cigar traumas drained into some psychic sump at puberty, sank and left only an oily slick that catches the light in distorted ways. The warbly Polynesian music's way clearer up here. He starts up the steep hill on Brainerd Rd., which terminates at the Enfield line. Maybe Lenz can't move straightforwardly south at all past a certain time. The acclivity is not kind to asphalt-spreader's boots. After the initial crazed-gerbil-in-brain phase of early Withdrawal and detox, Bruce Green has now returned to his normal psychorepressed cerebral state where he has about one fully developed thought every sixty seconds, and then just one at a time, a thought, each materializing already fully developed and sitting there and then melting back away like a languid liquid-crystal display. His Ennet House counselor, the extremely tough-loving

Calvin T., complains that listening to Green is like listening to a faucet with a very slow drip. His rap is that Green seems not serene or detached but totally shut down, disassociated, and Calvin T. tries weekly to draw Green out by pissing him off. Green's next full thought is the realization that even though the hideous Hawaiian music had sounded like it was drifting up northward from down at the Allston Spur, it's somewhat louder now the farther west he moves toward Enfield's Cambridge St. dogleg and St. Elizabeth's Hospital. Brainerd between Commonwealth and Cambridge St. is a sine wave of lung-busting hills through neighborhoods Tiny Ewell had described as Depressed Residential, unending rows of crammed-together triple-decker houses with those tiny sad architectural differences that seem to highlight the essential sameness, with sagging porches and psoriatic paint-jobs or aluminum siding gone carbuncular from violent temperature-swings, yard-litter and dishes and patchy grass and fenced pets and children's toys lying around in discarded attitudes and eclectic food-smells and wildly different patterned curtains or blinds in a house's different windows due to these old houses are carved up inside into apartments for like alienated B.U. students or Canadian and Concavity-displaced families or even more alienated B.C. students, or probably it looks like the bulk of the lease-holders are Green-and-Bonkesque younger blue-collar hard-partying types who have posters of the Fiends In Human Shape or Choosy Mothers or Snout or the Bioavailable Five[3] in the bathroom and black lights in the bedroom and oil-change stains in the driveway and that throw

---

3. *Popular corporate-hard-rock bands, though it shows where Bruce Green's psychic decline really started that, except for TBA$_s$, these bands were all truly big two or three years past, and are now slightly passé, with Choosy Mothers having split up entirely by now to explore individual creative directions.*

their supper dishes into the yard and buy new dishes at Caldor instead of washing their dishes and that still, in their twenties, ingest Substances nightly and use *party* as a verb and put their sound-systems' speakers in their apartments' windows facing out and crank the volume out of sheer high-spirit obnoxious-ness because they still have their girlfriends to pound beers with and do shotguns of dope into the mouth of and do lines of Bing off various parts of the naked body of, and still find pounding beers and doing bongs and lines fun and get to have fun on a nightly after-work basis, cranking the tunes out into the neighborhood air. The street's bare trees are densely limbed, they're a certain type of tree, they look like inverted brooms in the residential dark, Green doesn't know his tree-names. The Hawaiian music is what's pulled him southwest, it emerges: it's originating from someplace in this very neighbor-hood somewhere around W. Brainerd, and Green moves up-river toward what sounds like the source of the sound with a blankly horrified fascination. Most of the yards are fenced in stainless-steel chain-link fencing, and occasional yard-dogs whine or more commonly bark and snarl and leap territorially at Green from behind their fences, the fences shivering from the impact and the chain-link stuff dented outward from pre-vious impacts from previous passersby. The thought that he isn't scared of dogs develops and recedes in Green's midbrain. His jacket creaks with every step. The temperature is steadily dropping. The fenced front yards are the toy-and-beer-can-strewn type where the brown grass grows in uneven tufts and the leaves haven't been raked and are piled in wind-blown lines of force along the base of the fence and unpruned hedges and overfull wastebaskets and untwisted trash bags are on the sagging porch because nobody's gotten around to taking them down to the E.W.D. dumpster at the corner and garbage from the overfull receptacles blows out into the yard and mixes with the leaves along the fences' base and some gets out into the street and is never picked up and eventually becomes part of the composition of the street. A nonpeanut M&M box is like intaglioed into the concrete of the sidewalk under Green, so bleached by the elements it's turned bone-white and is only barely identifiable as a nonpeanut M&M box, for instance. And, looking up from identifying the M&M box's make, Green now espies Randy Lenz. Green has happened upon Lenz, way up here on Brainerd, now strolling briskly alone up ahead of Green, not close but visible under a functioning streetlight about a block farther uphill on Brainerd. There's some disincentive to call out. The incline on this block isn't bad. It's cold enough now so his breath looks the same whether he's smoking or not. The tall curved streetlamps here look to Green just like the weaponish part of the Martian vessels that fired fatal rays in their conquest of the planet in an ancient cartridge Tommy Doocy'd never tired of that he labeled the case "War of the Welles." The Hawaiian music dominates the aural landscape by this point, now, coming from someplace up near where he sees the back of Lenz's coat. Someone has put Polynesian-music speakers in their window, pretty clearly. Creepy slack-key steel guitar balloons across the dim street, booms off the sagging facades opposite, it's Don Ho and the Sol Hoopi Players, the grass-skirt-and-foamy-breakers sound that makes Green put his fingers in his ears while at the same time he moves more urgently toward the Hawaiian-music source, a pink or aqua three-decker with a second-floor dormer and red-shingled roof with a blue and white Quenucker flag on a pole protruding from a window in the dormer and serious JBL speakers facing outward in the two windows on either side of the flag, with the screens off so you can see the woofers throbbing like brown bellies hula-ing, bathing the 1700 block of W. Brainerd in dreadful ukuleles and hollow-log percussives. All the blunt fingers in his ears do is add the squeak of Green's pulse and the underwater sound of his respiration to the music, though. Figures in plaid-flannel or else floral Hawaiian shirts and those flower necklaces melt in and out of lit view behind and over the window-speakers with the oozing quality of large-group chemical fun and dancing and social intercoursing. The lit windows make slender rectangles of light out across the yard, which the yard is a sty. Something about Randy Lenz's movements up ahead, the high-kneed tiptoed skulk of a vaudeville fiend up to no good at all, keeps Green from calling out to him even if he could have made himself heard over what to him is a roar of blood and breath and Ho. Lenz moves through the one operative streetlight's cone across the sidewalk and over to the stainless chain-link of the same Quenucker house, holding something out to a Shetland-sized dog whose leash is attached to a fluorescent-plastic clothesliney thing by a pulley, and can slide. It's cold and the air is thin and keen and his fingers are icy in his ears, which ache with cold. Green watches, rapt on levels he doesn't know he has, drawn slowly forward, moving his head from side to side to keep from losing Lenz in the fog of his breath, not calling out, but transfixed. Green and Mildred Bonk and the other couple they'd shared a trailer with T. Doocy with had gone through a phase one time where they'd crash various collegiate parties and mix with the upper-scale collegiates, and once in one February Green found himself at a Harvard U. dorm where they were having a like Beach-Theme Party, with a dumptruck's worth of sand on the common-room floor and everybody with flower necklaces and skin bronzed with cream or UV-booth-salon visits, all the towheaded guys in floral untucked shirts walking around with lockjawed *noblest oblige* and drinking drinks with umbrellas in them or else wearing Speedos with no shirts and not one fucking pimple anyplace on their back and pretending to surf on a surfboard somebody had nailed to a hump-shaped wave made of blue and white papier-mâché with a motor inside that made the fake wave sort of undulate, and all the girls in grass skirts oozing around the room trying to hula in a shimmying way that showed their thighs' LipoVac scars through the shimmying grass of their skirts, and Mildred Bonk had donned a grass skirt and bikini-top out of the pile by the keggers and even though almost seven months pregnant had oozed and shimmied right into the mainstream of the swing of things, but Bruce Green had felt awkward and out of place in his cheap leather jacket and haircut he'd dyed orange with gasoline in a blackout and the EAT THE RICH patch he'd perversely let Mildred Bonk sew onto the groin of his police-pants, and then they'd finally got tired of the *Hawaii Five-0* theme and started in with the Don Ho and Sol Hoopi CDs, and Green had gotten so uncomfortably fascinated and repelled and paralyzed by the Polynesian tunes that he'd set up a cabana-chair right by the kegs and had sat there overworking the pump on the kegs and downing one plastic cup after another of beer-foam until he got so blind drunk his sphincter had failed and he'd not only pissed but also actually *shit* his pants, for only the second time ever, and the first public time ever, and was mortified with complexly layered shame, and had to ease very gingerly into the nearest-by head and remove his pants and wipe himself off like a fucking baby, having to shut one eye to make sure which him he saw was him, and then there'd been nothing to do with the fouled police-pants but crack the bathroom door and reach a tattooed arm out with the pants and bury them in the living room's sand like a housecat's litterbox, and then of course what was he supposed to put on if he ever wanted to leave that head or dorm again, to get home, so he'd had to hold one eye shut and reach one arm out again and like strain to reach the pile of grass skirts and bikini-tops and snatch a grass skirt, and put it on, and slip out of the Hawaiian dorm out a side door without letting anybody see him, and then ride the Red Line and C-Greenie and then a bus all the way home in February in a cheap leather jacket and asphalt-spreader's boots and a grass skirt, the grass of which rode up in the most horrifying way, and he'd spent the next three days not leaving the trailer in the Spur, in a paralyzing depression of unknown etiology, lying on Tommy D.'s crusty-stained sofa and drinking Southern Comfort straight out of the bottle and watching Doocy's snakes not move once in three days, in their tank, and Mildred had given him two days of high-volume shit for first sulking antisocially by the keg and then screwing out and abandoning her at seven months gone to a sandy room full of tanly anomic blondes who said catty things about her tattoos and creepy boys who talked without moving their lower jaw and asked her things like where she "summered" and kept offering her advice on no-load funds and inviting her upstairs to check out their Dürer prints and saying they found overweight girls terribly compelling in their defiance of culturo-ascetic norms, and Bruce Green lay there with a head full of Hoopi and unresolved pain and didn't say a word or even have a fully developed thought for three days, and had hidden the grass skirt under the dustruffle of the couch and later savagely torn it to shreds and sprinkled the clippings over Doocy's hydroponic-marijuana development in the tub, for mulch. Lenz goes in and out of Green's focus several times within a dozen andante strides, still out in front of the Canadian-refugee-type house that's drawn Green on, Lenz holding a little can of something up over one side of the fence's gate and dribbling something onto the gate, holding something else that suddenly engages the dog's full attention. For some reason Green thinks to check his watch. The pink or orange clothesline quivers as the leash's pulley runs along it as the dog comes up to meet Lenz inside the gate he's slowly opened. The huge dog seems neither friendly nor unfriendly toward Lenz, but his attention is engaged. The leash and pulley could never hold him if he decided Lenz was food. There's bitter-smelling material from his ear on Green's finger, which he can't help but sniff. He's forgotten and left the other finger in his ear. He's now pretty close, standing in a van's shadow just outside the pyramid of sodium light from the streetlight, like two houses down from the source of the grisly sound, which all of a sudden is in the silence between cuts of Ho's early *Don Ho: From Hawaii with All My Love*, so that Green can hear baritone Canadianese party-voices through the open windows and also the low lalations of baby-talk of some sort from Lenz, "Pooty ooty doggy woggy" and whatnot, presumably directed at the dog, who's coming over to Lenz in a sort of neutrally cautious but attentive way. Green has no clue what kind of dog it is, but it's big. Green can remember not the sight but the two very different sounds of the footfalls of his Pop the late Mr. Green pacing the Waltham living room, the crinkle of the paper bag around the tallboy in his hand. It's well after 2245h. The dog's leash slides hissing to the end of the Day-Glo line and stops the dog a couple paces from the inside of the gate, where Lenz is standing, inclined in the slight forward way of somebody who's talking baby-talk to a dog. Green can see that Lenz has a slightly gnawed square of Don G.'s hard old meatloaf out in front of him, holding it toward the straining dog. Lenz has the

blankly intent look of a short-haired man with a Geiger counter. The hideously compelling Ho starts again with the total
abruptness that makes CDs so creepy. Green's got one finger
in one ear, shifting around slightly to keep Lenz's lampshadow
from blocking the view. The music balloons and booms. The
Nucks have turned it way up for "My Lovely Launa-Una Luau
Lady," a song that's always made Green want to put his head
through a window. Part of the instrumentals sounds like a
harp on acid. The hollow-log percussives are like a heart in
your extremest-type terror. Green fancies he can see windows
in the houses opposite vibrate from the horrific vibration.
Green's having way more than one thought p.m. now, the
squeak of the gerbil-wheel starting to crank deep inside. The
undulating shiver is a slack-steel guitar that fills little Brucie's
head with white sand and undulating tummies and heads that
resemble New Year's subsidized parade balloons, huge soft
shiny baggy wrinkled grinning heads nodding and bobbing as
they slowly inflate to the shape of a giant head, tilted forward,
straining at the ropes they're pulled by. Green hasn't watched
a New Year's parade since the Year of the Tucks Medicated
Pad's, which had been obscene. Green's close enough to see
that the Hawaiianized Nuck house is 412 W. Brainerd. Blue-
collar-type cars and 4x4s and vans are all up and down the
street packed in in a somehow partyish attitude, as in parked
in a hurry, some of them with Canadian lettering on the plates.
Fleur-de-lis stickers and slogans in Canadian on some of the
windows also. An old Montego cammed out into a slingshot
dragster is parked square in front of 412 in a sort of menacing
way with two wheels up on the curb and a circle of flowers
hung jauntily over the antenna, and the ellipses of dull fade in
the paintjob of the hood that show the engine's been bored
out and the hood gets real hot, and Lenz has gotten down on

one knee and breaks off some of the meatloaf and tosses it underhand to the ground inside the leash's range. The dog goes over and lowers its head to the meat. The distinctive sound of Gately's meatloaf getting chewed plus the ghastly music's zithery warbling roar. Lenz now rises and his movements in the yard have a melting and wraithlike quality in the different shades of shadow. The lit window farthest from the limp flag has solid swarthy guys in beards and loud shirts passing back and forth snapping their fingers under their elbows with flower-strewn females in tow. Many of the heads are thrown back and attached to Molson bottles. Green's jacket creaks as he tries to breathe. The snake had leapt from the can with a sound like: *spronnnnng*. His aunt at the Winchester breakfast nook, in dazzling winter dawnlight, quietly doing a word-search puzzle. Two dormer windows are half-blocked by the throbbing rectangles of the JBLs. Green's the type that can recognize a JBL speaker and Molson-green bottle from way far away.

A developed thought coheres: Ho's voice has the quality of a type of: *ointment*.

Any displaced and shaggy Nuck head in these windows chancing to look out into the yard now would be able to probably see Lenz depositing another chunk of meat in front of the pet and removing something from up near his shoulder under his topcoat as he's melting stealthily all the way around behind the dog to sort of straddle the big dog from the rear, easing the last of the loaf down in front of the dog, the big dog hunched, the crunch of Don's cornflake topping and the goopy sound of a dog eating institutional meat. The arm comes out from under the coat and goes up with something that looks like it would glitter if the windows' yardlight reached far enough. Bruce Green keeps trying to wave his breath out of the way.

Lenz's fine coat billows around the dog's flanks as Lenz braces and leans and gathers the hunched thing's scruff in one hand, and straightens up with a mighty grunting hoist that brings the animal up onto its hind legs as its front legs dig frantically at empty air, and the dog's whine brings a lei-and-flannel shape to the lit space above one speaker overhead. Green doesn't even think of calling out from his shadowed spot, and the moment hangs there with the dog upright and Lenz behind it, bringing the upraised hand down in front and hard across the dog's throat. There's a lightless arc from the spot Lenz's hand crossed; the arc splatters the gate and the sidewalk outside it. The music balloons without cease but Green hears Lenz say what sounds like "How *dare* you" with great emphasis as he drops the dog forward onto the yard as there's a high-pitched male sound from the form at the window and the dog goes down and hits the ground on its side with the meaty crunch of a 32-kilo bag of Party-Size Cubelets, all four legs dog-paddling uselessly, the dark surface of the lawn blackening in a pulsing curve before its jaws that open and close. Green has moved unthinking out of the vanshadow toward Lenz and now thinks and stops between two trees by the street in front of 416 wanting to call to Lenz and feeling the strangled aphasia people feel in bad dreams, and so just stands there between the treetrunks with a finger in one ear, looking. The way Lenz stands over the hull of the big dog is like you stand over a punished child, at full height and radiating authority, and the moment hangs there distended like that until there's the shriek of long-shut windows opening against the Ho and the dire sound of numerous high-tempo logger's boots rushing down stairs inside 412. The creepily friendly bachelor that lived next to his aunt had had two big groomed dogs and when Bruce passed the house the dogs' toenails would scrabble on the wood of the front porch and run with their tails up to the anodized fence as Bruce came by and jump up and like sort of *play* the metal fence with their paws, excited to see him. To just like set eyes on him. Lenz's arm with the knife is up again and ungleaming in the streetlight's light as Lenz uses his other hand on the top of the fence to vault the fence sideways and tear-ass uphill up Brainerd Rd. in the southwest direction of Enfield, his loafers making a quality sound on the pavement and his open coat filling like a sail. Green retreats to behind one of the trees as beefy flannel forms with leis shedding petals, their speech grunty-foreign and unmistakably Canadian, a couple with ukuleles, spill out like ants over the sagging porch and into the yard, mill and jabber, a couple kneel by the form of the former dog. A bearded guy so huge a Hawaiian shirt looks tight on him has picked up the meatloaf's baggie. Another guy without very much hair picks what looks like a white caterpillar out of the dark grass and holds it up delicately between his thumb and finger, looking at it. Yet another huge guy in suspenders drops his beer and picks up the limp dog and it lies across his arms on its back with its head way back like a swooned girl, dripping and with one leg still going, and the guy is either screaming or singing. The original massive Nuck with the baggie clutches his head to signal agitation as he and two other Nucks run heavily to the slingshot Montego. A first-floor light in the house across Brainerd lights up and backlights a figure in a sort of suit and metal wheelchair sitting right up next to the window in the sideways way of wheelchairs that want to get right up next to something, scanning the street and Nuck-swarmed yard. The Hawaiian music has apparently stopped, but not abruptly, it's not like somebody took it off in the middle. Green has retreated to behind a tree, which he sort of one-arm-hugs. A thick girl in a horrible grass skirt is saying "Dyu!" several times. There are obscenities and heavily accented stock phrases like "Stop!" and "There he goes!" with pointing. Several guys are running up the sidewalk after Lenz, but they're in boots, and Lenz is way ahead and now disappears as he cuts like a tailback left and disappears down either an alley or a serious driveway, though you can still hear his fine shoes. One of the guys actually shakes his fist as he gives chase. The Montego with the twin cam reveals muffler problems and clunks down off the curb and lays two parentheses as it 180s professionally around in the middle of the street and peels out up in Lenz's direction, a very low and fast and no-shit car, its antenna's gay lei tugged by speed into a strained ellipse and leaving a wake of white petals that take forever to stop falling. Green thinks his finger might be frozen to his ear's inside. Nobody seems to be gesticulating about anything about maybe an accomplice. There's no evidence they're looking around for any other un-wittingly guilty accessory-type party. Another wheelchaired form has appeared just behind and to the right of the first seated backlit form across the street, and they're both in a po-sition to see Green up against the tree with his hand to his ear so it looks like he's maybe receiving communiqués from some kind of earpiece. The Nucks are still milling around the yard in a way that's indescribably foreign as the one Nuck staggers in circles under the weight of the expired dog, saying some-thing to the sky. Green is getting to know this one tree very well, spread out against its lee side and breathing into the bark of the tree so his exhaled breath won't plume out from behind the tree and be seen as an accomplice's breath, potentially.

AT NIGHT

BY DAVID RYAN

Back Bay

(Originally published in 1998)

He sits there and regards the waitress, wondering what she would think if she knew he occasionally followed her home; if she knew about the Window Trick in her Fenway flat; if she knew how her breath sometimes sped in the dark; how once he touched her sleeping throat and her back arched, or how she then rolled over. And what if she woke and saw him, his silhouette stiff against the wall lit by moon and perhaps a streetlight spilt in against his shadow; what if she heard his breath on her ear, discovered an estranged print of his foot, a piece of cast mud, a matted leaf or a fresh stain on the floor? He reviews the list repeatedly and his coffee chills.

She belched in her sleep once.

How many times had he imagined her on the bearskin rug in the pamphlet?

Through the window of the restaurant, across Newbury Street, a woman talks into a pay phone by the wine shop. Sunlight glints off the chrome of the old phone bank, though if he tends to squint with the sun, he squints without it too. And he feels this gives him away; it displays his attempt to conceal his weaknesses.

He believes she does not see him, does not notice his

deep-set eyes, the flaps of skin wrinkled around them. He is young for such old-set eyes.

His coffee is weak as tea.

Summer brings out the cleft at the base of their calves, tanned skin shaved smooth—a few razor scrapes, or a nick—to the mid-thigh, droplets of perspiration clinging to the down above.

The woman at the pay phone waves her free hand against the sun impatiently. The other hand clutches the phone to the side of her mouth. He imagines a chance conversation. He catches himself moments later speaking to the empty chair that faces him. As if to reconcile this indiscretion, he lines up a bubble in the window glass, positions it to her ankle, then rides his eye up along her leg.

Pow.

In the autumn, they bundle up. There comes a time during the course of a day when they must bundle down, the cold comforter slipping up, softly, caressing their prickly goose-pimpled thighs. Outside, the dry morning smell of cedar and orange leaves rises from the chill.

Winter conjured the bearskin rug from the pamphlet he keeps in his top drawer. The fur, matted and stained in the center, glows white from the sun and blue snowdrifts that shine through the window. He imagines large umbrella flash-lamps set outside the photograph that add to the artifice of a snow-lit day in the pamphlet's room. The glossy cover tells him to *Ski Colorado*. In the pamphlet, Colorado is a mountain range two inches tall. The bearskin rug on the back flap is larger than the mountain on the front.

In the spring, everything was wet and animals copulated.

In the summer, the dew dried. The sun burned it off by a certain hour in the morning, the sky lit differently from the other seasons; though often the film remained, covered the air like a moist tarp.

He's grinning until the waitress spoils it, catches him with his teeth showing, asks if he'd mind paying now seeing as— she waves her hand over to several people who wait by the door—they want to sit and your coffee's been long going. If you don't mind. She is too aggressive awake. A cheap bracelet shakes on her wrist. He wishes he could take one of the metal charms from it, touch it to his mouth and suck. He has seen her take it off her wrist before she retires, though only now has he found pleasure in his mouth from the idea.

"A minute," he says. He wants to say, *I know how you sleep.* A minute and a glance suffice, however. He is the center of that glance, the implications of it. In her unwitting world, he is God.

She walks off to the *future table* with her hands raised shrug-level. He's already singing a fire-song inside his head.

The restaurant, not much more than a coffee shop, is air-conditioned. No sound comes from the unit, just the sound of spoons and conversation. With his eyes closed, it sounds to him as if the spoons are speaking. He imagines the street outside burning up, now sees the woman at the phone, a grate outside shoots hot air under her dress, ballooning it up, her long legs rising, lengthening . . . To watch them struggle, their free hand no longer waving off the sun but pushing into the thin, flowered fabric, trying to hold the dress down while their legs grow long underneath. Oh, to watch them blush like that all day: her hand still crimped down against her brown leg; the back of her thigh turned toward him. Tomorrow the phone she holds in her hand will look like the black box they remove from the charred debris of airplanes. It will leave its coke all over fingers. It will stain pants, shirts, fingertips, and the gaze of eyes. Bricks will hold the smoke splattered over them like shadows fused to the surface.

He had more than once been told his features were strong, but he knew by the pause that indicated the search for euphemism that his features were not fairly or truthfully found in the word.

He crushes a dollar and sets it on the table. He passes the *table of the future*, gives them a thumbs-up, then churns his middle finger from it like some sleight of hand. He laughs, pushes the door open into the hot sun. He stops in the heat as though he has forgotten what he is doing, or where he is going. He leans against the wall of the coffee shop and squints at her again, bolder this time because he is in the open air and only across the street. The train underground did it, the T caused the wind to push their skirts up through the grate like that.

He reaches up and sniffs his finger; it smells like sulfur, like the safety matches he keeps in his pocket. The irony in the words *safety* and *matches* makes him think. He squints and laughs. He attracts attention this way; he forgets, then remembers, he was put on this earth for everyone to see, like the gutted cat in science class years ago that wore the glass tube full of honey-colored fluid. He occasionally forgot they could see him, like the time he was very small and first realized he was not invisible. Dirty trick.

Tomorrow, those hands will blacken if they touch that phone. A crowd will gather and know *how it is:* it was his way of being invisible.

His erection softens; she has hung the phone on its cradle. She walks away, her skirt now settled against her sides, pushed by the wind slightly so that a long vertical dip has formed between her legs.

In that science class, he threw the lit alcohol burner down, and said it was an accident as students scattered and the flames spread around his feet like a burst water balloon. It was a beautiful gush, blue and pure, scalding hot. It burned off the alcohol, then left a mark in the linoleum that said, *Walter did it*.

The rest of the school year he sat next to his teacher up front, facing the class. He could look up the girls' skirts, sitting in the front there like that, but instead stared right through them at the cat floating frozen at the back of the room: mouth open, caught with its guts hanging down in the anemic yellow liquid, dangling like a skin brassiere from a clothesline . . . or thinking of how he yelled *Timber!* from his bed with his little voice as smoke filled the stairwell and how he climbed out of the comforter and how the beam from the attic came down sparking the banister and how he saw his mother in their Dorchester duplex, saw her mouth freeze open, heard her shriek between the ash and smoke that cloaked her like static-charged laundry. Cinders were floating like snowflakes . . . or how when he opened the window, a ball of heat rushed at him and left his arms bubbled under gauze for weeks. "One fried little peanut," he heard whispered from the hall as he danced in a big circle, flames consuming his childhood, his family; yes, his, he supposes, though at times nothing is clear. They went up like paper boats in the winter, when the wood was peeling from itself and dry; they went up like origami swans dangled over a candle.

He runs his tongue across his lips. He watches the big eye in front of him blinking. He squats and scratches his back against a brick wall. He kills time until nightfall, passes down Newbury, cuts through Copley Square. He buys a soft drink. He circles a city block several times. He walks and walks, Copley to South End, South End to no-man's-land then west to the edge of Roxbury where before turning back he finds a shoe in a gutter. This shoe he ties to his belt. He spits twice. He comes back by way of Mass Ave. Back, then deeper to where the city softens, the trees are large, the streets cooler. The neighborhoods that look nothing like where he grew up.

With night fallen, he can get down to it. Certain nights he must wait for hours until the right moment. But he can be very patient. He can persuade time at her apartment window, or—once she falls asleep—he can climb inside with the Window Trick and listen to her breathe. He could count the stars and wait for them to fall if he wanted, but he does not do this. He stuffs the rag inside the jar instead. Clots of the remnant mayonnaise bob suspended in the gasoline. He screws the lid on and pulls a strip of cloth through the hole he has punched, forming a wet wick. A little gasoline leaks onto his scarred hand. It feels cool in the night air. He will sit still and wait in the dark for the right moment. He tilts the jar upside down and drizzles more gasoline on the scars. It feels good, the smell comforts him. Tomorrow the building that holds the pay phone will not be a building, only a pile of sticks and brick.

He climbs the wooden steps that lead to the small porch under her window. At the top, he sees his face clearly in the shiny dark of the glass. He tricks the window and steps inside. Her nose is snoring. Her mouth has filled the room with breath. He picks up the bracelet from the night table and touches a charm onto his tongue. He stands there and listens to her breathe.

ABOUT THE CONTRIBUTORS

No Author
Photo

KENNETH ABEL is the author of the highly praised *Bait* and *The Blue Wall*. *Down in the Flood* is his third in the critically acclaimed Danny Chaisson thriller series; previous titles include *Cold Steel Rain* and *The Burying Field*. He lives in Columbus, Ohio.

Lynn Wayne

LINDA BARNES, winner of Anthony and American Mystery awards, has written seventeen novels, twelve featuring 6'1" redheaded Boston private investigator Carlotta Carlyle. Her most recent Carlyle novel, *Lie Down with the Devil*, was named one of the best mysteries of 2008 by *Publishers Weekly*. *The Perfect Ghost*, a nonseries novel, will be published in 2013.

Elizabeth Brown

JASON BROWN is the author of two books of short stories, *Driving the Heart and Other Stories* and *Why the Devil Chose New England for His Work*. His short fiction has appeared in *Harper's*, the *Atlantic*, *Best American Short Stories*, NPR's *Selected Shorts*, and many journals and anthologies. He teaches in the MFA program at the University of Oregon.

Jon Laprade

JAIME CLARKE is the author of the novel *We're So Famous;* editor of *Don't You Forget About Me: Contemporary Writers on the Films of John Hughes* and *Conversations with Jonathan Lethem;* and coeditor of *No Near Exit: Writers Select Their Favorite Work from Post Road Magazine*. He is a founding editor of the literary magazine *Post Road* and has taught creative writing at UMASS-Boston and Emerson College. He is co-owner of Newtonville Books, an independent bookstore in Boston.

J.M. Clarke

MARY COTTON is the pseudonymous author of nine novels for young adults, six of them *New York Times* best sellers. She is also a fiction editor for the literary magazine *Post Road,* and is coeditor of *No Near Exit: Writers Select Their Favorite Work from Post Road Magazine*. She is co-owner of Newtonville Books, an independent bookstore in Boston.

ANDRE DUBUS (1936–1999) is considered one of the greatest American short story writers of the twentieth century. Over an illustrious career, he wrote a total of six collections of short fiction, two collections of essays, one novel, and a standalone novella. He was awarded the *Boston Globe*'s Lawrence L. Winship Award, the PEN/Malamud Award, the Rea Award for the Short Story, and the Jean Stein Award from the American Academy of Arts and Letters.

GEORGE HARRAR is the author of the literary mystery *The Spinning Man*, described by the *New York Times* as "elegant and unnerving." Among his dozen published short stories, "The 5:22" won the Carson McCullers Prize and was selected for inclusion in *Best American Short Stories 1999*. In 2013, Other Press will publish his psychological drama *Reunion at Red Paint Bay*. Harrar lives west of Boston with his wife, Linda, a documentary filmmaker.

GEORGE V. HIGGINS (1939–1999) was the author of more than twenty novels, including the best sellers *The Friends of Eddie Coyle, Cogan's Trade, The Rat on Fire,* and *The Digger's Game.* He was a reporter for the *Providence Journal* and the Associated Press before obtaining a law degree from Boston College Law School in 1967. He was assistant attorney general and then an assistant US attorney in Boston from 1969 to 1973. He later taught creative writing at Boston University.

CHUCK HOGAN is the *New York Times* best-selling author of several acclaimed novels, including *Devils in Exile* and *Prince of Thieves*, which was awarded the Hammett Prize and was adapted into the Oscar-nominated film *The Town*. His nonfiction has appeared in the *New York Times* and *ESPN The Magazine*, and his short fiction has twice been anthologized in *Best American Mystery Stories*. He lives outside Boston with his family.

DENNIS LEHANE is the author of the Patrick Kenzie and Angela Gennaro mystery series (*A Drink Before the War; Darkness, Take My Hand; Sacred; Gone, Baby, Gone; Prayers for Rain,* and *Moonlight Mile*), as well as *Coronado* (five stories and a play) and the novels *Mystic River, Shutter Island, The Given Day,* and *Live By Night.* Three of his novels have been made into award-winning films. In 2009, he edited the bestselling anthology *Boston Noir* for Akashic Books.

Theresa Salgado

BARBARA NEELY writes novels, short stories, and plays wherever she can. Her first novel in the Blanche White series won three of the four major mystery awards for best first novel. Neely's short stories have appeared in anthologies, magazines, university texts, and journals. She is currently working on a stand-alone novel and a play.

Charles Gross

JOYCE CAROL OATES, editor of *New Jersey Noir* (2011), is the author most recently of the story collection *The Corn Maiden* (Mysterious Press) and the novel *Mudwoman* (Ecco/HarperCollins). Her earliest fascination with Boston and its historic environs sprang from her experience as a nineteen-year-old undergraduate in the Harvard Summer School, living in an antiquated residence in the Harvard Yard during a particularly hot and torpid summer some decades ago.

John Earle

ROBERT B. PARKER (1932–2010) was the author of seventy books, including the legendary Spenser detective series, the novels featuring Jesse Stone, and the acclaimed Virgil Cole–Everett Hitch westerns, as well as the Sunny Randall novels. Winner of the Mystery Writers of America Grand Master Award and long considered the undisputed dean of American crime fiction, he died in January 2010.

Susan Breen

DAVID RYAN's fiction has appeared in *BOMB, NERVE, Mississippi Review, Denver Quarterly, Cimarron Review, Tin House, Alaska Quarterly Review, New Orleans Review, Hobart, 5_Trope,* and the W. W. Norton anthology *Flash Fiction Forward,* among others. He is a recipient of a MacDowell Fellowship and a recent arts grant from the state of Connecticut.

Linda Carrion

HANNAH TINTI grew up in Salem, Massachusetts. She is the author of a story collection, *Animal Crackers* (which includes "Home Sweet Home"), and a novel, *The Good Thief.* She is also cofounder and editor in chief of *One Story* magazine. Recently, she joined the National Public Radio program *Selected Shorts,* as their literary commentator.

DAVID FOSTER WALLACE (1962–2008) wrote the novels *The Pale King, Infinite Jest,* and *The Broom of the System,* as well as the story collections *Oblivion, Brief Interviews with Hideous Men,* and *Girl with Curious Hair.* His nonfiction includes *Consider the Lobster, A Supposedly Fun Thing I'll Never Do Again, Everything and More,* and *This Is Water.*